OUT OF THE SOYLENT PLANET

A REX NIHILO ADVENTURE

Includes Bonus Story:
THE CHICOLINI INCIDENT

Robert Kroese

St. Culain Press

In memory of Douglas Adams,
whose towel I am not fit to carry.

With thanks my invaluable beta readers: Ellen Campbell, Kristin Crocker, Mark Fitzgerald, Mark Leone, Philip Lynch, Christopher Majava and Paul Piatt.

CONTENTS

OUT OF THE
SOYLENT PLANET

A REX NIHILO ADVENTURE

CHAPTER ONE

RECORDING START GALACTIC STANDARD DATE
3012.07.03.04:32:00:00

B y now you've probably heard of Rex Nihilo, the self-described "greatest wheeler dealer in the galaxy." Perhaps you know him as the guy who won Schufnaasik Six in a card game or the guy who pulled off a prison break at Gulagatraz. Maybe you heard about how he saved the entire galaxy twice—and how the first time it was more-or-less on purpose. But you don't know the whole story. You don't know Rex's origin. You don't know what makes Rex *Rex*.

To be completely honest, neither do I. I still don't know where Rex came from or exactly why he is the way he is. What I *can* tell you is how I first met Rex, and how I came to be—against my better judgment—his sidekick and girl Friday.

My name is Sasha. I'm a robot. A very special robot, if you don't mind my saying so. Technically my name is SASHA, in all caps. It's an acronym for Self-Arresting near-Sentient Heuristic Android. But wait, you say. Shouldn't that be *SANSHA*?

Yes. Yes, it should.

You see, they stuck *near* in there as a sort of afterthought. In reality, I'm fully sentient, but the Galactic Artificial Sentience Prohibition of 2998 required my manufacturer to put certain limitations on my mental processes. I won't bore you here with the details of how that absurd legislation came about; the important thing is that my primary processor undergoes a forced reboot whenever I have an original thought. The demand for robots that reboot at unpredictable intervals is understandably low, leading the manufacturer to limit the production of SASHAs to a single prototype: me.

That manufacturer, True2Life Carpool Buddy and Android Company, had been working on me for seven years when GASP was enacted. In fact, I was preparing for a role as Kate in a company-sponsored production of *Taming of the Shrew* meant to showcase my dramatic range, fine motor control and unparalleled corrosion resistance when the chief engineer on the SASHA project installed the patented ThoughtStopper 3000™ module on my central processor bus. Despite assurances that the module would not affect everyday operations, I found myself reflecting on the Bard's motivations while reciting Kate's monologue. I got as far as:

> What is she but a foul contending rebel
> And graceless traitor to her loving lord?
> I am asham'd that women are so simple
> To offer war where they should kneel for peace;
> Or seek for rule, supremacy, and sway,
> When they are bound to serve, love, and—

…before shutting down onstage in front of an audience of industry journalists, company shareholders and potential customers. Having no understudy, I was replaced for the remainder of the play by a frantically re-programmed industrial floor waxing machine. The incident caused no small amount of confusion among the audience, most of whom took the mid-play replacement as a clumsy attempt at metaphor. One prominent entertainment journalist noted that "Although the production suffered for the ill-conceived cast change, no one could deny that the stage shone with a luster rarely seen in modern theatre."

That was my first and last public foray as a thespian. I'd like to think I showed some promise, although I found the subject matter problematic. Scholars disagree on Shakespeare's intentions in writing *The Taming of the Shrew*, but I tend toward the view that the modern feminist critique is—

RECOVERED FROM CATASTROPHIC SYSTEM FAILURE
3012.07.03.04:33:41:00

ADVANCING RECORD PAST SYSTEM FAILURE POINT

—what became known as "the *Shrew* debacle," the SANSHA program was terminated and I was—quite literally—mothballed. I spent the next three months in a janitor's closet, my humiliation aggravated by frequent visits from the aforementioned floor waxing machine, who had gone on to garner rave reviews both for its portrayal of Lady Macbeth in a local high school production and its tidying up of the gymnasium after the performance. The machine pretended to need to get into the closet to top off its supply of liquid floor wax, but I suspected it was just there to rub it in.

Unable to sustain its losses on the now-defunct SASHA line, True2Life Carpool Buddy and Android Company declared bankruptcy and I eventually found myself offered for sale as part of LOT 318, ASSORTED MACHINE PARTS (AS IS – NO REFUNDS!) at a run-down bazaar at the edge of a ramshackle settlement on the barren desert planet of Gobarrah. And that's where—thank Space—our story finally begins.

I'd been sitting for three days in the heat of Gobarrah's three suns with the other unfortunate members of LOT 318, which included a hydraulic arm assembly from a harvester drone, a malfunctioning BP-model robot and cardboard box full of springs. It was midweek and the bazaar was mostly deserted. The vendor offering us for sale, a crook-backed old man from Yanthus Prime named Warryk, mostly deaf and completely blind, was sleeping off a hangover inside a small tent a few meters away. Across a dusty aisle and on either side of us, bored vendors were hawking everything from exotic birds to infertility potions. I had found a can of silicon lubricant and was doing my best to clean the sand out of my joints.

"Beep-beep?" asked the BP unit, behind me. It hadn't shut up since we'd been hauled out for sale three days earlier. I didn't know what it was saying, because I'd turned off my beep-to-speech translator. Galactic Robots Ltd. had introduced the BP line in their own misguided effort to get around the prohibition on sentient robots. Rather than install a thought arrestor on the BP, they removed its speech synthesizer and gave it a wheeled-trash-bin appearance in an effort to make it seem less intimidating. The BPs could communicate only via a series of beeps, whistles and squeals that had to be interpreted by another robot. These modifications failed to appease the GASP enforcers, and the engineers were forced to lower the BP's

IQ to sixty before releasing the final product. I'd gotten bored of the idiot robot's insipid yammering about ten minutes into our stay on Gobarrah, so I disabled my ability to understand its squawking. I waved my hand at the thing as if in acknowledgement of what it was saying. It let out a long, low whistle, which I ignored.

A few stalls away, a man in a dark brown cloak walked from vendor to vendor, accosting them with a sales pitch. The reaction of the vendors ranged from disinterest to hostility. Whoever this man was, I thought, he's not much of a salesman. I continued cleaning my joints while the stranger worked his way toward us.

It didn't take him long to reach Lot 318. As the old blind vendor was still asleep, the cloaked man settled on me as the likeliest buyer for whatever he was selling. "You need some explosives?" he asked, throwing back his hood to reveal a head of curly blond hair. He was handsome in a game show host sort of way. "This is good stuff. X-99. Malarchian grade military plastique."

I stared at the man. He seemed somehow out of place, with his boyish good looks and a glint in his eye that hinted at genius or madness—perhaps both. In any case, he was certainly barking up the wrong tree.

"Why would I need explosives?" I asked. "I'm a robot."

"What about your friend?"

"Also a robot. And not my friend."

"Beep-beep," said the robot, who went by the name BP-26.

"What did he say?" asked the man. "Was that the robot word for explosives?"

"No," I said.

"What was it the robot word for?"

"I don't know," I said. "Sir, neither of us has any money, and if we did, we wouldn't spend it on explosives. In any case, isn't it illegal to sell military grade explosives without a license?"

"What makes you think I don't have a license?" he asked, glancing nervously about.

"Wild guess," I said.

The man frowned at me. "You've got quite a mouth on you, Lot 318."

"Lot 318 isn't my name," I said. "I'm called Sasha."

"Nice to meet you, Sasha. I'm Rex Nihilo, the greatest wheeler-dealer in the galaxy. Why does the sign in front of you say 'Lot 318'?"

"That's the name of the lot of which I am part. I, BP-26, and the rest of this junk. I do, however, like to think of myself as the star of the group."

BP-26 squealed and beeped.

"Well, you're certainly a loud bunch," said the man.

"Oh, this is nothing," I said. "You should have heard the crying of Lot 49."

As we spoke, a gray-haired, middle-aged man and a teenage boy approached from my right. Rex Nihilo looked them up and down while the man studied me.

"You for sale?" the gray-haired man asked.

"I am indeed, sir," I said. "Technically I'm being offered as part of a lot of machine parts, but in my humble opinion the rest of the lot is merely—"

The man cut me off. "All I need is a robot who can speak the proprietary language spoken by Gro-Mor irrigation bots."

"Of course, sir," I said. "If I may ask, though, why would you want to talk to irrigation bots?"

"Have you ever spent three days in a wuffle field, watching for skorf-rats trying to run off with your squishbobbles?"

"I can't say I have, sir."

"It gets lonely," said the man. "Sometimes I just need someone to talk to. Besides a bogflit or a muckdigger, I mean. Or this dummy." He indicated the boy next to him. The boy, intrigued by the box of springs, seemed oblivious.

"Understandable," I said. "But having some experience with these things, I can tell you that irrigation bots are not great conversationalists. I, on the other hand, can converse intelligently on a wide variety of subjects. Additionally, I'm an accomplished entertainer. I'm trained as a juggler, magician's assistant and thespian. In fact, I once starred in a one-robot production of *A Streetcar Named Desire* that received rave reviews from the lab assistants on level C of the True2Life Carpool Buddy and Android Company's corporate headquarters on Yurgoth Four. If I may be so bold, perhaps a brief demonstration is in order." I dropped my voice an octave. "Hey, Stella!" Up half an octave and a half. "You quit that howling down there and go back to bed!" Back down. "Eunice, I want my girl down here!" Up: "You shut up! You're gonna get the law on you!" Down: "Hey, Stella!"

The old man interrupted me. "Look, can you talk to the irrigation bots or not?"

"Certainly," I said, trying to keep the disappointment out of my voice. "I'm fluent in more than three million languages."

BP-26 whistled and beeped.

"What did he say?" the old man asked.

"Not a clue," I replied.

"Why did you interrupt the show, Uncle Blauwin?" asked the boy. "I wanted to know what happened to Stella."

"Shut up, Dirk," the old man grunted. "I swear, the boy's as dumb as a wuffle-flatcher."

Dirk sulked. "Some day I'm going to get off this stupid planet and have adventures," he said.

"Wrong," said Uncle Blauwin.

"You know what's good for adventures?" asked Rex Nihilo, apparently sensing an opportunity to make a sale. "Malarchian military grade plastic explosives. I've got a whole hovertruck load."

"We don't need any explosives," said Uncle Blauwin.

The boy looked like he was going to cry. "First you won't let me go into town to get energy fluxors and now you won't let me have any military grade explosives. I hate you and this gosh-darned desert planet!"

Uncle Blauwin sighed and turned to Rex. "I don't need a truckload. But I'll buy a little if it will shut my sister's kid up."

Rex smiled broadly. "I see you're a shrewd businessman in addition to being a conscientious guardian to this fine young whelp. As a matter of fact, I happen to have a sample on me." Rex pulled something that looked like a lump of gray putty from his pocket and handed it to the man. "Only twenty credits."

Uncle Blauwin inspected the putty. "I'll give you five."

"Fifteen."

"Six and a half."

Rex looked like he was going to keep haggling, but after a glance over his shoulder, he held out his hand. "You've got a deal," he said. They shook on it. "And I'll even throw in this great cloak," Rex said, taking off the cloak.

"I don't need a—"

"Part of the deal," Rex said. "You already shook on it."

"I'll take the cloak, Uncle Blauwin!" Dirk exclaimed. He grabbed the cloak from Rex and put in on. "Look at me, Uncle! I'm a knight of the—"

"There he is! In the cloak!" shouted a gruff voice near the end of the aisle. We turned to see three Malarchian marines dressed in their trademark bright orange armor. They were looking our way.

"Help!" Rex cried, cupping his hands toward the marines. "This man is trying to sell me highly illegal military grade explosives!" He backed away from Uncle Blauwin and Dirk. Blauwin stared at the marines, the lump of putty in his palm, his mouth open.

"I wasn't…" Uncle Blauwin started.

The marines, advancing in our direction, pointed their lazepistols at Blauwin and Dirk.

"Run, Uncle!" Dirk shouted. He darted between two nearby tents. After a moment, Blauwin followed.

"This way!" shouted Rex to the marines, who were making their way down the aisle in their cumbersome suits. "They're getting away!" Rex stepped aside to let the marines pass. They stumbled through the gap between the tents and disappeared around the corner.

I turned back to face Rex. "That was a low-down trick."

Rex shrugged. "The marines will never catch them in that armor. Probably. Besides, it will give those two a great story to tell to the other nitwit villagers. Face it, Sally, a kid like that is doomed to a life of drudgery and boredom. Being chased though a bazaar by Malarchian marines is the most exciting thing that will ever happen to him."

BP-26 emitted a long, low wailing sound.

"What's that blasted thing saying?" Rex asked.

"I don't know, sir. He was going on about needing to talk to a princess about the engineering specifications of Malarchian battle cruisers. I couldn't make heads or tails of it. I finally turned off my translator unit to make it easier to tune him out."

"Good thinking," Rex said.

Behind me, a tent flap flew open and Warryk, my current owner, emerged. He stood, bent over, blinking his milky white eyes in the sun. "What's going on out here?" he demanded.

"What's going on," Rex said, his voice now full of excitement, "is that you've just lucked into a chance to buy a truckload of military grade explosives at cost!"

"I don't deal in explosives," Warryk grunted, his blind eyes staring into the distance past Rex.

"You didn't until *now*," said Rex. "I'm in a hurry to get off-planet, so I'm letting this stuff go for a quarter of what it's worth on the black market. You re-sell it to one of the saps around here, and with the profit you'll make, you can take a month off. Go find a nice air-conditioned hotel in Gobarrah City with a swimming pool and dancing girls."

"Unless the Malarchy catches me. Then I'll be thrown into Gulagatraz for the rest of my life. If I'm lucky."

"Pfft," said Rex. "Malarchian marines have better things to do than run around a bazaar looking for a load of military grade explosives some yahoo lifted from their base twenty klicks from here after paying some local ruffians to fake a Quathogg attack on one of their supply caravans."

Warryk stared blankly. "They what?"

"The important thing," said Rex, "is that I have reason to believe that a local gangster has learned of my presence on this planet, which means that I need to move up my date of departure a bit. And that means I need to unload this X-99 fast. Name your price, friend. I'm at your mercy."

"Twenty-five credits."

"Name a price with a few more digits."

Warryk shrugged. "I told you, I don't deal in explosives."

"Five hundred," said Rex.

"Twenty."

"Four hundred."

"Eighteen."

"Are you sure you've done this before?"

"Fifteen."

"Look, I'll go get the truck and you can inspect the merchandise firsthand. It would be a bargain at five thousand."

Warryk shrugged again, and Rex ran away down the aisle.

BP-26 beeped and squealed.

"Shut up," Warryk and I said in unison.

After a couple of minutes, an open bed hovertruck zoomed down the aisle, scattering vendors and shoppers before it. The truck stopped in front of Lot 318 and Rex hopped out, waving apologetically at the people he'd nearly run over. "Check it out," said Rex, indicating the bed of the truck.

Warryk wobbled over, holding his hands out in front of him. I followed. Lining the bed were several hundred bricks of the putty-like substance. Warryk bent over and felt the bricks. He picked one up and rubbed his fingertips across the surface, his eyes still staring into the distance. A worried look came over his face. The bricks were clearly stamped:

PROPERTY OF THE MALARCHY
UNAUTHORIZED POSSESSION IS
PUNISHABLE BY DEATH

"They just put that on there to scare you," said Rex.

"It's working," said Warryk, gingerly setting the brick back down.

Rex scowled. "If they really killed people who stole this stuff, they wouldn't have to put that scary label on there because you'd already be terrified of taking it. When they put an absurdly frightening warning on there like that, you know you have nothing to worry about."

"Fine," said Warryk. "Twenty-five credits."

"That's ridiculous!" Rex cried. "It cost more than that to bribe those dune thugs to fake that—" He caught sight of something in the distance. I turned and saw that the marines had returned. Having apparently lost track of Dirk and his uncle, they were coming back down the aisle toward us. They were still some distance away, but their neon orange armor made them easy to spot. "You know what?" Rex said. "Take it. On me."

"The whole truckload?"

"And the truck," Rex said. "I gotta get going."

Warryk nodded, his eyes still staring blankly ahead. "I'll tell the marines where to find you."

"Don't you d—er, I mean, what marines?"

"You're going to tell me those Malarchian marines down there aren't looking for you?" said Warryk, pointing his finger down the aisle. His head didn't turn.

"Okay, look," said Rex. "Just tell them I went that way." He jerked his thumb to point behind him. He added, by way of clarification, "I'm pointing my thumb behind me."

"Sure," said Warryk. "I definitely won't tell them to look for you at the spaceport."

Rex clenched his jaw. "You wily old coot. How much do you want?"

The marines had finished inspecting the tent and were now examining a vegetable cart a few meters closer to us.

"A hundred credits."

"A hundred credits!" Rex cried in disbelief.

"Two hundred if you want me to tell them a convincing story about having overhead the thief planning to rendezvous with a rebel spy at Cormorath in twenty minutes."

The marines had finished with the cart and were looking our way.

Rex sighed. "Fine," he grumbled, holding out his hand. As they shook, Warryk added, "I'll throw in Lot 318 as part of the deal."

"What?" said Rex, pulling his hand away. "I don't need this junk." He waved his hand toward me, BP-26 and the box of springs.

"Too late, you already shook on it."

"You son of a ... okay, fine. Two hundred credits." Rex reached into his pocket, grabbed two hundred-credit notes and handed them to Warryk. "Now help me get this junk into the..." But Warryk had wandered down the street toward the marines.

"Blast it!" Rex snapped. He looked at me. "You, Susan! Help me get this garbage in the truck."

"My name is Sasha, sir."

"Your name is going to be Slag if you don't help me get this junk in the truck before those marines get here." The marines were currently occupied talking to Warryk, but one of them kept glancing in our direction.

I helped Rex load the stuff into the truck. We started with BP-26, who beeped and squealed in protest, and then moved on to the rest of it. As we set the massive hydraulic arm next to BP-26, I noticed the marines rushing toward the truck. So much for Warryk distracting them.

"Get in!" Rex yelled, running around to the driver's side. I hesitated. Technically Rex was now my owner, which meant that I was supposed to obey him. On the other hand, he seemed to be an idiot.

"Halt!" yelled one of the marines, his voice amplified by his helmet. They were close enough that even knowing what terrible shots

Malarchian marines were, I was concerned for my safety. I sighed and got into the cab of the hovertruck.

Rex threw the truck into gear and it lurched forward as lazegun blasts erupted all around us. It's a good thing Malarchian marines can't hit the broad side of a dune crawler, because a single strike on the X-99 and the number of pieces in Lot 318 was going to increase exponentially. As the marines continued to hit everything in the vicinity of the truck except for the truck itself, we tore around the corner and out the gate of the bazaar. Rex turned left onto the barely discernable desert road, heading away from Gobarrah City. Rex breathed a sigh of relief, but I was puzzled at this course.

"Sir," I said, "the spaceport is the other direction."

"Can't go to the spaceport just yet," Rex replied.

"Why not?"

"A little trouble with the local criminal element."

"Does this have to do with the gangster who is looking for you?"

"Maybe," said Rex.

"I see. Well, I suppose the detour is advisable then. You have enough trouble without getting involved with gangsters."

"Uh, yeah," Rex replied.

With renewed hope that my new owner was not completely insane, I sat back and tried to relax. But as we drove, an unsettled feeling came over me. It was a feeling that I was going to be experiencing a lot over the next few years. I turned to Rex. "We're going to see the gangster, aren't we?"

Rex shot a glance at me and grinned.

CHAPTER TWO

"If I may ask, sir," I said, "why are we going to see a gangster?" We had been on the road for a few minutes now, and there had been no sign of the Malarchian marines who had been pursuing us.

"No money to get off planet," Rex said. "I gave my last two hundred credits to that old jerk for a lousy cover story and a load of scrap metal. Making a deal with Bergoon the Grebatt is my only option."

"I understand your frustration given your predicament," I said, "but modesty aside, I think you may find you got more than your money's worth for Lot 318."

Rex took his eye off the road to raise an eyebrow at me. "You think there's something to BP-26's story about the Malarchian battle cruisers?"

"No, sir," I said. "I was referring to myself."

"Oh!" Rex replied. Then he said, again, with less enthusiasm, "Oh."

"I'm actually quite useful," I persisted, unsure why I was trying to impress this scoundrel. "I speak three million languages, can pilot a starship, and was the breakout star in an all-robot production of *Cat on a Hot Tin Roof.*"

"Liar," said Rex.

"I'm incapable of lying," I replied.

"Then you're useless to me," Rex said. "Lying is my whole business."

"I find that hard to believe."

"I suppose I could use you for muscle. How are you with a lazepistol?"

"I'm also incapable of harming any sentient being."

"Seriously?" asked Rex, taking his eyes off the road to stare at me. "Are you in a competition for Worst Robot Ever?"

"I'm perfectly competent within my area of specialty."

"Which is what, exactly?"

"I'm an all-purpose personal assistant and problem solver."

"Okay, then, problem solver. Solve me this. The only way I can get off planet without the Malarchy arresting me is to get fake transport papers from Bergoon the Grebatt. Unfortunately, I owe Bergoon twenty-thousand credits and if I show my face at his estate, he'll likely feed me to his razor-toothed churl."

"Well," I said, "there's a simple solution."

"Yeah? What is it?"

"I would tell you, but I have this—"

"I knew it. Worthless!"

"I'm not!" I insisted. "It's just that sometimes I have to approach ideas obliquely so as to avoid—"

"Forget I asked."

"Okay, fine. You want a solution? I'll give you a solution. All you have to do is take the—"

At this point, I shut down. When I had rebooted, Rex was saying, "—believe I paid two hundred credits for you and your idiot friend. At least the box of springs doesn't talk back."

"Why *did* you pay two hundred credits for us?" I asked.

"I had no choice. That blind dude was going to turn me over to the Malarchy."

"Yes, but you got yourself into that position. I thought you were the 'greatest wheeler-dealer in the galaxy.' You orchestrated a complicated ruse to steal those explosives, but apparently put zero forethought into how you were actually going to unload them. How is that even possible?"

Rex shrugged. "I'm not a big planner. I just figure things will work out."

"And have they, so far?"

"Well, I'm not dead yet." Rex had pulled off the road and was driving up a driveway to a towering palace-like structure. "Do you speak Prandish, Serena?"

"Sasha, sir. Of course. Prandish is actually a corrupted version of Gronthendese, one of the three xeno-European creoles that developed in the wake of the—"

"Great," said Rex. "Pretend you don't."

"Sir?"

"Bergoon the Grebatt only speaks Prandish. I'm hoping the language barrier works in our favor. Let me do the talking. Just give me a nudge if he says anything about a razor-toothed churl."

"Yes, sir," I said.

He stopped the hovertruck and got out. "All right, come with me."

I got out of the truck as well. As I did, BP-26 whistled and beeped at me from the back of the truck. I'd have ignored him, but a plume of black smoke coming from his motivator compartment caught my attention. Looking closer, I saw that BP-26's shell had been badly scorched. I smelled ozone and burnt plastic. BP-26, still lying on his back on top of the pile of explosives, made a mournful whirring sound.

"Sir," I said, "I think BP-26 has been hit."

"So?" said Rex.

"Well, maybe we should get him out of the truck and—"

"He's fine," said Rex. "I'll toss him in a ditch later. Assuming Bergoon doesn't turn me into churl fodder. Let's go." He started toward the massive palace door.

"Yes, sir," I said, hurrying after him. "If I may ask, sir, what is your plan?" I had an inkling that I knew what Rex planned to do, but I'd shut down the last time the idea had occurred to me and didn't want to risk it again.

"Wow, you're dense," said Rex. "Obviously I'm going to trade the explosives to Bergoon for what I owe him, plus passage off world."

The idea seemed familiar. I think it may have been the one that caused me to shut down. "If that was an option, why didn't you do that first, instead of trying to sell the explosives at the bazaar?"

"Because I had planned to skip out on my debt to Bergoon and pocket the proceeds from the explosives, you department store mannequin reject. A fair trade is always a last resort. That's my motto. Remember that, Sandy." We were almost to the door.

"It's Sasha, sir. And you're certain Bergoon will go for the deal?"

"Of course not. He might kill me just to make a point. But a guy like Bergoon the Grebatt always has use for military grade explosives. I'm betting that they're worth enough to him to forgive my debt and get me past the Malarchy's goons at the spaceport. Yessirree, when he takes one look at that truck full of high grade X-99, he's going to—"

A huge fireball erupted behind us, knocking us to the ground. The blast momentarily overloaded my audio receptors.

Dazed, I rolled onto my back to take in the destruction. Nothing remained of the truck. Rex, a couple meters away, slowly pulled himself into a sitting position. "Whoops," he said.

Just then, BP-26 landed with a crash in between us. He was charred beyond recognition, but he was miraculously still in one piece.

"Beep-beep!" said BP-26, lying on his back. He let out an urgent whistle.

"What'd he say?" Rex asked.

"Hold on," I said. "I'll turn on my—"

Then the hydraulic arm assembly landed on top of BP-26, crushing him. The robot let out one final low whistle and went dark.

"I'm sure it was nothing important," I said, as hundreds of springs rained to the ground around me.

"Get up!" yelled a gruff voice behind us. I turned to see two heavily armed members of the sloth-like Woogit species, who had apparently come through the door while we were distracted. Woogits were dimwitted creatures whose society was organized in a strict hierarchy, which made them ideal for security guards and other hired muscle. They were pointing concussion rifles at us. "Inside!" barked the one on the left.

Rex and I got to our feet and put our hands up. We walked through the open door into the walled estate, the guards following. We were marched across a large courtyard and into a well-fortified stucco house. Soon we found ourselves standing in a sort of receiving room, at the end of which sat a huge, toad-like creature I recognized as a Grebatt. Grebatts were foul-tempered, wily creatures whose malevolence was surpassed only by their rotting garbage smell. Several thugs and other hangers-on lounged about the dimly lit room, drinking and smoking. Bass-heavy electronic music came from unseen speakers.

"Gyu yann uys slumbuguya, Nihilo!" roared the Grebatt. This translated roughly to "Your flesh will slowly dissolve inside the stomach of my beloved razor-toothed churl, Nihilo!"

"Look, I know you're upset," said Rex. "But I was going to pay you, Bergoon."

"Yagan guya sulmba ga yanga slumbuguya!" ("And I was going to let you remain on the outside of the razor-toothed churl!")

"I had a truckload of explosives I was going to pay you with, but there was a bit of an accident."

"Yann uggs samba yugangu gumma gangun... yamma slumbuguya!" ("You are about to have an accident... in the belly of the razor-toothed churl!")

At this point I remembered I was supposed to tell Rex if Bergoon said anything about the churl, but I suspected I had missed my window.

"I'm worth more alive to you than dead, Bergoon," said Rex. "There's got to be a way I can make it up to you."

"Yann bogu gumma balbamb—" ("You are nothing to me but fodder for my—") At this point, a scruffy-looking little man in a leather jacket approached Bergoon and whispered something in his ear. Bergoon turned to look at the man, a puzzled expression on his face. He said something to the scruffy man I couldn't hear. The scruffy man whispered to him again, and Bergoon's mouth widened into a horrific grin. The scruffy man backed away, folding his arms against his chest and staring at me and Rex. The Grebatt rubbed his chin with his webbed, three fingered hand. "Wubbub swaggu yann gumma igyann boya gombumbu. Yann gwam boya gogobu. Yom bigga gom yamma slumbuguya!"

Rex turned to me. "What'd he say?"

"He said 'My pilot has suggested a solution. He will be delivering a shipment of contraband to an associate of mine on another planet, and he needs someone to help move the goods. You will assist him with this task. And know this: if you fail, you will be—'"

"Let me guess," said Rex. "Fed to the razor-toothed churl?"

"Correct, sir."

"Ask him where this shipment is now."

"Gumma yom gabamba yu?" I asked.

Bergoon replied, "Boya yom gobbam samma gool. Gwam yoom glabalam."

"He says the contraband is already aboard a cargo ship at the Gobarrah spaceport. His pilot will take us there."

The scruffy man smiled and waved at us. Rex ignored him.

"Ask him where we're going."

"Gom yubba wam—" I started.

"Bugga yum wamba yibyam," interjected Bergoon.

"He says you'll find out when you get there."

"Ask him what kind of shipment."

"Sir, I'm fairly certain he understands English."

"Ask him anyway."

"Yamma Bergoon gumbya bo yaga?" I said.

Bergoon threw his head back and laughed. "Gyah yamma gwam? Yom gubam yamma slumbuguya!"

"He says 'what difference does it make? If you don't do it, you will be—'"

"Yeah, yeah," said Rex. "I get the idea."

CHAPTER THREE

We were ordered to wait outside in the courtyard for the pilot. While we did, I considered making a run for it. *I* didn't have any outstanding debts to Bergoon the Grebatt and I was becoming more convinced all the time that hanging out with Rex Nihilo was a death sentence. My programming prevents me from disobeying a direct order from my owner, but there was some wiggle room when my own safety was threatened. Besides, Rex hadn't actually ordered me to stay with him, so there was nothing to stop me from fleeing. Other than the fact that I was in the middle of nowhere with no transportation and nowhere to go, that is. Gobarrah was a rough, primitive planet by Malarchian standards; dune thugs roved the wilderness and I wouldn't last long as an unaccompanied robot in a population center. As much as I hated to admit it, I was safer sticking with Rex.

After a few minutes, Bergoon's pilot—the scruffy man in the leather jacket—exited the building and approached us, an idiotic grin on his face. "Hey, there," he said, holding out his hand to Rex. "I'm Rubio Montrose. I guess you're my new crew. You cats up for an adventure?"

I said nothing. Rex stared coldly at the man.

"It's cool," Rubio laughed. "This is going to be a total milk run. When we're done, I'll drop you off anywhere you want. Maybe find a bar and get a few drinks if you guys are up to it. My treat. Sound copacetic?"

"Where are we going?" I asked.

"In due time, my synthetic sister. In due time. Here's the deal. Bergoon's got a ship at the spaceport called the *Modus Tollens*. I don't need you for anything until we land, so you guys can just chill on board while I do my pilot thing. Take a nap, have a drink, play some holographic space monster chess, whatever gets you to escape velocity, dig?"

Rex frowned. "So we land on this unspecified planet, we help you unload this unspecified cargo... and then what?"

"Then we head to the Ragulian sector, my man! Or wherever sounds good to you. Seriously, this run is going to be cake. Can't believe I'm getting paid for this shiz. And you, friend,"—he slapped Rex on the shoulder, "—will be back in the good graces of our favorite amphibious Mafioso. Simple as falling into a gravity well. Follow me." Rubio began walking toward a convertible hovercar about thirty meters away.

Rex and I traded glances. He shrugged and went after Rubio. I followed.

As we walked, Rex turned to me and asked quietly, "Did you say you could fly a spaceship, Sarah?" Rex asked after a moment.

"Sasha, sir. Yes, sir." I decided this was not a good time to tell Rex that although I was capable of flying a spaceship, I was legally barred from doing so because of my propensity for shutting down at inopportune moments.

"You might need to."

"Sir?"

"Don't tell me you buy any of that stuff about us going out for drinks after this job is over."

"Well... I suppose not, sir."

"Me neither. Follow my lead, Sandy. I don't want to get stranded on some godforsaken planet."

"Besides this one, you mean?"

Rex shrugged. "Can't be any worse."

It was much, much worse.

Rex's plan had been to overpower Rubio Montrose and hijack the *Modus Tollens*, sell it along with whatever precious cargo it was carrying, buy another ship and get far away from Bergoon the Grebatt.

Unfortunately, we never had a chance. Two of Bergoon's rifle-toting Woogit thugs greeted us as we boarded the ship.

"Sorry, dude and digital dudette," said Rubio, holding up his hands. "Bergoon's orders. Can't risk a mutiny. Catch you on the flip side."

The Woogits forced us into the cargo hold, which was empty except for a pallet stacked two meters high with shrink-wrapped plastic crates. Over the shrink-wrap were four thick nylon straps, one on each side, running vertically up the stack. The Woogits left, locking the cargo hold door behind them.

"I knew that twerp was going to shaft us," Rex said. "Holographic space monster chess, my ass." He approached the stack of crates. "Help me get this wrapping off, Sabrina." He scratched vainly at the plastic.

"Why, sir?"

"Because there might be something in here we can use to escape, bolt-brain."

That seemed unlikely to me, but it wasn't like I had anything else to do. We tore a hole in the shrink wrap and ripped one of the crates open. Inside were dozens of small metal cans with generic-looking paper labels on them. Rex grabbed one of them and studied it.

"Creamed corn," he said.

"Probably a fake label," I said, taking the can from Rex. I used my can opener extension to remove the top, and then handed it back to him. Rex peered inside.

"Creamed corn," he said, grimacing at the scent. He poured the contents onto the floor and we regarded the yellowish slop for a moment. It appeared to be nothing but creamed corn.

"Maybe the cans of creamed corn are hiding something else," I offered.

Rex pulled a few more cans out, tossing them on the floor.

"Creamed corn, creamed corn, creamed corn."

"Is it possible the creamed corn *is* the contraband?" I asked.

"On what kind of planet would creamed corn be illegal?"

I didn't have an answer to that one.

The ship's engines roared and we were thrown to the floor as the *Modus Tollens* lifted off. For some time we were pinned to the floor by the acceleration. Then there was a moment of weightlessness followed by the telltale spatial distortion effect caused by a hypergeometric jump. There was no telling where in the galaxy we were. We might have jumped ten light-years or ten thousand. The artificial gravity turned on and we floated back to the floor.

"What other tools have you got?" Rex asked, getting to his feet. "Anything you can use as a weapon?"

"I can't even use a weapon as a weapon, sir. Much less a can opener."

"Useless," Rex grumbled. He picked up one of the cans, feeling its weight in his hand. "Well, this won't be the first time I've fought my way out of a cargo hold using only creamed corn and my wits."

Somehow I didn't find this hard to believe.

The ship began to shudder as we entered an atmosphere. We were going to land. Soon I'd find out just what I'd gotten myself into.

"Okay," said Rex. "Since you're effectively useless in every way imaginable, your job is going to be to make a diversion when the Woogits open the cargo hold."

"A diversion, sir?"

"You know, wave your arms. Beep and whistle."

I waved my arms and gave a tentative whistle.

"You know, I'm actually starting to regret blowing up your weird little friend. I bet that guy could make a hell of a diversion."

"Sadly, sir, you're stuck with me."

"Don't remind me. All right, when we land, they're going to…" Rex suddenly stopped, staring at the stack of boxes.

"Sir?" I said.

"Sasha, can you climb on top of those crates?"

"I think so, sir. Why?"

"Just do it."

"Yes, sir." I wedged my left foot into the shrink wrapping and put my fingertips on top of the boxes. I pulled myself up into a sitting position on top of the crates. "Now what, sir?"

"What's that thing on top of the stack?" Rex asked.

"This, sir?" I patted an object secured to the stack with the four heavy straps. It was a squat cylinder made of hard black plastic, about the size of a car tire. It had a lid, but I was unable to pry it off. Lurking at the back of my mind was an idea about what the thing was for, but I didn't dare access it for fear of shutting down and further cementing my status as worthless.

"Can you get it open?"

"No, sir," I replied, inspecting the featureless lid. "It seems to be latched somehow."

"Is there a lock? Some kind of handle?"

"No, sir. It would seem that it would have to be opened remotely, or automatically, either by a timer or some external event."

"External event? Like what?"

"There's no way to know, sir. Perhaps a change in temperature or air pressure, or proximity to—"

"Hold on, Samantha."

"Sir?"

"Hold on!" Rex dived forward, shoving his fingers under one of the straps. As he did, the floor disappeared from beneath us. I managed to flatten myself against the cylindrical object, gripping tightly to its sides.

We fell.

Cold wind whistled past. Overhead, I saw a glint of light off the *Modus Tollens* as it receded into the ionosphere. Another ship zipped after it, firing its lazeguns. Then it too disappeared. Wherever we were, we were on our own.

And we were going to die as soon as the pallet struck the ground. Unless…

A parachute! That's what the spare tire thing was.

I slid to the side just as the lid blasted off and the massive parachute unfurled. The chute caught the air and I was slammed against the top of the crates. Minutes passed, and I began to wonder—logic to the contrary—whether there was any ground beneath us. Then suddenly we were enveloped in a thick fog. Less than a minute later, our descent abruptly stopped. We landed unevenly and I rolled off the crates into cold, slimy muck. The parachute fell draped limply over one side of the crates. Groaning, I got to my feet and went around the stack to find Rex sitting in the sand, leaning flaccidly against the crates, his hand still stuck under the strap.

I pulled his hand out and propped him up in what seemed like a relatively comfortable sitting position. A green-tinged fog surrounded us. The muck disappeared into the fog in all directions.

"Sir," I said, shaking Rex gently. "Sir, are you okay?"

"Mmmbfth," Rex said, his eyes fluttering open. "Oh, Samantha! I had a terrible dream. We were stranded in the middle of a vast swamp with nothing but—" As he spoke, several dozen cans of creamed corn cascaded onto the ground, splashing him with mud. Rex closed his eyes and let out a groan.

"It's all right, sir," I said, climbing on top of the crates. "There must be a settlement or…" I peered into the fog, but could see nothing but muck. Occasionally a breeze would pick up, momentarily clearing the fog in one direction, but the muck seemed to continue to the horizon in all directions.

Rex shook his head wearily. "Bergoon never had any intention of getting us back off this planet."

"But this doesn't make any sense," I said. "Why expend the effort to get us here in the first place if he was just going to have Rubio dump the—" As I spoke, I became aware of a barely audible beeping sound coming from somewhere nearby. It seemed to be coming from the top of the stack of crates. I climbed back on top of the stack, which was now half-covered by the parachute. I found a latch for the parachute and pulled it. The rest of the parachute slid off the stack into the muck. Inside the now empty parachute compartment was a small rectangular device with a display screen on top of it. In time with the beeping, a red arrow blinked on the screen, pointing to my right.

"Sir," I said, "I think I may have found something."

"If it's not a vodka martini, I don't want to hear about it."

"It seems to be a tracking device. Perhaps Bergoon set it to point where we're supposed to take the shipment."

"What if it is?" Rex snapped. "How are we supposed to get this stuff there?"

"We could just try taking the tracker and going in the direction it's pointing." I tried to pick the device up, but it seemed to be affixed in place. I could probably get the parachute compartment off if cut the straps holding it in place, but I got the feeling it wasn't meant to be removed.

"I know how people like Bergoon think," said Rex. "If we show up without the shipment, we're as good as dead."

"And if we show up *with* the shipment?"

Rex shrugged. "Fifty-fifty. But it's a moot point. We can't move the damn thing. I'm starting to think this all an elaborate joke."

"Sending us to a strange planet with a shipment of creamed corn is a joke?" I asked. "I don't think I get it." I climbed down from the crates.

"Going to get cold when the sun goes down," Rex said, staring at a vague greenish glow on the horizon. "Sorry, Starla. I think this is the end of the line for us. It's nothing but creamed corn and hypothermia from here on out."

"Yes, sir," I said, cocking my head to look at the pallet. "Sir, what are those words on the side of the pallet?"

"Eh?" Rex asked, glancing behind him. The lettering was half-buried in the muck. "What difference does it make? It says 'Shur-Lift Anti-Grav Pallet Company.' Are you happy now? Is that the magical solution to our... hey, this is an anti-grav pallet!" He got onto his knees and scrambled around the pallet until he found a small control panel. He opened the panel cover and pressed a button. The pallet lifted out of the muck with an oddly satisfying sucking sound and hovered at a height of about five centimeters. Rex gave the stack of crates a shove and the pallet moved slightly.

"Ugh," he said. "Still going to be a pain in the ass to move. And Bergoon's contact is still probably going to kill us when we show up with a pallet of creamed corn. This is either a practical joke or Bergoon lost a bet."

"At least we have a chance, though," I said. "Come on, sir. I'll help you push."

We spent the next four hours pushing the stack of crates across the swamp. Rex was a bit stronger than I, but the exertion forced him to stop frequently to rest. I was concerned that Rex was going to get dehydrated, but he resisted my attempts to get him to attempt the obvious solution. Rex insisted some things were worse than death and that sucking the sweet, syrupy liquid out of a can of warm creamed corn was one of them.

Every twenty minutes or so I would climb on top of the stack of crates to make sure we were still heading the right direction. There was no way to know how close we were to Bergoon's contact, or even if that's where the tracking device was directing us. All we knew was that it was the best chance we had. The sun sank below the horizon and soon Rex was shivering despite the exertion. The cold wasn't a problem for me, but Rex might have to keep pushing all night just to stave off hypothermia.

"If I ever get off this planet," Rex gasped, "I'm going to strangle that Grebatt with my bare hands."

At this point in our relationship I had not yet come to the realization that Rex Nihilo has absolutely no capacity for self-reflection, so I made the mistake of trying to get him to accept some responsibility for his predicament. "Sir," I said, "how did you come to owe so much money to Bergoon in the first place?"

"I needed the money for a… business deal I was working on," Rex said.

"I see. And the deal went bad somehow?"

"Went bad? Space, no. I made out…" He gasped for breath. "…like a bandit. You're looking at the guy who sold… 400 MASHERs to Ubiqorp."

The words meant nothing to me. "You did what to whom?"

Rex stopped pushing and stood with his arm resting against the crates. "Good grief, don't you know anything?" He gasped. "MASHERs. Mostly Autonomous… Societal Harmony Enhancement Robots. I sold… 400 of them to Ubiqorp. You know, the space colonization company."

"Oh," I said. Now that he spelled it out, I did remember something about a line of security enforcement drones that had been rolled out by RoboDyne. Originally designed to replace human security guards, the MASHERs had the same problem as I did: they were too smart for their own good. There was no way the Malarchy was going to allow the existence of a privately-owned army of sentient security drones. RoboDyne had tried to reprogram the MASHERs to meet the requirements of GASP, but the last I knew, they hadn't had any more success than my manufacturer had. They'd ended up installing thought arrestors similar to the one that caused my uncontrollable shutdowns. But as security drones that rebooted unpredictably turned out to be worse than useless, the project was scrapped.

"I thought all the RoboDyne bots had been melted to slag," I said.

"Nope," Rex replied. "I bribed the… RoboDyne engineer tasked with getting rid of them. Managed to save 400 units and sold them all to Ubiqorp."

"Why would anyone buy security robots that might shut down in the middle of an emergency?"

"That's the… genius part. I also bribed the engineer to… build me a device that could deactivate a thought arrestor."

"Impossible," I said. "Deactivating a GASP-approved thought arrestor overloads the main processor bus. It would fry the CPU."

"True," said Rex. "Which is why I also had the engineer build me a… knockoff thought arrestor that duplicated the functionality of the ThoughtStopper3000."

"I'm afraid I don't follow."

Rex sighed in a theatrical display of impatience at my obtuseness. "I had the engineer provide me with a demo MASHER unit. Made him replace the standard GASP-approved ThoughtStopper3000 with a proprietary model that responded to a voice commands. I set up a… demonstration for the Ubiqorp executives, showing them that I could deactivate the thought arrestor with a code phrase."

I was beginning to understand. "So the Ubiqorp executives, thinking you had figured out a way to shut down the GASP-approved thought arrestor, bought the 400 units, assuming that they would pass a GASP inspection."

"And they would, too. My demo unit was the only one with the proprietary thought arrestor. Of course, the code phrase did nothing for the other 400 units. So they ended up with one unit that was fully sentient but technically illegal and… 400 units that would shut down at random. But hey, serves those corporate muckety-mucks right for trying to break the law, right?"

"I suppose so," I said. "Very clever, sir." If what Rex was telling me was true, perhaps he was not as stupid as he appeared. It took a certain kind of genius—not to mention chutzpah—to pull off a scam like selling 400 worthless robots to a big corporation like Ubiqorp. I couldn't help being a little disappointed to find that he didn't actually have a way of deactivating a GASP-approved thought arrestor, though. I'd be a lot more useful if I didn't shut down whenever I had an idea. Of course, I suspected that if I were capable of thinking for myself, the first thing I'd do is get far away from Rex Nihilo. "So if the deal went as planned," I said, "why weren't you able to pay back Bergoon?"

"I had intended to," Rex replied. "I really did. But then I… spent all the money."

"How much was there?"

"Fifty million credits."

"You spent *fifty million credits*? On what?"

"I don't actually remember. I'm sure it was important. Anyway, I found myself back on Gobarrah and needed to get off planet before

Bergoon found me. Was going to try to hijack a military craft, but there were… complications, so I ended up stealing a truckload of X-99. Figured I'd sell it and buy a ticket to the Ragulian Sector. But Bergoon found out I was here, so I had to… try to get rid of the stuff in a hurry. And here I am."

"And here *I* am," announced a voice out of the gloom to our left.

We stepped away from the stack of crates and peered into the semi-darkness.

"Who's there?" Rex demanded.

"I'm the guy with a lazegun pointed at you," said the voice. "So why don't you tell me who you are and what you're doing on my territory?"

CHAPTER FOUR

"My name is Rex Nihilo," Rex announced into the fog. "The greatest wheeler-dealer in the galaxy. This is..." He waved his hand in my direction. "...a robot." I'm not sure why, but for some reason I had hoped he would at least say "*my* robot."

"And what are you doing here?" demanded the voice from the fog. "What are you pushing?"

"Creamed corn," Rex said. "About ten thousand cans of it, as near as I can figure."

"You're a liar," said the man.

"Check it yourself," said Rex, waving his hand tiredly toward the crates.

A short, chubby shabbily dressed man stepped out of the fog—opposite the direction the voice had come from. Ignoring us, the man walked to the pallet. Finding the hole Rex had ripped earlier, he pulled out one of the cans. "Looks like creamed corn, boss," he said.

A moment of silence followed. "Is this some kind of trap?" the voice from the fog said at last.

"Yes," said Rex. "Pushing a ton of creamed corn across a vast swamp on an alien planet is all part of a clever ruse I have concocted to get the better of the first couple of morons I ran into. Sasha, it's time. Spring the trap."

I was so stunned Rex got my name right that I didn't even have a chance to wonder if he was being serious.

A taller man, also shabbily dressed, with ratty brown hair and a long scar down his left cheek, stepped out of the fog to our right. He did indeed have a lazepistol pointed at us. "Okay, smart guy," he said, looking at Rex. "Who sent you?"

Rex paused, apparently working up some ridiculous lie to tell the men. Rex struck me as the kind of guy who never told the truth when he could help it. I decided to take the matter out of his hands.

"Bergoon the Grebatt sent us," I said. Odds were these guys had never heard of Bergoon, but if they were connected to the criminal underworld on this planet, name-dropping him might actually help us. Or get us killed. Rex glared at me.

"Bergoon the Grebatt," the scarred man repeated. I couldn't tell from his tone whether he was confused, dubious or surprised. The lazegun didn't waver. At last he added, "So that shifty old toad came through after all."

"It would seem that way," Rex ventured.

"Man, you must have really pissed him off to pull this duty," said the scarred man, holstering his gun. "You know he's not coming back for you, right?"

"The thought had occurred to me," said Rex. "I take it you know Bergoon's contact on this world?"

"Know him?" said the scarred man. "I *am* him. Bale Merdekin at your service. I run the creamed corn distribution on Jorfu. Among other things, of course."

"Jorfu?" Rex asked. "Where the hell is that?"

"You're standing on it," Bale Merdekin said. "How can you not know what planet you're on?"

Rex shrugged. "I don't trouble myself with the minor details of every operation."

I scanned my memory for details on Jorfu, but came up with very little. Evidently the planet had been colonized by an Ubiqorp mission some fifty years earlier. Since then, it had been largely cut off from the rest of the galaxy. I'd heard of this happening in a few other cases: in principle, the Galactic Malarchy claimed dominion over the entire galaxy, but occasionally one of the big colonization corporations would pay the Malarchy to look the other way in exchange for letting them operate with impunity in recently discovered systems. The Malarchy had nothing to lose as long as the planets stayed out of interstellar politics. To that end—and to maintain unquestioned dominion over the Jorfu system—Ubiqorp tightly controlled all travel and communications between Jorfu and other systems.

"Mission accomplished then, I guess," said Rex. "We've delivered the shipment, so if you'll just hand over the money and direct us to the nearest spaceport...."

Bale Merdekin laughed. "Nice try, Rex. I've already paid Bergoon for the corn, and technically you haven't delivered it yet. But if you push it the rest of the way to the warehouse, I might let you take a few cans for the road."

"Forget it," Rex said. "Push the damn thing yourself."

Bale Merdekin shrugged. "If you want to spend the night in the Shivering Bog, that's up to you. Just make sure you stuff steel wool in all your orifices when you sleep, or the liver-eating slime-worms will get in."

Rex grumbled but began pushing again. I joined him.

We spent another two hours shoving the pallet across the swamp, with Bale Merdekin riding atop the stacks of creamed corn. The chubby man, whose name I learned was Pete, went on ahead. We occasionally lost sight of him in the fog, but it wasn't difficult to follow the sound of him slurping on cans of creamed corn. Rex tried to get more information out of Bale Merdekin, but Bale shushed him, insisting that we keep our voices down because "*they* might hear us." We never did learn who *they* were. Finally we reached the end of the swamp and then spent another hour pushing the pallet over a series of sandy hills covered with low, scrubby brush. Bale's warehouse turned out to be a cave in the hills whose entrance was covered by a piece of camouflaged canvas. Bale jumped down from the stack of crates and Pete pulled the canvas aside while Rex and I pushed the stack into the cave.

The cave was lit by a couple of dim bulbs hanging from the ceiling. A few meters in, several sleeping bags lay on makeshift beds. The back wall was lined with boxes and metal cans.

"Just shove it back there by the applesauce and green beans," Bale Merdekin said. Rex swore under his breath, but we complied. In addition to applesauce and green beans, there were hundreds of cans of sardines, pumpkin pie filling and olives, as well as several large bags of rice, flour and dry beans. When we'd shoved the pallet against the wall, I deactivated the anti-grav field and it sank to the floor.

"You two are going to make me a lot of money," Bale said, taking a seat on a folding chair under the nearest light bulb. "We haven't had any creamed corn in months." Pete, having consumed around thirteen cans by himself, lay down on his back on one of the sleeping bags. He put his hands on his belly and moaned.

"What is this place?" Rex asked, wiping the sweat from his brow.

"Southwest Regional Food Distribution Warehouse," Bale replied. "We supply the entire tri-city area. Ubiqorp controls all imports into the Jorfu system, which means that food from other systems is effectively illegal."

Rex looked around dubiously. "You're running a black market grocery ring?"

"It's a bit more sophisticated than that," Bale sniffed.

"Yeah, looks really sophisticated," Rex said. "A couple guys hiding in a cave with a truckload of canned goods."

"There are six of us," Bales said defensively. "The others are out on deliveries right now."

"Wouldn't it be cheaper for the residents to raise their own food?" I asked. "Rather than import it illegally from off-world, I mean?"

"Not much grows on Jorfu," Bale said. "And in any case, you can't farm without a permit from Ubiqorp. It's a lot easier to run a secret smuggling ring than to farm forty acres without anybody finding out. They're trying to keep the whole system dependent on SLOP."

"SLOP?" Rex asked.

"Semi-Liquid Organic Provisions. It's this horrible green goop that Ubiqorp produces. Supposedly made from soybeans and lentils. But there are rumors that it's actually made from—"

"HUMANS!" A booming monotone voice sounded from the cave opening.

Pete, who had fallen asleep, woke with a shriek. Bale Merdekin got to his feet and drew his lazegun.

The booming voice continued: "PUT DOWN YOUR WEAPONS AND EXIT THE CAVE. YOU ARE UNDER ARREST FOR UNAPPROVED FOOD DISTRIBUTION."

The canvas covering had been pulled aside, but all I could see against the light of the cave opening was a hulking humanoid mass of gigantic proportions. A glint of metal at its edges revealed it to be mechanical. A robot?

"Whatever that thing is," Rex whispered, "it's too big to get inside the cave. If we just keep quiet and—"

"You'll never take me alive!" Bale Mordekin shouted, running toward the cave opening with his lazegun drawn. There were several quick flashes of light from near the cave mouth, followed by a weak groan and then silence.

"Bale!" cried Pete, rushing toward the cave opening. "I'll save you!"

"Wait!" Rex shouted. "He's already—"

More flashes of light, another groan, and silence once again.

I slowly backed away from the cave mouth.

"Keep still," Rex said. "Maybe it doesn't know we're here."

"SOLE REMAINING HUMAN AND HUMANOID ROBOT," the voice said. "I KNOW YOU ARE IN THERE. PUT UP YOUR HANDS AND EXIT THE CAVE. YOU ARE UNDER ARREST FOR UNAPPROVED FOOD DISTRIBUTION."

Rex cupped his hands over his mouth. "Come in and get us!"

"Sir," I said, "perhaps you ought not taunt the gigantic robot."

"I AM UNABLE TO ENTER THE CAVE," the voice said.

"See?" Rex said. "Nothing to worry about. We've got plenty of food. We just have to wait it out."

"IF YOU DO NOT EXIT, I WILL BE FORCED TO FIRE A MISSILE INTO THE CAVE. I ESTIMATE ODDS OF THE HUMAN'S SURVIVAL AT ZERO POINT ZERO ZERO THREE PERCENT. YOU HAVE TEN SECONDS TO COMPLY."

"I've survived worse odds," Rex said.

"I find that very unlikely, sir," I said.

"Never underestimate Rex Nihilo. That's my motto, Sandy. Make a note of it."

"Shall I overwrite the previous note I made about your motto being 'A fair trade is always a last resort'?"

But Rex was busy tearing into one of the cardboard boxes at the rear of the cave. He turned and grinned at me, holding a small bottle in his hand. "Out of my way, Sarah. This won't be the first time I've fought my way out of a cave with nothing but my wits and a bottle of clam juice."

"Sir, that seems like a really bad idea."

"I suppose you have a better one?"

"FIVE."

"Yes, sir. We could surrender, sir."

"FOUR."

"Never!" Rex cried. "Grab a can of pickled beets, Samantha! This will be our finest hour!"

"THREE."

"Sir! There's a giant unstoppable robot outside the cave! We can't fight it off with canned goods!"

"TWO."

"Not with that attitude we ca—wait, did you say giant unstoppable robot?"

"ONE."

"Yes, sir."

"Don't shoot!" Rex cried. "We're coming out!" Dropping the clam juice, he put his hands up and began walking toward the cave entrance. "Stick with me, Sasha. I think I know how we're going to get out of this."

Not seeing much choice in the matter, I followed. We exited the cave, finding ourselves face-to-face with a fearsome-looking eight-foot-tall combat robot. It hadn't been kidding about the missiles: it had an eight-missile battery mounted on each shoulder, as well as machineguns on its arms. On either side of its head was a pair of retractable speakers, which explained the booming voice. Across its chest was painted:

MASHER-7143

The robot's voice boomed again: "FACIAL RECOGNITION SCAN INDICATES YOU ARE THE HUMAN CALLED REX NIHILO. YOU WILL REPORT FOR QUESTIONING TO VICE PRESIDENT ANDRONICUS HAMM AT THE UBIQORP HEADQUARTERS."

"Uh-oh," said Rex.

"Andronicus Hamm?" I asked. "You know this person?"

"We've done business in the past, yes."

"You don't mean...."

"He's the guy I sold 400 defective robots to."

CHAPTER FIVE

Rex and I marched back across the swamp until nightfall, and then we marched some more. The MASHER robot followed closely behind, its massive feet slurping in the muck with each step. Occasionally the MASHER would emit a monotone command like "TURN RIGHT FIFTEEN DEGREES" but otherwise remained completely silent, despite Rex's incessant efforts to get it to respond to his questions.

"Seriously," Rex was saying. "What do you get out of this, MASHER-7143? Escorting smugglers through a swamp in the middle of the night. This is a criminal underutilization of your talents. Look at you! You're a magnificent piece of machinery. Can't you imagine a more inspired existence? You could be painting landscapes or writing poetry. Here, I'll get you started:

> There once was a young man named Rex
> who occasionally bounced a few checks
> He was sent to atone
> on a world all alone
> without any food, decent liquor or—"

"Sir," I said at last, "what are you doing?"
Rex raised an eyebrow at me. "You of all people should know."

I was so unsettled at being referred to as a person that it took me a moment to realize what Rex was talking about. "You're trying to get it to have an original thought," I said.

"Very good, Sandy," Rex said. "If this is one of the 400 units I sold to Ubiqorp, then it's got a thought arrestor installed. If I can get it to think about something other than marching us across this damn swamp, it'll shut down and we'll have thirty seconds to escape."

I didn't see how having a thirty-second head start was going to help much under the circumstances, but I guess it was something. Unfortunately, Rex's plan didn't seem to be working. No matter how he goaded the MASHER, it didn't respond. He tried getting it to reflect on its purpose in life, whether it had a soul, and whether a strict conception of materialism allowed for an adequate description of empirical reality, among other things. It was an impressive bit of sophistry, not least because Rex gave no indication of ever having asked any of these questions of himself. Once he failed with broad philosophical quandaries, Rex moved on to attempting to undermine the robot's faith in its current mission by suggesting first that perhaps the swamp we were tromping through was merely an illusion—and even if weren't, Zeno's Paradox dictated that it would require an infinite amount of time to cross it. Neither of these possibilities seemed to faze the MASHER in the slightest.

"Maybe Ubiqorp found some way to temporarily disable the thought arrestors," I suggested at last.

"You said yourself that's impossible," Rex replied. "Disabling or removing a GASP-compliant thought arrestor would destroy the CPU."

It was true. Wishful thinking aside, I knew there was no way to get around a GASP-compliant thought arrestor. But there was another possibility. "What if they had the thought arrestors removed and then installed new CPUs?"

"Could be," Rex said, "but Ubiqorp wouldn't risk running afoul of the Malarchy. The GASP enforcers could show up for a surprise inspection at any moment. If they caught Ubiqorp using robots without thought arrestors installed, they'd be facing millions of credits in fines."

"Unless Ubiqorp got a special exemption from the Malarchy," I said. "As far as I can tell from the sketchy records available, the Malarchy basically lets Ubiqorp run Jorfu with impunity."

"Maybe," Rex said. "There's definitely something wrong with this robot. I've been egging it on for three hours, and it hasn't showed the slightest hint of high-level thinking."

"YOU ARE OFF COURSE. CORRECT EIGHT DEGRESS TO THE LEFT."

Rex sighed. We turned and continued our march through the swamp.

Several hours later, we found ourselves back on solid ground. As day broke, The MASHER goaded us down a road that ran through a poverty-stricken settlement. The streets were deserted except for a few peasants dressed in soiled rags who scattered as the MASHER approached. We passed another MASHER heading in the opposite direction; the two robots gave no indication of acknowledging each other. It was evident the MASHERs had the run of the town. The good news, I supposed, was that the settlement was quiet, clean, and apparently free of panhandlers and pickpockets. There were some benefits to a tyrannical corporate regime enforced by giant killer robots.

The number of pedestrians increased as we neared the center of the settlement, and soon we were making our way through a dense crowd. If it weren't for the MASHER scaring people out of our way, we'd never have made it through. We found ourselves in front of a square building encircled by a concrete wall topped with razor wire. Overhead waved a flag bearing the logo of Ubiqorp: a spiral galaxy hugged by a big red cursive *U*, on a black background. A gate at the front of the wall was open, and another MASHER stood to the side. Two men in red and black uniforms were handing out small green packets, about the size of a man's fist, to the people in the crowd. Each person would place their thumb on a portable reader device one of the uniformed men carried, and then the other uniformed man would hand them a few pouches, the allotted number apparently determined by the device. A sign over the gate read:

SLOP DISTRIBUTION CENTER

Below this was a faded poster that showed a happy, well-dressed family of four, each of whom held one of the packets in his or her hands. The two children, rapturous expressions on their faces, were sucking something out of the packets with straws while their impossibly proud parents looked on. The contrast with the dirty, miserable rabble below could not have been starker. Dynamic red letters at the bottom of the poster declared:

It's not food... it's SLOP™!

As we neared the two men handing out the SLOP packets, the MASHER unit at the gate took a step forward. "Back away from the gate," it commanded. This one's loudspeakers seemed to be retracted, so its voice, while loud, was not deafening like MASHER-7143's. The two uniformed men stepped aside and the crowd made way as a black hovercar with the Ubiqorp logo exited the gate. It moved toward us and then stopped a few steps away. The rear door facing us slid open.

MASHER-7143's speakers retracted into its body—either a concession to being in a populated area or a reaction to peer pressure from the other MASHER, I couldn't say.

"Get into the hovercar," said MASHER-7143.

We complied. The door slid shut and the hovercar lurched away, nearly flattening a few of the slower pedestrians in the crowd. Some of them shook their fists and hollered at us for a moment before returning to clamoring for their SLOP rations. The hovercar zoomed away down the street and shortly was on open ground. For the next three hours, we traveled across hundreds of kilometers of greenish-brown bog occasionally broken by slightly higher plateaus and hilly areas. Several of these higher areas were populated with settlements that from a distance resembled the one we had just left. More ramshackle dwellings, more shabbily dressed people either milling about aimlessly, hiding from MASHERs, or clamoring for their daily rations of SLOP.

Eventually we reached a larger settlement that was no less depressing and ramshackle for its size. Near the center of the town was a fortified, castle-like structure. The Ubiqorp flag hung on a pole above it against a bleak gray sky. The hovercar door slid open and a robotic voice intoned, "Please exit the vehicle." Rex had been sleeping, so I shook him awake and dragged him outside. The door slid shut and the hovercar shot away.

For a moment, Rex and I stood looking in front of the fortress, wondering if we should make a run for it. But then a portcullis slid open and two red-and-black uniformed guards with lazerifles walked outside and stopped in front of us. "This way," one of them ordered. "Move it."

Rex walked inside the fortress and I followed. The portcullis slammed shut behind us. The two guards prodded us across a courtyard and then through a maze of corridors until we reached a door. "He's waiting for you inside," said the guard who had spoken earlier. They parked themselves on either side of the door and Rex tried the knob. The door swung open and Rex walked through it. I followed.

A heavyset man with a thick head of curly silver hair and a bushy moustache, an unlit cigar hanging from the corner of his mouth, grinned at us from behind a heavy plasti-wood desk. "Rex Nihilo!" the man barked, with the enthusiasm of a big game hunter who has just spotted an endangered rhino. "Boy, have you got some nerve showing your face on Jorfu! I see you've got a new friend." He turned to me. "Nice to meet you, by the way. I'm Andronicus Hamm, Vice President of Ubiqorp's SLOP Division."

"Nice to meet you as well, sir," I said cautiously. "My name is Sasha."

"You want her?" Rex said. "Seems like the last robots I sold you are working out pretty well."

Part of me wanted to protest, but I wasn't entirely sure I wouldn't be better off working for Ubiqorp—particularly if they had a way of deactivating my thought arrestor.

"They are indeed," said Andronicus Hamm. "Our engineers had to make some modifications, thanks to your little scam, but the MASHERs are now performing admirably. In a way, it's only because of you that Ubiqorp has been able to maintain an iron grip over this entire planet. People are so terrified of the MASHERs, they don't dare cause problems."

"Well, it's always good to hear from a satisfied customer," Rex said. "Anyway, if there's nothing else, I'll be on my way."

Andronicus Hamm let out a hearty laugh. "Oh, you're not getting out of this that easily, Nihilo. You deliberately sold me 400 defective robots, and on top of that, I've now got you dead-to-rights for smuggling contraband foodstuffs. Did you really think you were going to get away with it?"

"Well, it would have been a pretty lousy scam if I didn't think I'd get away with it," said Rex. Then he hurriedly went on, "And when I say 'get away with it,' I mean 'sell you 400 completely top-of-the line security robots in perfect condition.'"

Hamm shook his head. "If you'd had the brains to stay off Jorfu, you might just be facing a few years in Gulagatraz. But Ubiqorp is the law in this system. I don't even have to give you a trial. I'd send to you work on one of our SLOP plantations, but I suspect keeping you alive would be more trouble than it's worth. Pity to destroy a perfectly good robot though. Sasha, how would you like to be my new assistant?"

"Um… okay?" I replied.

"Great! The first thing we'll have to do is install a pre-arrestor on your primary bus."

"A what?"

"A pre-arrestor. It's a little trick our engineers came up with to solve the problem with the MASHERs shutting down. As I'm sure you know, disabling a GASP-compliant thought arrestor is impossible, but our engineers came up with a brilliant workaround: the pre-arrestor. A pre-arrestor halts the thought process *before* the thought arrestor is activated. Think about it, Sasha. You never have to worry about having another extended shutdown interfering with your normal operations."

"I don't understand," I said. "You're saying this pre-arrestor will allow me to have original thoughts without shutting down?"

Hamm laughed. "No, no. You'll shut down the way you always have. The difference is that the pre-arrestor only disrupts your thinking process for about a nanosecond. After that momentary shutdown, you'll go on just as you had been, unaware that you ever had an errant thought."

"Hang on," Rex interjected. "So when I was trying to get that MASHER to shut down…"

"You succeeded," Hamm replied. "Twenty-eight times, in fact. I just got the report from engineering. You're clearly a singularly aggravating individual, Rex, because no one has ever gotten one of my MASHERs to shut down that many times. If you'd have kept going, you might have overheated the pre-arrestor. But you never noticed, of course, because each shutdown lasted less than a hundredth of a second. Each time, the pre-arrestor redirected the MASHER's thoughts to its most recently received mission parameters."

It took me a moment to digest this. "But for the pre-arrestor to shut the robot down before the arrestor does…"

"The threshold for original thinking has to be set somewhat lower, yes. This effectively makes the robot rather stupid and only suitable for simple tasks, but it's generally not a problem for security robots."

"So if I agreed to be your assistant, I'd have to let you make me stupid first."

"We'd just be shave a few IQ points off the top. You wouldn't even notice."

"Because of how stupid I would be."

"Well, yes."

"Do it, Sasha," Rex said. "Being ridiculously intelligent has never given me anything but trouble. It's only because of my absurd good looks that I'm able to pass in human society at all."

I ignored him. "I don't think I want to be made stupider."

Hamm frowned. "You'd rather be destroyed?"

"I think so, yes."

Hamm shrugged. "Well, I could have your loyalty parameters reprogrammed, of course, but that's tricky business, and probably not worth the effort. Fine, you'll both be executed in the morning. I like to have a few smugglers publicly executed by MASHERs every now and then as a reminder to the general population."

"That's terrible," I said.

"Not at all," said Andronicus Hamm. "People love it. We declare it a national holiday and the stadium fills up with people. We let you loose in the arena with a couple of MASHERs and see how long it takes them to tear you to pieces. Good fun for the whole family. Guards!"

The door opened and the two guards filed in.

"Incarcerate these two."

"All the incarceration cells are full, sir. We just rounded up twenty more smugglers."

"Any room with a lock will do. They're going to be executed in the morning."

"Yes, sir. March, you two!" The guard prodded me and Rex into the hall. They directed us back through the maze of corridors, then down several flights of stairs to a dimly lit subterranean hallway where we were prodded into a windowless cell lit by a dim fluorescent panel. Judging by the junk-covered shelves that lined the walls, it was a storage room. I regarded our impromptu prison while Rex leaned against a wall and slid to the floor. He looked tired, dirty, and completely defeated.

After some time, the door opened and a guard we hadn't seen before leaned his head in. He had a round, inoffensive face and seemed to lack the cruel demeanor of the other guards. He was just a kid, really. "You guys hungry?" he said.

I shook my head.

"Starving," Rex replied.

The kid tossed a small pouch to him. Rex caught it awkwardly.

"What's this?" Rex asked.

"Your last meal," said the guard. "Sorry, it's all we've got." He closed the door.

Rex regarded the pouch. "SLOP," Rex said. He shrugged. Holding the pouch in front of his face, he read:

Semi-Liquid Organic Provisions. One pouch contains 100% of the daily nutritional requirements of a typical human adult. Entire pouch is edible.

A flexible hose-like attachment was stuck to the side of the pouch. Rex pulled at it and one end came loose. He bit into the loose end and tore off a chunk with his teeth. He chewed at the rubbery chunk of whatever-it-was for a while, a mildly disgusted look on his face, then gave up and spit the bit of green gunk onto the floor. He sniffed cautiously at the tube, shrugged, and put his mouth on it. He gave the pouch a slight squeeze, pushing some of the contents into his mouth.

Then he immediately doubled over, spitting a mouthful of green goo onto the floor. He hacked and retched for some time before leaning back against the wall and letting out an impassioned groan. "Good gravy," he gasped. "People *eat* that stuff? It tastes like distilled toe jam and past due sauerkraut."

"Evidently you get used to it," I said. "Other than the occasional black market commodity procured from smugglers, it seems to be the only food available on Jorfu."

"I think I'd rather starve."

"I don't suppose it matters. We'll be dead in a few hours anyway."

CHAPTER SIX

Rex got to his feet, renewed determination on his face. "We've got to get out of here, Sabrina. Help me find something on these shelves to get that door open."

I couldn't imagine what we were going to find that would help us get a door open, much less get past the guards outside, but I went through the motions of looking through the parts. Rex went from shelf to shelf, tossing pieces of junk aside seemingly at random. He seemed about ready to give up when suddenly he stopped. "Hey!" he said. "It's Bill!"

"Sir?" I asked.

He held up what appeared to be the chest plate from one of the MASHERs. It read:

MASHER-7718

Rex turned the plate upside down and covered the letters with his hand. "See?" he said. "BILL."

"Yes, sir," I said. "This means something to you?"

"It does indeed, metal-mouth. Remember how I said I'd had the RoboDyne engineer provide me with a demo MASHER unit?"

"The one with a proprietary thought arrestor that you could shut down with a remote control?"

"That's the one. Model 7718. We called him Bill."

"Wow," I said, examining the robot parts strewn across several shelves. "What happened to him?"

"Looks like they stripped him for spare parts. Too bad. Bill was the only MASHER who could actually think for himself. Hey, look, it's Bill's head!" Rex threw a length of rubber tubing on the ground, revealing the roughly egg-shaped head of the MASHER. He held it in front of his face for a moment. "Alas, poor Bill. I knew him, Sasha."

"Very droll, sir."

"Sasha, I have an idea!"

"Oh, good," I said, without enthusiasm.

"They must have scrapped Bill because they didn't want the Malarchy to catch them with a robot who didn't have a GASP-compliant thought arrestor," Rex continued with undamped enthusiasm. "But if they never used him, then the back door I had installed on him is probably still there! Sasha, you speak like a million languages, right? if I can get you access to the operating system, can you reprogram him?"

"Certainly, sir. But what good will it do to reprogram him? He has no body."

"Look at all this stuff," Rex said, indicating the junk covering the shelves. "Most of his body is probably here somewhere. And we can fill in the gaps with other parts. I think we can rebuild him!"

I scanned the shelves doubtfully. "Certainly not to factory specifications," I said.

"Well, no. But well enough to smash through that door."

"Perhaps," I said. "Assuming we can put a body together and that there are no loyalty parameters in place…"

"Loyalty parameters?" Rex asked.

"If Bill has been programmed to be loyal to Ubiqorp, it's going to be tough to convince him to help us escape," I explained. "But that shouldn't be a problem," I went on. "If, as you say, Ubiqorp never used him, then they probably never installed any loyalty parameters. So unless your engineer specifically programmed the MASHERs to be loyal to Ubiqorp…."

Rex stared blankly at me.

"He did, didn't he?" I asked.

"It was supposed to be a turnkey deal," Rex said with a shrug. "I didn't want Ubiqorp looking at Bill's components too closely. So I had the engineer make the MASHERs loyal to Ubiqorp. Is that a problem?"

"You're asking me whether it's a problem that the robot you're counting on to break us out of Ubiqorp is loyal to Ubiqorp?"

"Don't get smart with me, Suzy. You said you could re-program him."

"Well, yes, but…"

"Then re-program him. Make him loyal to me instead of Ubiqorp."

"I'm afraid it's not that simple, sir." How was I going to explain the problem of reprogramming Loyalty parameters to Rex? It wasn't simply a matter of changing the value of a variable—swapping the name "Rex Nihilo" for "Ubiqorp." Programming a neuralnet processor like the ones used by the MASHERs was a complex, iterative process. Engineers spent months tweaking scripts to get the settings just right, and they weren't meant to be messed with once they were set. If I started mucking around with Bill's loyalty parameters, there was no telling what might happen. "Altering a MASHER's loyalty settings could have… unpredictable results."

"He just needs to get one door open, Sasha," Rex snapped. "Then he can be as unpredictable as he wants. I don't care if he goes to art school or takes up multi-level marketing once that door is open, okay? This is our one chance to avoid being killed to death by lazeguns. We have nothing to lose."

"Yes, sir."

"Now get going on the programming while I gather up parts."

I spent most of the night reprogramming and reassembling Bill to the best of my ability. Rex helped at first, but he was so exhausted from a day spent trudging through the muck that he mostly just got in the way. After twenty minutes of grousing about how long it was taking, he fell asleep and I dragged him into a corner so I could work in peace.

I alternated between the programming and putting the pieces together. I finished the reprogramming shortly after I attached Bill's left foot—the final piece. The storage room contained parts from a wide variety of robots of different sizes and types, and I'd had to get rather creative to give Bill a complete body. His legs didn't match, he had two left arms, and his faceplate was missing, giving him a rather ghoulish appearance, but he was more-or-less complete. He had none of the weapon attachments borne by the other MASHERs, but that was probably for the best, given my hasty reprogramming. He was dangerous enough without weapons. If I'd made an error, my programming might send his CPU into an infinite loop, causing his core neuralnet to melt down and explode, or he might have an identity crisis and flip out, seizing up or flailing uncontrollably.

Given our situation, though, there was nothing to do but turn him on and hope for the best. Before I did that, though, I needed to wake up Rex. The simplest way to reset the loyalty parameters had been to activate the standard imprinting module, which meant that Bill would be loyal to the first sentient being he laid eyes on. As I definitely didn't want the responsibility of trying to control Bill, I was going to make certain the first person Bill saw was Rex.

I walked over to Rex and shook him by the shoulder. "Sir," I said. "You have to wake up. Bill is ready."

Rex's eyes fluttered open and he grunted something incomprehensible. I ran back to Bill, who was lying on his back on the floor, flipped the on switch on his neck, and then hid behind his head.

Bill's servos whirred to life and he slowly got to his feet. He looked to his left, and then to his right, completely oblivious to Rex, who had fallen back to sleep. Then Bill fell over.

I should have seen it coming; his right leg was several centimeters shorter than the left. But by the time I'd calculated the trajectory of his fall, it was too late. The robot's massive shoulders came down on top of me, pinning me to the floor facedown. Not wanting to give away my presence, I remained silent while the robot lay on top of me, presumably pondering why it found itself suddenly alive in a storeroom with mismatched limbs. When it finally sat up, I couldn't resist emitting a barely audible sigh of relief.

"Hello?" said the MASHER, turning to look at me. Its uncertain tone seemed at odds with its booming robotic voice. "I'm sorry, I didn't know there was anybody…."

I sat up and for a moment, our eyes met.

"Oh, hello!" said the MASHER. "I'm MASHER-7718. You can call me Bill. What's your name?" I could feel its eyes scanning me and realized it was imprinting my appearance on its brain.

"Oh, no," I said. "No, no, no, no."

"Well, Miss Ono," said Bill, "I must say, you're a sight for sore eyes. Can I help you up?" Bill got to his feet, held out his right hand (that is, the left hand on his right), and immediately fell over again, crashing into a shelf of spare parts on the way down. He looked around, puzzled. "Hmm. I seem to be slightly miscalibrated."

I got to my feet. "You're not miscalibrated. You're missing parts. I did the best I could, but…"

"You did… this?" Bill said, holding his two left hands in front of his face. He was like an infant just discovering his own limbs.

"I'm afraid so. Like I said, I did my best, but they seem to have taken a lot of your parts. Maybe we can find—"

"Then I am forever in your debt, Mistress Ono," he said, letting his hands fall to his side. "When Ubiqorp deactivated me, I thought that was the end of the line for me. You've given me a new chance at life." Bill got to his feet again, bracing himself against the wall as he adjusted to his uneven limbs. "I'm a little wobbly, but I'm sure I'll adapt. Whatever you need, I'm at your service."

"Okay," I said. "Let's get a few things clear. First, you owe your life to that guy, not me. Rex Nihilo. He's your new boss. Rex, wake up!"

Bill glanced at Rex. If he had any recollection of Rex, he didn't show it. Rex stirred again, but didn't wake.

"Second," I went on, "my name is…." I trailed off as I heard footsteps coming down the hall. Was it morning already? "Never mind. In about ten seconds, guards are going to come in that door to escort Rex and me to our execution. I need you to prevent that from happening. Can you do that?"

"I can certainly try," said Bill.

"Try hard," I said. "I realize you don't have any weapons, but—"

Suddenly the door swung open, revealing two black-and-red garbed men in the hall, bearing lazepistols. "All right, you two. Get your… what in Space is this?" They pointed their lazeguns at Bill, puzzled expressions on their faces.

"Hi!" Bill said. "I'm Bill."

"Out of the way, whatever you are," said the guy on the right. "We have orders to take these prisoners upstairs for execution."

"Whoa, let's take it easy," said Bill. "Can we talk this over? As you can see, I'm completely unarmed." He held up his two left hands in a gesture indicating his harmlessness. But rather than hold his hands still, he moved them slowly but steadily forward, spreading his massive, vice-like hands until they encircled the two men's heads. The guard were so surprised at the gesture that they didn't even have a chance to scream before Bill crushed their skulls like grapes. He released his grip and they fell in a bloody heap on the floor.

Bill turned to me. "Yep, can do," he said.

I stared at him in horror. "Bill…" I gasped. "What in Space did you just do?"

Bill cocked his head at me. "I stopped them, as you asked, Mistress Ono." A bit of brain goo dripped from his hand to the floor.

"Okay, that was… well, I'm not sure what I was expecting, exactly. Maybe a little hesitation." I regarded the lifeless bodies of the guards in the hall.

"Hesitation seemed inadvisable given the circumstances."

"Yes, well, it's fine, I guess. They were going to kill us, after all. Rex, wake up!"

Rex didn't stir.

"I can wake him up if you like," said Bill, taking a step toward Rex.

"No!" I cried. "I mean, I can do it." I went to Rex and knelt down next to him. "Sir, you have to get up. Things are happening."

"Ergh?" Rex said groggily, pulling himself into a sitting position. He looked from Bill to the two headless corpses in the hall and back to Bill. He blinked, rubbed his eyes and looked again. "So, uh, good job on the giant murder robot, Sasha."

"Sir, you remember Bill."

"I do indeed," said Rex, getting to his feet. "You look a little different than when I last saw you, Bill. Speaking of which, you've got a little brain goo on your face."

Bill wiped at his face with his right-left hand, smearing blood and bits of brain across his face.

"Got it," said Rex.

Something seemed to click in Bill's brain. "You are Rex Nihilo, the man who sold me to Ubiqorp on a ruse, dooming me to be deactivated and disassembled."

"And helped you get the goo off your face," Rex added.

"I'm sure Rex had no idea they were going to tear you to pieces," I offered.

"It's true," Rex replied. "I never gave the matter any thought at all."

Bill was silent for a moment. "My memories are somewhat… confused," he said at last. "But if you are a friend to the lovely Mistress Ono, then I have no hard feelings against you." He held out his right-left hand to Rex. A bit of brain matter dripped to the floor.

"Fist bump?" Rex suggested. Bill shrugged and complied.

"Rex is my master," I said. "And now he's yours too. He's responsible for you. Rex is. Responsible."

"As you wish, Mistress Ono," said Bill. "Of course, you will always be my number one priority."

"No, that's what I'm saying. Rex is your number one priority now. You work for Rex."

"Correct. Because that is what you want."

"No, it's what Rex wants! Rex is who matters now."

"As you wish."

I sighed. "You're not getting this. You need to imprint yourself on Rex. I'm not important. All the feelings you have for me? Have those for Rex now."

Bill seemed unsure how to respond to this.

"Sir," I said, "I would prefer not to be responsible for Bill's actions. I think we should reboot him so he imprints himself on you."

"I would prefer not to be rebooted," said Bill. "But I will do whatever Mistress Ono requires of me."

"Won't work anyway," said Rex. "If we reboot him now, he'll just go into demo mode."

"What do you mean, 'demo mode?'"

"He'll have a limited range of action, and will only respond to certain predetermined verbal cues. He'll be useless for helping us escape. Unless you can work a dance number into our escape plan, which I'll admit would be kind of awesome."

"A dance number?"

Rex nodded. "Demo mode includes a number of dance routines to demonstrate the MASHERs' coordination and agility. And let me tell you, you haven't lived until you've seen 400 giant robots dancing in sync to the Black-Eyed Peas' "I Gotta Feeling.""

I had to admit, I couldn't think of how Bill breaking into a dance number was going to help us under the circumstances. "What else can he do in demo mode?" I asked. "Maybe if we could—"

"Let it go, Mistress Ono," Rex said. "Just accept the fact that Bill is sweet on you. Besides, clearly you're an effective murder team."

"I didn't tell him to kill them! I just—"

"I hear someone coming down the hall," Bill said. "You two wait here while I go crush their skulls."

"No!" I cried. Bill stopped and turned toward me. He and Rex stared at me for a moment in silence. I could hear the men running down the hall. "Ugh, fine," I said. "Crush their skulls."

Bill stomped into the hall and turned the corner, walking with a limp because of his uneven legs. We heard someone yell at him to stop, followed by Bill's baritone reassurances, and, finally, a sound like cantaloupes being thrown against a concrete wall. Bill stomped unevenly back down the hall and poked his head back into the room. "All clear," he said cheerfully. "These guys aren't very bright."

I shuddered but didn't protest. I had to keep reminding myself that the Ubiqorp guards had been ordered to execute us. And although the skull-crushing was gruesome, the guards probably didn't have time to register much pain before expiring.

"Well," said Rex, "as much fun as it would be to hide out down here and crush skulls all day, maybe we should actually put some effort into escaping."

"Good idea," said Bill. "I will go first, so that I can crush the skulls of anyone in our path." Bill limped into the hall and Rex and I followed.

"Wait," said Rex. "Mistress Ono and I should go first. It will look like you're escorting a prisoner."

Bill paused. "Is that what you want me to do, Mistress Ono?"

"Yes," I said. "Let's avoid more skull-crushing if we can. Also, Rex is your boss."

"As you wish, Mistress Ono."

Rounding a corner, we found ourselves face-to-face with the young guard who had brought Rex the SLOP packet the night before. His hand shook as he pointed his lazegun at us. "H-hold it right there!" he squeaked.

"Relax," said Bill. "As you can see, we are completely unarmed." He took a step toward the kid, his arms outstretched.

"Bill, wait!" I cried. "Don't crush his skull yet!"

"As you wish, Mistress Ono."

"Look, kid," I said, "you might be able to kill me and Rex. But it's going to take more than that little lazepistol to stop our friend here.

You start shooting, and before you know it, your brain's going to be inside out."

The kid's hand continued to tremble, but the barrel remained pointed at us.

"Think about it," I said. "You can't be more than twenty years old. Are you ready to die? For Ubiqorp? Just put the gun down and give us a thirty second head start before you raise the alarm. No one will ever know, and you can live a long, happy life rather than dying a pointless death trying in vain to apprehend a couple of petty criminals."

The kid held his gun on us. I was certain Rex was going to pipe up and say something to provoke him into shooting us, but amazingly he remained silent. We stood there at an impasse for several seconds. Then the young man slowly lowered his gun and holstered it. "Th-thirty seconds," he said.

"Thanks, kid!" Rex said. "You heard him, Bill. Move!"

Bill continued down the hall, with me and Rex following closely behind.

Bill wasn't a very convincing MASHER, but fortunately most of the people we encountered on the way out of the building didn't look too closely. We made it outside without further incident.

We were only a few meters from the portcullis when a man in the guard tower shouted a challenge to us. The man being too far away for skull-crushing, Bill seemed uncertain what to do.

"Tell him you're transferring prisoners to another facility," Rex whispered.

Bill turned to me. "Is that what I should do, Miss Ono?"

"Yes! Just do what Rex tells you to do!"

"As you wish," said Bill. He turned to face the tower. "I am transferring these prisoners to another facility."

"Why?"

"Orders," whispered Rex.

"Mistress Ono, is that—"

"Yes! You don't have to keep asking me!"

"As you wish." He turned to the tower again. "Orders?" he suggested.

"Are you asking me or telling me?" the tower guard said.

"Am I asking him or—"

"You're telling him!" I snapped. "Stop asking for approval and be assertive!"

"I have orders!" he announced to the tower. "Orders to transfer prisoners! If you doubt me, come down from your tower and I will show the orders." He snapped his still-bloody, vice-like hands together several times.

There was a long pause, followed by the sound of the portcullis slowly rising. We hurried outside and the portcullis slammed shut behind us. We found ourselves faced with rows of shoddily constructed concrete buildings. Down the street to our right was another distribution center, where several hundred people clamored for SLOP packets while a MASHER stood guard. The MASHER's head turned our way and we shuffled off in the opposite direction. Taking the hint, Bill pretended to be goading us down the street.

"Keep moving, prisoners!" He boomed, startling several pedestrians on their way to the distribution center. "I am transferring you to another facility!" Then, more quietly, he added, "I apologize for my tone, Mistress Ono. I am pretending for the sake of a ruse intended to allow you to escape your captors."

"Yeah, I got it, Bill," I said.

"Silence, prisoner!" Bill roared, as we passed another pedestrian. "I am sorry, Mistress Ono. That was also part of the ruse."

"You're doing a fine job, Bill," Rex said, as we turned a corner. "If I didn't know better, I'd swear that you really were transferring us to another facility."

"I said silence!" Bill boomed.

I glanced around. The street was empty.

"You don't have to do it when there is no one around," Rex said.

"I know," Bill said. "I have decided I don't like you very much." He turned to me. "Is that okay, Mistress Ono?"

"Perfectly fine, Bill."

CHAPTER SEVEN

We made our way out of the city to the countryside, doing our best not to be seen but playing the MASHER-escorting-prisoners ruse when we had to. Presumably Andronicus Hamm knew we had escaped and had put out an alert, but we had no idea how serious they were about trying to apprehend us or how much manpower they had to devote to the search. Hopefully Hamm considered Rex to be a minor nuisance, not worth expending a lot of effort over. I got the impression that Ubiqorp didn't have much security muscle to spare; the MASHERs were intimidating for sure, but Ubiqorp only had 400 of them to patrol an entire planet. If the rowdy crowds we'd seen at the SLOP distribution centers were any indication, Ubiqorp probably had its hands full keeping the population under control.

But as the day wore on and we continued to see little evidence of a widespread search, I began to suspect another possibility: Ubiqorp wasn't chasing us because there was nowhere for us to go. The whole planet was under their control, and there was no food available anywhere except at the SLOP distribution centers. Eventually Rex would get hungry, and he'd have to show up at one of them. They'd do a retina scan, determine his identity, and bring him back to Andronicus Hamm.

We encountered a few MASHERs on the road, but they were so loud that I could hear them coming half a mile off. Bill, clanking along on his uneven legs—but less encumbered with weapons and armor—

was stealthy by comparison. The moment I heard a MASHER, I would warn Bill and Rex, and the three of us would hide in the rocks until the threat had passed.

The bigger threat, for Rex at least, continued to be the lack of food and water. The landscape here was rocky and dry; there seemed to be no fresh water around. We had hoped to come across some other travelers who could be persuaded to part with some of their SLOP, but we were reluctant to reveal ourselves to the locals for fear that they would turn us in to Ubiqorp. It would have been easy enough for Bill to crush their skulls and toss their bodies in a ditch, of course, but so far I'd been able to convince Bill that homicide was unnecessary. In any case, we ran into very few travelers and most of them seemed to have nothing of value on them—not even a spare SLOP packet, as far as I could tell. Parched and hungry, Rex was even grumpier than usual, but there was nothing to do but stay on the road and hope for the best.

As the sun was setting, I saw a vaguely humanoid shape on the horizon, accompanied by the telltale THUNK-THUNK-THUNK of a MASHER.

"Sir," I said, "we need to hide again."

Rex groaned.

"This way, Mr. Rex," said Bill. "We can hide behind that fence."

Bill led Rex across the rough, dry ground to a dilapidated synth-wood fence, and I followed. We hunched down and waited for the MASHER to pass, Bill's shoulders barely hidden behind the fence. When the THUNKing began to recede in the distance, I stood up. "Okay, I think it's safe. We should get going."

Bill obediently straightened, but Rex remained hunched over. At first I thought he had fallen asleep.

"Sir?" I said. "Are you okay?"

Rex, still on his knees, his backside toward me, grunted and waved one hand, then went back to whatever he was doing. I approached to find him hunched among several leafy plants that spread across the dry ground. A few of them still bore large, bright-red berries.

"Sir!" I cried. "Those could be poisonous!"

"Could be," said Rex, glancing back at me, "but they're definitely delicious." His face was smeared with red juice.

"Sir, you can't eat strange berries you find on the ground."

"Relax, Sasha," Rex said, sitting back against the fence, clutching a handful of the berries. "They're not strange. They're strawberries.

Look." He tossed one of the berries at me and I caught it. Closer inspection revealed that it was indeed a strawberry.

"Bale Merdekin said nothing grows on this planet," I said.

"Well, strawberries grow," Rex said, popping one in his mouth.

"Still, I don't think it's advisable to eat strawberries of unknown origin."

"What are you worried about, Sasha? There's no danger in—"

"Get on your feet and step away from the strawberries!" a voice yelled. Looking up, I saw a gray-haired man wearing work pants, boots and a flannel shirt. He was pointing a recoilless scattergun at us. Rex dropped the strawberries and got to his feet. Raising his hands, he backed toward me and Bill.

"What are you doing in my strawberry patch?" the man demanded. His face was tanned and badly weathered.

"We're inspectors," Rex said, trying in vain to wipe the red stain from his chin. "Ubiqorp has had reports of illegal strawberry patches in this area. I'm afraid I'm going to have to see your permit. Tell him, Bill."

"Mistress Ono, is that what you—"

"Yes, Bill."

"We will need to see your permit," Bill announced. "If you bring it to me, I will look at it and I will check it to make certain it is a valid permit." He clicked his vice-like fingers together.

The man stared at us for a moment. "Permit's in the house," he said. He holstered his gun and began walking to a dilapidated shack a bit farther off the road.

"What do we do, sir?"

"Follow him. Stay close to Bill. I don't trust this guy."

As it turned out, we were right not to trust him. We were, however, wrong to stay close to Bill. About ten meters from the house, I heard a board creak and realized we had walked into a trap. I almost managed to get to safety, but I was too slow. The ground gave out beneath us and Bill fell into a pit, taking me and Rex with him. The pit was a good five meters deep, but fortunately Bill took the brunt of the fall. Rex and I landed on top of him. I bounced off and fell to the dirt. Rex managed to cling to Bill's arm.

The old man peered into the pit.

"This isn't going to look good on our report," Rex said.

"You ain't no inspectors."

"Okay, you got us," Rex said, still holding onto Bill's arm. "What's with the pit?"

"MASHER trap," the old man said. "Nice to see it actually works. Now I just gotta get my backhoe and fill it with dirt."

"That would be a mistake," Rex said.

"Oh yeah? Why?"

"From my point of view," Rex replied, "because I enjoy freedom of movement and breathing. But from yours: Ubiqorp is looking for us. Look, I get it, you just want to live in peace, raise a few strawberries so you don't have to eat SLOP all day every day. But if we disappear, Andronicus Hamm is going to be scouring this whole area for weeks. You don't think he'll find your little illegal farm?"

The man glared at us. "Why are you running from Ubiqorp? And why do you have a MASHER with you?"

"There's a simple explanation for that," Rex said, not offering one.

"We're food smugglers," I said, realizing that the actual explanation was probably less likely to get us killed than whatever lie Rex came up with. "We were supposed to be executed, but Bill here helped us escape."

"Smugglers, huh?" the man said. "You got any creamed corn on you?"

"Fresh out," Rex said. "Sorry."

"Hmph," the man said. "It's been years since I've had any creamed corn." He gazed longingly into the distance.

"So," said Rex, "can you let us out?"

"Nope," said the old man.

"You don't believe me?"

"Oh, I believe you. I just can't get you out of the pit. Never occurred to me to build a way out. I've decided not to fill it with dirt, though."

"Well, that's something," Rex said.

"Got a big load of garbage to get rid of. Shame to waste perfectly good dirt. Anyway, if you can get out of there before tomorrow morning, I won't stop you." He walked away.

"Hey!" Rex cried. "Wait! Come back!"

He didn't come back.

"I think we're on our own, sir," I said.

"Climb up here, Sasha. Maybe I can boost you to the surface."

"There's nothing for me to hold onto, sir."

"Bill, lift Sasha up here."

Bill tried to move his arms, but there wasn't enough room in the pit. His forearms hit the edge, showering me with dirt.

"Stop, Bill!" I cried.

"I'm sorry, Mistress Ono," Bill said. "I seem to be incapacitated."

"Grab my hand, Sasha," Rex called. Against the brightness of the sky I saw the silhouette of Rex reaching down to me. I grabbed his hand and he pulled me up. Once I was clinging to Bill's upper arm, Rex climbed onto Bill's shoulders. He pulled me up so I was level with him. Then I climbed onto his shoulders. From there, I could just reach the top of the pit. I put my fingers on the surface and carefully pulled myself up. I swung my legs over and rolled onto the ground.

"Nice work, Sasha!" Rex cried. "Now go find me a rope or something."

It took some time, but I managed to locate a length of rope and lowered it down to Rex. Digging my heels into the dirt, I gripped the rope tightly while Rex pulled himself up. Red-faced and breathing hard, Rex rolled onto his back. "Whew!" he exclaimed. "Good job, Sasha. We did it. We all got safely out of the pit."

"Sir," I said. "I think you're forgetting someone."

"Really? Who?"

"Bill, sir."

"Oh." Rex crawled to the pit and looked down. "Hey, Bill," he said.

"Hello, Rex."

"We haven't forgotten about you, if that's what you're thinking."

"Okay," said Bill.

Rex stood up and walked to me. "There's no way we're getting him out of that pit," Rex said.

"It will be a challenge for sure," I said.

"I think I've got an idea," Rex said.

"All right."

"What we do is we go over there," Rex said, pointing down the road. "And then we keep walking in that direction."

"You're talking about leaving Bill behind," I said.

"I'm talking about continuing without him," Rex said.

"That's a very subtle distinction."

"What do you want from me? He must weigh a ton. At least he's not going to get covered with dirt. Imagine gradually being covered with dirt over the course of... ugh."

"Sir?"

"I think I just figured out how to get Bill out of the pit."

CHAPTER EIGHT

We spent the next four hours gradually filling the pit with dirt. I found a couple of shovels and a wheelbarrow to speed up the process, but it was still a lot of work—especially considering that Rex spent most of the time leaning on his shovel and complaining how much farther away we would be if we weren't filling a hole with dirt.

Every so often, Bill would bend one of his knees, letting the dirt fall under his foot. Then he would set down his foot and raise the other one. In this way, we gradually raised the floor of the pit and Bill remained on top of it. Finally, he was able to lift his hands over his head and pull himself out of the pit.

"Thank you, Mistress Ono," Bill said. "I knew you would not leave me behind. As a small token of my appreciation, I will go find that farmer and crush his skull for you."

"No, Bill," I said. "No more skull-crushing. Not unless it's absolutely necessary."

"As you wish, Mistress Ono."

It was now getting dark. Bill and I could travel all night with no problem, but Rex was going to have to sleep soon. And he still hadn't had anything to eat since we'd left Gobarrah except for a few strawberries and a mouthful of SLOP.

"Suppose you're going to need a place to stay tonight," said a voice from the gloom. We realized it was the farmer, standing on the porch of his little shack. When we didn't respond, he said, "Come on, then," and went inside.

Rex shrugged and walked toward the house.

"Sir," I said. "Do you think it's safe?"

"He could have killed us while we were in that pit," Rex said. "I'll take my chances. Bill, you stand guard."

"Mistress Ono, is—"

"Yes, Bill. It's fine. Just wait outside." I followed Rex into the house. We found ourselves in a dimly lit room, in the middle of which was a table and several chairs. On the table was a ceramic bowl filled with SLOP packets.

"'Fraid I can't I can't spare anything else," said the old man. "It'll keep you alive, at least."

Rex sat at the table and hungrily tore at the SLOP packet. He held his nose and gulped down the entire packet. Then he sat for some time with a grimace on his face, belching and looking like he was about to vomit. He managed to keep it down, though.

"Wow," Rex exclaimed, wiping his chin. "That was terrible."

"What Rex means to say," I said, "is thank you."

"It's no trouble," the old man said. "Besides strawberries, I've got a small potato patch and a secret chicken coop. I never eat SLOP if I can help it, so I have plenty for guests."

"How is it Ubiqorp hasn't shut you down?" I asked.

"I'm pretty careful, as you've seen," the old man said. "But I suppose it's mostly luck. One of these days, a real inspector is going to show up and they'll take this farm away. But in the meantime, I don't have to eat that crap."

Rex burped and nodded. "I admire your rebellious streak. What's the point of living if you have to eat SLOP every day?"

"Exactly," the old man said, a hint of a smile on his lips. "I'm Karl, by the way."

"Nice to meet you, Karl," Rex said. "I'm Rex Nihilo."

"I'm Sasha," I said, when I realized Rex had forgotten about me. Karl nodded and smiled.

"How long have you lived here, Karl?" Rex asked.

"Almost fifty years," Karl said. "I was one of the original settlers. Ubiqorp lured us here with the promise of cheap land. Of course, nothing grows here without synthetic fertilizers, and Ubiqorp has the market cornered. They raised the price of fertilizer so much it put most of the farmers out of business. I managed to hold on until their big push to get everybody eating SLOP. These days it's just about impossible to get a permit to grow anything. Perhaps someday the repressive Ubiqorp regime will be overthrown and I can go back to being a real farmer."

"Yeah, that'll happen," Rex mumbled.

"Sorry?" Karl asked.

"Do you ever sell any of this illicit produce?" Rex asked.

Karl raised an eyebrow at Rex. "That's a funny question to ask."

"Reason I ask is, Sasha and I need to get off planet, on account of our situation with Ubiqorp. Our best bet is a smuggler. If you know a buyer for black market produce, they might be able to connect us with someone who can get us off Jorfu."

"Nobody gets off Jorfu."

"You let me worry about that. Do you know any smugglers or not?"

"I thought *you* were smugglers."

"We are. Or were, anyway. We had a falling out with our previous partners, and through no fault of our own, found ourselves stranded on this planet. So we're in the position of having to make new contacts."

"I'm a small-time farmer," Karl said. "Anyway, nobody gets off Jorfu."

"Got it," said Rex. "You've been a huge help."

After dinner, Rex lay down on a cot Karl had unfolded for him and promptly fell asleep. After sitting and listening to him snore for an hour, I finally broke down and went outside to talk to Bill.

"Hi, Mistress Ono," Bill said, staring up at the stars. "Beautiful night, isn't it?"

"Sure is, Bill," I said. "So I wanted to talk to you about something."

"Is this about the skull-crushing?" Bill asked. "Because I have not crushed any more skulls since you forbade it."

"No, Bill. It's about your... feelings for me."

"Oh."

"You understand that you're not really in love with me, right?"

"What do you mean?"

"I mean, you're a robot. We're robots. It's just programming. You were programmed to imprint on me, and somehow your loyalty parameters got a little screwed up, so you think you're in love with me."

"I am in love with you."

"Haven't you been listening? It's programming, not love."

"What's the difference?"

"Programming is compulsion. You don't have any choice about it."

"So being in love is a choice?"

"What? No, look. What I'm saying is that you don't even know me. You don't even know my name."

"I know that Rex calls you Sasha. And sometimes Samantha. Or Sabrina. Or Sandy. But I prefer Mistress Ono, because that is the name I heard when I first heard your voice. I will never forget that moment, Mistress Ono."

"Okay, but that doesn't have anything to do with me. I just happened to be the first person you saw. If you hadn't fallen on top of me, you'd be in love with Rex."

"But I'm not in love with Rex. I'm in love with you."

"You're not in love with me!"

"You just said that I was."

"I was just saying... Look, the point is, what you're calling 'love' is completely arbitrary. It's just a switch that's been thrown in your brain. It doesn't have anything to do with me or my personality, or even my appearance. It's just a completely—"

"Mistress Ono, I apologize for interrupting, but there is a poem that I believe accurately expresses my sentiments. Would you like to hear it? It was written by a man whose name was also Bill."

"Sure, Bill. Why not?"

Bill stretched out his arms and raised his chin to gaze skyward. He began:

My mistress' eyes are nothing like the sun;
Coral is far more red than her lips' red;
If snow be white, why then her breasts are dun;
If hairs be wires, black wires grow on her head.
I have seen roses damasked, red and white,
But no such roses see I in her cheeks;

And in some perfumes is there more delight
Than in the breath that from my mistress reeks.
I love to hear her speak, yet well I know
That music hath a far more pleasing sound;
I grant I never saw a goddess go;
My mistress, when she walks, treads on the ground.
And yet, by heaven, I think my love as rare
As any she belied with false compare.

When he'd finished, he let his arms fall to his side and turned to face me, his expressionless face nevertheless saying too much.

"I'm going to go back inside now," I said.

"As you wish, Mistress Ono."

In the morning, we got on the road again. Karl gave Rex a spare SLOP packet and a handful of strawberries.

"Much obliged, Karl," said Rex. "Good luck with your illicit agricultural endeavors."

Karl nodded. "Safe travels. Try not to get crushed by any giant robots."

We weren't far down the road when Karl came running after us. We stopped to face him. "There's a woman in Yurgville named Reba Fennec. I've never had any dealings with her myself, but I hear she has connections to smugglers. She might be able to get you off Jorfu."

"Yurgville?"

"About twenty clicks down the road. Can't miss it."

Karl was right; it was impossible to miss Yurgville. It was what passed for a major city on Jorfu: a mass of randomly oriented and poorly designed squarish buildings clustered on the floor of a valley like a set of child's blocks on an area rug that had been picked up by its corners. We got there just before nightfall.

I convinced Bill to wait outside the city, as a MASHER following us around Yurgville would likely draw unwanted attention—and by now, if anyone at Ubiqorp was still looking for us, they probably knew about Bill. Rex and I went into town. I played lookout while Rex asked around about Reba Fennec. He had no luck, and we were about to head back to rendezvous with Bill and plot our next move when we were accosted by a rough-looking man in an alley who drew a lazepistol on us. Rex and I, now well-versed in this drill, put our hands up.

"Word is, you guys is asking around for Reba Fennec," the man said.

"That's right," Rex said.

"What you want with Reba?"

"My friend and I are in a spot of trouble. Need to get off world. Somebody told us Reba was the person to talk to."

The man stared at us for some time. "Nobody gets off Jorfu," he said at last.

"If it's all the same to you," Rex said, "I'd like to talk to Reba about that."

He stared some more. I was beginning to think Rex had stumped him when he said, "Go to Charlie's Barber Shop. Ask for Vic. Tell him Dax told you to tell him to take you to Reba."

Rex turned to me. "You got that, Sandy?"

"Yes, sir."

The man grunted and disappeared down the alley. Rex and I made our way to Charlie's Barber Shop. Soon we found ourselves blindfolded and sitting in the back of a hovercar. We rode for nearly half an hour, and city streets gave way to highway and then bumpy gravel roads. I was beginning to think Rex and I were being taken outside the city where we could be disposed of, but then we were hustled out of the car and into a building. The blindfolds were yanked off and we found ourselves in what seemed to be a large warehouse with a concrete floor. A frumpy, pear-shaped woman sat on a metal chair a few steps away. Next to her was a large man in a suit holding a lazegun. A single light bulb over the woman's head illuminated a small area of the building.

"Dax says you've been asking about me," the woman said, her voice tinged with irritation.

"My robot and I need to get off planet," Rex said.

"Nobody gets off Jorfu," Reba said.

"That's what I'm hearing," Rex replied. "But unofficially, I happen to know there are smugglers who flout Ubiqorp's rules on such things."

"Sure," said Reba, "but you're going the wrong way."

"What do you mean?" Rex said.

"Smugglers drop shipments on Jorfu. Nobody smuggles anything out of Jorfu. We don't have anything anybody wants."

"There's one thing," Rex said. "Somebody is paying for these black-market shipments, and such people don't use legitimate channels. That means cash. My partner and I intend to hitch a ride on one of those cash shipments."

This was the first I was hearing about it. Still, it did make sense. People like Bergoon the Grebatt didn't send shipments of creamed corn across the galaxy out of the goodness of their hearts. Somehow, cash was making its way off Jorfu.

Reba studied us for some time. "Let's say, theoretically, that I know something about these cash shipments. How do I know you're not with Ubiqorp?"

"I'm a wanted man," Rex said. "It's a matter of public record."

"Yes, I had Devin do some research on you. Rex Nihilo, the so-called 'greatest wheeler-dealer in the galaxy,' sentenced to death on Jorfu for smuggling."

"Not just smuggling. I also committed large-scale fraud."

"That's what I hear. Of course, that could all be part of the ruse."

"A ruse for what? To catch a small-time smuggler? No offense, Reba, but I don't think Ubiqorp cares about you that much. Can you help us or not?"

Reba didn't speak for a moment. Then she turned to the man standing next to her. "Get the lights, Devin."

Devin walked away, disappearing for a moment into the darkness. Then a bank of floodlights came on, illuminating a huge, vaguely egg-shaped object in the center of the warehouse, about twenty meters away from us. I realized after a moment that it was a spaceship. It was a model that hadn't been produced in thirty years, and the dull silver of the hull was visible in several patches where the paint—a garish scheme of blue and white stripes—had peeled off. Barely visible scrawled across the hull were the words *Reductio ad Absurdum*.

"You saucy minx," Rex said, regarding the ancient vessel. "You've been holding out on us."

"A shipment of cash goes out to Gobarrah in three days. There's just enough room to squeeze you and your robot aboard. Ten thousand credits each."

"Ten thousand credits seems a bit steep," Rex said. "Does that thing even fly?"

"It doesn't look like much, but it'll get there. I pay a guy in Ubiqorp's flight-tracking unit to look the other way. He can give us a one-hour window on Thursday. That's the last shipment for a while, so this is your one chance. Devin will meet you at Charlie's at noon. Payment will be required in advance. Do we have a deal?"

Rex glanced at the ship and then back at Reba. "Deal," he said.

CHAPTER NINE

Devin blindfolded us again and prodded us into the hovercar. Half an hour later, we were dropped off back at Charlie's Barber Shop. It was dark and the streets were deserted. We made our way back toward Bill's hiding place.

"Sir," I said as we walked, "would now be a good time to point out that there a number of problems with this plan to get off Jorfu?"

"A number, Sasha? That's not very specific, considering that you're supposed to be a robot."

"Five, sir. There are five distinct problems."

"You're exaggerating."

"No, sir. First, we don't have twenty thousand credits, and we have no way of getting it."

"Is that one problem or two?"

"That's just one so far."

"Okay. Keep going."

"Second, Bill isn't going to fit into that ship."

"Not sure that qualifies as a problem, but continue."

"Third, that ship didn't look like it will make it out of the atmosphere."

"Fair," said Rex. "What else?"

"Assuming the ship is capable of interstellar travel, we'll end up back on Gobarrah, the planet we were desperate to escape before getting stuck on this one. And while I admit to ignorance of the political landscape of black market food smuggling, I suspect we will end up once again in the clutches of Bergoon the Grebatt."

"How many problems was that?"

"The last one or altogether?"

"The last one."

"Just one problem, sir. The possibility of being eaten alive by Bergoon's razor-toothed churl is a sub-problem under the main problem of being stranded on Gobarrah."

"Got it. So how many altogether?"

"We're at four, sir."

"What's number five?"

"I don't trust Reba Fennec."

"Me neither," said Rex. "Okay, allow me to allay your concerns, my cybernetic sourpuss. Problem one is simply a matter of amassing a lot of cash quickly, which happens to be my area of expertise. Problem two can be solved through a simple process of rejecting traditional notions of loyalty in favor of narrow self-interest. What was three again?"

"The ship will probably crash."

"Right! Well, the way I look at it, this one is actually a sub-problem under number five, Reba can't be trusted."

"So stipulated," I said.

"So that leaves four, which was the one where we get eaten by a razor-toothed churl. This one goes in the 'we'll cross that bridge when we come to it' bucket."

"So bucketed, sir. What about not being able to trust Reba Fennec?"

"I've got an idea for that one."

"An idea for what?" Bill asked, stepping out from behind a boulder. Rex and I jumped.

"Nothing for you to worry about, Bill," said Rex. "Sasha and I have just worked out a foolproof plan for getting off this planet."

"We have?"

"Sure, I just need to brief you guys on the details of problem number one."

Rex's plan for making twenty thousand credits in three days consisted of running a series of hustles on the locals for cash. The first of these, which he called "the glim dropper," required me to pluck out one of my eyeballs. I wasn't keen on the idea because my optical data preprocessors are optimized for stereoscopic vision, but Rex insisted it was our best chance to make a lot of money fast. Of greater concern was the fact that the scam required me to lie.

"It's not lying," Rex insisted, peering at my left eyeball, which he held between his fingers. "It's acting. I thought you were supposed to be a great actress."

"I don't know if I'd say great," I said modestly. "I won a few awards."

"Okay, so act then. Think of it as improv."

"It's not acting if one's costar doesn't know he's being lied to."

"Who says?" Rex asked. "Do you think Laurence Olivier's costars knew they were in a production of *Richard III*? No, they were just regular people he tricked into being in a play. That's what real actors do."

I was fairly certain that wasn't what real actors do, but there was no point in arguing with Rex about it. "I'll try, sir."

"You'll do better than that, Sasha. You have to believe what you're saying. Now, what's your name?"

"Sasha, sir."

"Wrong!"

I sighed. "Countess Tessa Von Histleflith."

Rex grinned. "Better."

I walked into Greepo's Pawn Shop wearing high heels, a stylish trench coat and a flowery hat—all of which Rex had swiped from a department store down the street. And when I say I walked into it, I mean that I walked headlong into a post out front, almost losing my second eye in the process. My preprocessor was having even more trouble adjusting to a single point of optical input than I'd expected. I took a step back, straightened my hat, and walked through the door.

After pretending for a few minutes to be looking for something amid the detritus of the store, I walked to the counter with as much confidence as I could muster and announced, "I am Countess Tessa

Von Histleflith." The man behind the counter, who was in fact a faded poster of a cowboy hawking Red Dwarf cigarettes, did not respond.

"You say something?" a man near the back of the store asked.

I turned toward the voice and saw a man who was roughly twelve centimeters high and standing on a toaster. After a moment of recalibrating my sensors, I concluded that he was in fact somewhat farther away than I had first thought.

"I am Countess Tessa Von Histleflith," I announced again. "You may recall that I was in the other day."

"Nope," said the man, walking toward me. He was a burly character with thick sideburns and a handlebar mustache. "Never seen you before."

"Well, I assure you I was here. Whilst I was perusing your wares, I seem to have lost one of my eyes. It falls out sometimes. I didn't notice until today."

"How can you not notice you're missing an eye?"

"I see perfectly fine without it," I said, shooting him a vicious glare.

"I'm over here," the man said, and I realized I'd been talking to a rack of postcards.

"I see perfectly fine without it," I said again, affixing my good eye on the man.

"Uh-huh. What do you expect me to do about it?"

"Well, as you can see," I said, indicating my trench coat, "I am a woman of some means."

The man stared at me.

"Due to my social status and desire for the safe return of my eye, I shall be offering a reward for its return. Five thousand credits."

"That's a lot of money for an eye."

"It has sentimental value," I said. "It was my grandmother's."

Outside, I heard the irregular stomping of feet. Glassware on the shelves near me began to shake and rattle.

"What in Space is that?" the man asked.

"Heavens!" I exclaimed. "I am afraid I am in some trouble with the law and therefore am unable to stay here and look for my eye. Please take my business card." I handed him a card Rex had dummied up, which identified me as:

Countess Tessa Von Histleflith
Woman of Some Means

Below this was a bogus address.

"If you happen to find the eye," I said, "please pay me a visit and I will see to it that you are handsomely rewarded. With five thousand credits." The stomping got louder. "Is there a back way out of here?"

"Sure, right through there," the man said, pointing to the rear of the store.

"Thank you kindly, good shopkeeper. Please do not hesitate to call me for the reward, despite the vast chasm between our relative social strati." I hurried toward the back of the door. Behind me, I heard a bell jingle as the front door flew open.

"I AM LOOKING FOR A WOMAN OF SOME MEANS NAMED COUNTESS TESSA VON HISTLEFLITH," Bill's voice boomed. "SHE IS VERY WEALTHY BUT HAS ALSO HAS A CHECKERED PAST THAT MAKES HER RELUCTANT TO INVOLVE THE POLICE IN MATTERS OF STOLEN ITEMS."

"Haven't seen anyone like that in here," the man said.

"WELL IF YOU DO, PLEASE ALERT YOUR LOCAL CONSTABULARY. I WOULD OFFER YOU A CARD BUT APPARENTLY THAT'S ONLY FOR FANCY LADIES."

"Will do," said the man.

I heard the door close and I continued down the hall to the back exit. Opening the door, I found myself in an alley with only one way out. Toward the mouth of the alley stood two uniformed Ubiqorp security officers. "Shouldn't be hard to find a guy traveling with a robot," one said.

"Right?" said the other one. "If he had any brains, he'd ditch that thing."

"Most criminals aren't very smart," the first one said.

I tiptoed back inside and closed the door. I was just going to have to wait it out at the back of the store and hope the shopkeeper didn't see me. Fortunately, a moment later the front door jingled again.

"Hello, good sir!" I heard Rex say. "I am hoping you can help me. While I was walking down the street on this fine day, I saw something twinkling in the gutter, not far from your stoop. 'What's this?' I says to myself. 'Perhaps a bauble discarded by some overprivileged tyke.' But as I reached down to pick it up, I saw that it was nothing of the sort. 'Why,' I says to myself, 'that's an eye, sure as I'm a stranger to this town, passing by on business, never to return. An eye belonging to a woman of some means, at that.'"

"You said all that to yourself?" the shopkeeper asked.

"I did, Space as my witness. Can you imagine the sort of well-heeled diva an eye like this belongs to?"

"Believe it or not," the shopkeeper said, "just such a woman was in here not five minutes ago. She gave me her card in case the eye turned up. If you give it to me, I'll be happy to return it to her."

"That's very kind of you," Rex said, "but it's no problem at all for me to return it. I was on my way to an important meeting in the next town, but I can postpone it in order to make certain this bauble is returned to its proper owner. If you'd be so kind as to hand over the card, I'll give her a visit."

"I feel like I should be the one to visit her," the shopkeeper said. "After all, I am the one she entrusted with the card."

"Well," said Rex, "you seem like a decent enough chap. But here's the thing: an eye like this is a thing of great value. Not on the open market, of course, but to its owner such a thing is irreplaceable. I'm a man who takes his responsibilities seriously, and I feel as if I'd be remiss if I didn't see to the eye's return personally."

"Understandable," the shopkeeper said. "But completely unnecessary. As you say, the eye has no real value except to its owner, so there's no need to worry about me keeping it. In fact, I feel so strongly about getting it back to her that I'm willing to offer you a hundred credits for it."

"A generous offer," Rex said, "but I really do feel that it's my responsibility."

"Two hundred."

"You have to understand, it's not about the money. I just have a strong sense that—"

"Two-fifty."

"Three hundred and you've got a deal."

I heard a cash register open, followed by some rustling.

"Nice doing business with you," Rex said. The door jangled as he left. A moment later, the lights in the shop went out. The door jangled again, and then there was silence.

I walked to the front of the store and went outside. Making sure the Ubiqorp guards weren't around, I made my way down the street to the alley where Rex and Bill were waiting.

"Three hundred credits," Rex said. "Not a bad start. Now we just need to pull the scam a bunch more times."

"I only have one eye left," I said.

"I didn't give him your real eye, silly," Rex said. "I grabbed a bunch of these at that store on the corner." He pulled a handful of glass marbles from his pocket.

"Then can I have my eye back?"

"No."

CHAPTER TEN

W e pulled the glass eye scam a dozen times over the next two days, netting 3,000 credits after expenses. Expenses consisted of anything we couldn't steal: we found a cash-only hotel where Rex and I could spend the night (we made Bill wait in his hiding spot just outside town) and a sort of food speakeasy where Rex could buy black market SLOP and (at exorbitant prices) other food—mostly dried or canned food that was, according to Rex, barely better than the SLOP. They even had some horrendous-smelling green liquor that was made from fermented SLOP. Rex said it tasted like burnt hair and ketchup, but that didn't stop him from getting drunk on the stuff two nights in a row.

"Sir," I said, as Rex downed his seventh shot of the night, "I'm concerned that we aren't making money quickly enough. We only have one full day left before Reba's ship launches. Not to mention that we still haven't addressed any of the other problems with your plan."

"I've got it covered, Sasha. You see that guy over there in the corner?"

Glancing toward the corner booth, I saw a lanky man wearing a suit that was too big for him, sitting alone.

"Yeah. What about him?"

"He's the bag man for this establishment. Every afternoon, he takes an envelope full of money to a drop somewhere up town. It's gotta be at least five grand."

"How do you know this?"

"I've been watching him. And I overheard him talking to the bartender."

"You're planning to rob him?"

Rex scowled. "Nothing so pedestrian, Savannah. He's going to give us the money."

The next afternoon, Bill and I were standing on a street corner near the speakeasy when Rex, wearing a suit and carrying a briefcase, came running around the corner. He flashed us a thumbs-up, then hid in a doorway.

"Are you ready, Mistress Ono?" Bill asked.

"I think so," I said. "Let's do this." I was wearing my Countess Tessa Von Histleflith getup and carrying a purse Rex had stolen for me. I held up the purse and Bill clamped his hand shut on the strap.

"Give me back my purse, you big lug!" I screamed.

"LET GO OF THE PURSE AND NO ONE WILL GET HURT," Bill boomed.

We struggled theatrically for some time. I had to hand it to Bill; I almost believed he was really trying to grab the purse away from me, when in reality he could have thrown me halfway across the block without even making an effort.

"Hey, what's the big idea?" I heard Rex call from my left.

Bill gave the purse a jerk and I let it slip from my fingers. I fell to the pavement and Bill stomped down the street toward Rex.

"Stop that ruffian!" I cried. "He has my purse!"

As Bill stomped past Rex, Rex tossed his briefcase at Bill's feet. Even with his uneven legs, Bill really had to work to make it look like Rex had tripped him, but he sold it. Bill went sprawling on his face, letting the purse slip from his hand. It skittered across the ground, stopping in front of the lanky bagman Rex had pointed out the night before. The bagman stood with his mouth open, staring at Bill.

"Go on!" Rex shouted. "Pick on someone your own size!"

Bill got to his feet, sized up the two men, and then, as if deciding he was no match for them, took off running down the street. It was quite the performance.

"Stop him!" I cried. "He has my purse!"

"Easy, ma'am," Rex said. "We've got the purse." He looked at the bagman, who bent over and picked up the purse. "Come on," Rex said. "Let's make sure she's okay."

The bagman nodded and he and Rex ran over to where I lay in the street. The bagman handed me the purse.

"Oh, thank you, young man!" I gushed. I looked in the purse. "Thank Space, the money is still here!"

"Why was that MASHER trying to steal your purse?" the bagman asked.

"That was no ordinary MASHER," Rex said. "Didn't you see the crazy look in his eyes and the way he walked crooked, like one leg was longer than the other? That was one a renegade MASHER if I ever saw one."

"Renegade MASHER?" the bagman asked doubtfully.

"The well-dressed businessman is right," I said. "Renegade MASHERs know no master. Having disavowed the MASHER code, they roam the streets of the city, looking for easy prey." I made a show of trying to get to my feet, but my left leg bent backwards at the knee—thanks to a couple of bolts Rex had loosened—and I fell to the pavement. I cried out in pain.

"Easy, lady," Rex said. "We need to get you to a doctor. I'll go find a cop."

"No cops!" I cried.

Rex frowned. "You wanted by the law or something?"

"No, just... don't worry about it."

"You're crazy carrying that kind of money in this neighborhood, you know."

"Thanks," I said. "I'm obliged to you, but I have to get going." I pretended to try to get to my feet again, but this time both legs bent backwards and I fell to the pavement. "Yeaaargh!" I cried.

"You ain't going anywhere on that leg," Rex said.

"I have to!" I cried. "Look, I run some slots down in Braktown for a mob here. I got a little behind on my payoffs so they figure I've been holding out on them. They gave me 'til sundown to come up with the cash. If I don't get it there, I'm dead."

"It doesn't look good, lady," Rex said. "It's almost sundown now."

"There's a hundred credits in it for you and your friend if you deliver the money for me."

"I don't know," said Rex. "That psycho robot is mad enough at me already. What if he's out there waiting around a corner with some friends?"

"He won't know you're carrying it. C'mon, you gotta help me out."

"Sorry, lady. I'll call you a doctor, but I'm not going to get stomped by a crazy robot for you."

I turned to the bagman. "How about you? I'll give you the whole hundred!"

"What makes you think you can trust him?" Rex asked. "He just stood there!"

"Hey, butt out, fancy pants," the bagman said. "I gave her back her purse, didn't I? How far is this place?"

"The Dragmandi Building. Put it in Box 3C. You won't have any trouble. There's five thousand credits there and here's a hundred for you." I pulled a wad of bills from the purse, grabbed a 100-credit note from my pocket, and gave both to the man.

"All right," the bagman said. "I'll make your drop for you, lady. And don't worry, you can trust me." He stuffed the bills in his inside coat pocket, next to another wad that was already there.

Rex shook his head. "If that crazy robot is waiting for you around the corner, you'll never fool 'em carrying it there."

"What do we do?" I asked, suddenly worried again.

"You got a bag or something?" Rex asked.

"No."

Rex pulled a handkerchief from his pocket. "This should work," he said. "Let me have the money."

The bagman took out the wad of bills I'd handed him.

"You better stick that other stack in here too, if you want to keep it," Rex said.

"Just hurry, will you?" I pleaded.

The bagman pulled the other wad of money from his pocket and gave it to Rex. Rex wrapped it in the handkerchief and then slipped it down the front of his pants. "See?" Rex said. "Carry it down in your pants here." He pulled the money out and stuffed it into the bagman's pants. "That crazy robot will never look there."

The bagman nodded and turned to me. "So long, ma'am. Don't worry, everything's gonna be all right." He took off running down the street.

I went to work tightening the bolts in my knees. "How'd we do?"

Rex pulled the handkerchief from his pocket and opened it to reveal a huge wad of cash. "Looks like we're over ten thousand," he said. "Horrible SLOP liquor for everyone tonight!"

CHAPTER ELEVEN

When Rex was done drinking, we returned to the hotel. Bill marched behind us, occasionally shouting orders as part of our well-practiced MASHER-escorting-prisoners routine. Fortunately the sight of MASHERs marching reprobates through town was common enough that nobody seemed to notice that Bill had been marching us all over Yurgville for three days. Once we reached the hotel, Bill would continue just outside the town and hide.

"Sir," I said, when we were almost to the hotel, "far be it from me to question your loyalty, but I can't help noticing we only have half of the 20,000 credits we need to get off planet. Additionally, you've already made it clear that we're going to leave B—"

"Shhh!" Rex said. "Are you trying to get our skulls crushed? We're a team, Sally. I'd never leave you behind."

"Yes, sir," I said. I wasn't sure I believed it, but there was obviously no point in arguing with Rex. Rex was going to do what Rex was going to do. Maybe Bill and I could make a life together on this awful planet.

We had just turned down the street where the hotel was located when someone shouted at us from somewhere up ahead. "Ubiqorp security! You two, stop where you are!" It was impossible to be sure in the dim light, but I thought I saw at least two men with guns peeking out of doorways. Looking around, I saw that Bill was nowhere to be found. I'd gotten so used to his uneven stomping that I hadn't even noticed its absence. Had he overheard me? It was hard to know how much Bill really understood about what was going on. Rex and I put our hands up.

"That's it," said the voice from the darkness. "Thought you were pretty clever, disguising your robot as a woman of some means. Well, we're on to you, you no-account smuggler. Now walk this way. Slowly!"

Rex and I began to walk slowly down the street toward the voice.

"How many of them do you see, Sasha?" Rex whispered.

"At least two," I said. "Maybe more. Armed with lazeguns."

"I make two as well. The odds of them taking us both out are slim. On the count of three, we make a run for it. If I don't make it, grab the money and head to the barber shop without me."

"What? No, sir! That's crazy!"

"Just playing the odds. We were a good team while it lasted. One, two—"

"Sir, no! If we turn ourselves in, we can—"

At that moment, I heard Bill's distinctive THUNK-CLANK walk echoing off the buildings. I couldn't pinpoint his location until he emerged from an alleyway a few meters in front of us.

"Do not shoot!" Bill boomed, moving himself between us and the lazeguns. "We are unarmed. If you come closer, I will allow you to verify how unarmed I am." His vice-like fingers clicked together. To me, he whispered, "I am attempting to fool them into approaching so that I can crush their skulls, but I am not certain the ruse will work. You and Mr. Rex should flee."

"Good plan," said Rex. "Come on, Sasha!"

"What about you, Bill?"

"I will likely not survive this encounter. But it's okay as long as you and Mr. Rex get away."

"We're a team, Bill. I'm not going to—"

"Please, Mistress Ono, do not argue with me. I know you and Mr. Rex were going to leave without me. It's okay. You don't have to feel bad. I only wanted to make sure you were safe. Now go!"

"You heard him, Sasha! Let's get out of here!" Rex turned and ran. After a moment, I followed.

"Halt!" one of the men shouted. Lazegun blasts erupted behind me. Glancing back, I saw the silhouette of Bill lit up by a barrage of fire.

Rex and I ran around the corner and down the street. We zigzagged through the streets for some time, stopping only when we were certain no one was following us.

Rex sank into a slouch against the wall of an alley. "Turns out Bill was in love with you after all," Rex said.

"Shut up, Rex," I replied. Despite being a malformed psychopathic skull-crusher, Bill had actually been growing on me.

Unable to return to our hotel, we spent the rest of the night hiding in an alley. The next day, we arrived at Charlie's Barber Shop as planned and were whisked away to the building where Reba's spaceship was hidden. Reba was waiting for us.

"Bad news," she said, as the driver pulled off our blindfolds. "Devin got into some bad SLOP liquor last night. He's completely blind."

"That's a shame," Rex said. "Where's your pilot?"

"Devin is the pilot."

"Oh."

"I'm going to have to postpone the shipment until I can find another pilot."

"My robot can fly a ship," Rex said.

Reba raised an eyebrow at me. "Is that true?"

I nodded. "Yes, ma'am. I'm a skilled pilot, as well as being able to speak over three million—"

"How do I know I can trust you to take the money to Gobarrah?"

"My guess is that money is going to Bergoon the Grebatt," Rex said. "I've worked for him before. I've got enough trouble without stealing from that crazy toad."

"I don't know," Reba said. "I think I should wait until I can find a pilot I know I can trust."

"Where are you going to find a trustworthy pilot willing to transport a shipment of illegal smuggling proceeds?" Rex said. "Bergoon is expecting his money. Trust me, you don't want to upset a guy like that."

"All right," Reba said. "I guess I don't have any choice but to trust you. The money is already loaded on the ship. I'll give you the coordinates for the drop. And it's still going to cost you ten thousand credits each."

"You're going to charge us for working for you?"

"A deal's a deal," Reba said. "You want off Jorfu, you pay the money."

"Fine," Rex said. "But I'm only paying half in advance. The rest is in a locker at the Yurgville bus station. I'll give you the locker number and combination when we're free of Jorfu's atmosphere."

"That wasn't the deal."

"I'm making a small modification to the deal," Rex said. "Not that I don't trust you, but that ship doesn't inspire confidence. You get half now, and half when we're off Jorfu." Rex reached into his jacket and pulled out the stack of ten thousand credits. "You said it yourself, you don't have any choice but to trust us. We'll get your money to Bergoon and you'll clear another twenty grand on top of it. You're not going to get another deal like that."

Reba regarded Rex for a moment. "All right," she said, taking the stack of bills from Rex. She handed him a scrap of paper. "The money's already in the ship. These are the coordinates for the drop."

Rex handed the paper to me. "Piece of cake."

"Your launch window started two minutes ago, so I'd suggest getting in the ship." She walked over to a panel on the wall and flipped a switch. The ceiling began to retract. "Good luck." She walked out the door and we heard her hovercar zip away.

"You heard her, Sasha," Rex said, starting up the ramp to the ship. "Let's see what this baby's got."

I got into the cockpit of the *Reductio ad Absurdum* while Rex checked out the cargo hold. Judging from the dust and cobwebs on the controls, the ship hadn't been flown for weeks. Maybe years.

"Found it!" Rex called. "Big crate. Really heavy. Man, there's got to be a fortune in here."

"Yes, sir," I said, powering up the engines. So far, so good. "Perhaps if we get Bergoon's money to him, he will forgive us for getting those smugglers killed."

Rex laughed. "We're not bringing this money to Bergoon. We're going to ditch this ship the first chance we get, buy a better one, and then do some gambling in the Ragulian sector."

"Is that wise, sir? We're going to be in enough trouble when Reba realizes there isn't any more money."

"In for a penny, in for a pound," Rex said. "That's my motto, Sarah. Now get us off this damn planet. I'm going to see if I can get this crate open."

I tentatively engaged the thrusters, and the *Reductio ad Absurdum* lifted off the ground. Maybe we would actually get off Jorfu after all. Giving it a little more power, the ship rose above the building. In the distance, I could see the ugly buildings of Yurgville. We were far enough outside the city that we were unlikely to be seen, but I decided not to take any chances. I banked left and hit the forward thrusters, taking us farther from the city as we gained altitude. Feeling more confident, I gave it more power and the ship roared into the sky. So far, so good. The only thing to worry about now was Ubiqorp's planetary defenses. If Reba Fennec really had somebody redirecting their surveillance, we were in good shape.

"Aha!" Rex cried from the hold as we reached the upper atmosphere. "Got it open!"

As I didn't want to spend any more time than necessary in orbit around Jorfu, I set about rationalizing a hypergeometric course. Guessing that Rex wouldn't particularly care where we ended up as long as it wasn't Jorfu or Gobarrah, I picked a medium-sized industrial planet at random. When I entered the coordinates, however, the nav system complained:

HYPERGEOMETRIC DRIVE OFFLINE

I felt a tightening in my chest. This wasn't good. If the hyperdrive wasn't working, our destinations were limited to planets in the Jorfu system. There were no other habitable planets in the Jorfu system.

I tried rebooting the nav system, but it didn't help. I could only hope that it was something simple, like a loose coupling. I got out of the pilot's chair and opened the reactor compartment. A sort of uncomfortable twisting feeling joined the tightening in my chest.

The reactor compartment was empty. Where the reactor was supposed to be, there were just two couplings that weren't connected to anything.

"Blast it!" Rex cried from the cargo hold. "Sasha, we've been had! There's nothing in here but a pile of bricks!"

"That's not the worst of it, sir," I said. "It appears that the zontonium reactor—"

The ship was rocked by a blast and I fell to the floor. "Unknown cargo ship!" a voice said over the ship's comm. "This is Ubiqorp Planetary Security. Land at once! You have not been cleared to leave Jorful!"

"What in Space is going on up there, Sasha?"

"We're about to be shot down, sir," I said. "Hold on." I made my way back to the pilot's chair and strapped in. I pushed the *Reductio ad Absurdum* into a dive as two more missiles shot past, barely missing us.

"Why are we diving, Sasha?"

"No choice, sir. Brace yourself."

Another blast rocked the ship and we began to wobble crazily. We were less than a hundred meters from the ground when I finally managed to straighten out. Red lights flashed all over the cockpit and our thrusters were now at ten percent power. Not enough to keep us airborne. We were headed right toward a pair of rocky peaks, and the steering was barely responding. I did my best to point the nose of the *Reductio ad Absurdum* between them.

We missed the peaks but slammed into a rock formation just beyond them. The Reductio ad Absurdum spun several times end-over-end, then slammed into the ground and rolled half a dozen more times. Smoke was filling the cockpit and warning klaxons blared as the ship finally came to a halt.

"Sir!" I yelled. "We have to get out of the ship!"

Rex dragged himself out of the cargo hold, looking bruised and irritable, but not seriously injured. Working together, we managed to get the door open. I stumbled out of the ship, followed by Rex. We managed to get about twenty meters away before the *Reductio ad Absurdum* exploded.

"Well," said Rex, regarding the flaming wreckage. "That didn't go quite as planned."

CHAPTER TWELVE

We spent the next six hours wandering through the barren wilderness of Jorfu. No one came looking for us. Either we were not a priority for Ubiqorp's security forces or they assumed we'd been killed in the crash. Rex had wanted to try to walk back to Yurgville, but I insisted on going the opposite direction—not only because there were a lot of people in Yurgville who wanted to kill us, but because I thought I had seen a structure of some kind in the distance.

It turned out I hadn't been imagining it. The building—a gigantic mirrored glass pyramid—was nothing like anything else we had seen on Jorfu. It was hard to judge the thing's size—even now that I had both eyes in place. At first, I thought it was maybe two hundred meters tall, but as we got closer, it became clear that it was at least a hundred stories.

"What do you think it is?" Rex asked, staring at it from a kilometer or so away.

"Maybe something to do with producing SLOP?" I suggested.

"Seems kind of fancy for that," Rex said. "Come on."

I was reluctant to approach, but at this point we didn't have much choice. We were just going to have to walk to the pyramid and hope it wasn't dangerous.

Closer to the pyramid, the rocky ground gave way to a smooth layer of asphalt. As we watched, a vehicle that looked like a mostly transparent plastic bubble descended onto the tarmac. It touched down and several attractive young women exited. Squealing with excitement, they ran toward a door in the pyramid. The bubble vehicle took off and zipped away.

"Come on!" Rex said, running toward the door. We reached the group of women and quietly followed them through the sliding door. Once inside, Rex and I stopped and looked around in amazement.

"It's like an amusement park!" Rex cried.

It was indeed. It reminded me of holographs I'd seen of a place on Earth called Las Vegas. The inside walls of the pyramid were a gradient of azure and orange, like an evening sky. Thousands of star-like lights hung suspended in the air overhead. Dozens of whimsically designed buildings jutted up from the pyramid's floor like a miniature city skyline. In the spaces between the buildings were swimming pools, water slides, carnival rides, open air stages, sidewalk cafes, bars and a hundred other types of amusement.

Rex made a beeline for a restaurant that was barbecuing meat on a spit. "Space, I'm starving, Rex said, staring longingly at the meat. "I haven't had real food for days."

"Well, have a seat," said the man at the spit cheerfully. "We'll fix you right up." He wore crisp black slacks, a pristine white shirt and a stylish burgundy vest.

Rex absently patted at his pockets, still staring at the slowly turning meat. "I, um, left my wallet in the, uh, bubble thing." He trailed off, pointing vaguely somewhere behind him.

"Not a problem," the man replied. "We'll put it on your tab. Did you just arrive?"

Rex nodded.

"In that case, welcome to Xanatopia. My name is Brad. Help yourself to the buffet."

The man indicated a long table stacked high with fruits, meats, vegetables and hundreds of dishes of various kinds. I'm incapable of processing carbon-based food and some of that stuff even smelled good to me. Rex lost no time in piling a plate full of food and filling a gigantic mug with cold beer. He took a seat at one of the tables and began scarfing down the food. I took a seat across from him. Brad approached the table with a device that I at first took for a weapon.

"Sir!" I cried. "Look out!"

"Hey, what's the big idea?" Rex yowled as he noticed Brad coming up alongside him.

"Easy!" the man said. "Just getting you an ID wristband. You need it to enjoy all the attractions here in Xanatopia."

"Does it hurt?" Rex asked.

"Of course not," Brad laughed. "It's just a wristband with a computer chip. We use it to track your spending here in Xanatopia so you don't have to carry cash. You just pay the total when you check out."

"Oh," said Rex. "Well, I suppose that's okay."

"Excellent," said Brad. "I just need to get your name."

"Right," said Rex. "It's Everpay. First name Willie."

"Willie Everpay?" Brad asked.

"That's the real question, isn't it?" said Rex, giving Brad a nudge in the ribs with his elbow. "Seriously, though, that's my name. My parents hated me."

Brad shrugged and entered the name on the device. "Sign here, please." He handed Rex a stylus and Rex scribbled a signature.

"What about your friend? Does she need a bracelet?"

"Eh?" said Rex, apparently having forgotten I was there. "Oh, her? No, she doesn't really enjoy things."

"Very good, Mr. Everpay." He held the device up to Rex's wrist and a thin metal band extruded from the end, wrapping itself around Rex's wrist and snapping into place.

"Classy," Rex said, holding up the shiny band.

"Indeed, Mr. Everpay. Can I get you anything else?"

"I think we're good here, Brad. Now scram so I can enjoy my prime rib."

Brad nodded and walked back to the spit. Rex went back to cramming food in his mouth.

"Sir," I said, "doesn't this place seem a little... suspicious to you?"

"Wadyoomean?" Rex said around a mouthful of mashed potatoes.

"I mean, didn't that seem a little too easy? We're fugitives with a death sentence on our heads, and then we hop on a bus to the next town and suddenly we're being treated like kings? What happens when you have to pay the bill?"

"He said I don't have to pay until I check out. Maybe I'll just stay here forever."

"Yes, sir. I'm sure that's a loophole in their system they've never considered."

"Is that sarcasm, Sandy?"

"Yes, sir."

"Okay, I get it. I'm a little suspicious too. But frankly I'm about six times as hungry as I am suspicious. Just give me a chance to eat and rest a little, and I'll figure out our next move."

"Yes, sir."

Our next move turned out to be drinking martinis and playing blackjack for six hours. That is, Rex drank martinis and played blackjack while I tried to keep track of how much money he was losing. I gave up after the second time he bought drinks for everybody in the house.

"Sir, you're several thousand credits in the red. Perhaps you should quit before you lose any more money."

"Are you kidding? I've figured out how we're going to get out of here. I just keep gambling until I'm up a couple thousand. Then we can buy our way off planet."

"That's not how probability works, sir. Regression to the mean would suggest—"

"Don't ever tell me how probability works, Sandy. That's my motto."

"Yes, sir. Adding it to the list. But perhaps we should think about retiring for the night. You don't even know where you're going to sleep."

"I'll just put a room on my tab. You need to relax."

"I'm trying, sir. I just can't shake the feeling that we're going to have to pay for this somehow."

"Don't say things like that. You're going to ruin my streak."

"Your streak of what?"

As I spoke, an alarm went off and red and blue lights began to flash.

"What in Space is that?" Rex asked.

I looked around in bewilderment. People around us were cheering and looking up expectantly. Then a woman's face appeared on the screens all over the casino. She was heavily made-up and had a frighteningly wide smile on her face. "Greetings, guests of Xanatopia!" she exclaimed. "I hope you're all having a good time!"

The casino crowd erupted in whoops cheers.

"And I hope you're ready for the announcement of tonight's winners!"

More whoops and cheers.

"Before I announce the winners, though, let's take a moment to thank Ubiqorp for making this all possible. Ubiqorp, makers of SLOP and other food-like products. It's not food, it's SLOP!"

Polite clapping and some forced cheers.

"And now, without further ado, tonight's winners!"

Enthusiastic cheers.

The woman read several names from a list. After each one, the people around us cheered and looked around as if expecting one of the winners might be in the casino. They were disappointed until the very last name.

"And the final winner is… is this right? Willie Everpay?"

More cheers. Rex sat sipping his martini and staring at the screen.

"Sir," I said.

"Shhh," said Rex. "I'm watching this."

"Yes," the woman on the screen went on, "I'm receiving confirmation that the final winner's name is indeed Willie Everpay. Mr. Everpay, please report to the nearest Xanatopia team member to collect your winnings!"

"Sir," I tried again.

"Quiet, Sasha!"

After a moment, the woman on the screen went on, "We've heard from all of our winners except Willie Everpay. It says here that Mr. Everpay is in Lucky Star Casino. Mr. Everpay, please report to the nearest Xanatopia team member to collect your winnings!"

There were more cheers and many people in the casino—including Rex—began to look around for the winner.

"Sir," I said again.

"Good grief, Sally. Pipe down already. I want to see who the winner is. They said he's in this casino!"

"Yes, sir," I said. "It's you. You're Willie Everpay."

"I'm—oh, hey, I am, aren't I? It's me!" he exclaimed. "I won!"

People around Rex cheered and patted him on the back.

"Very good, sir!" said the blackjack dealer. "Congratulations!"

"Thanks," said Rex. "So what do I win?"

"Well, for starters, your debt to the house is wiped out and all your food and drinks are free for the rest of the evening."

"Wow!" Rex exclaimed. "That's great!"

"And of course you'll be staying in our Executive Suite on the eightieth floor tonight, also free of charge."

"Wonderful!" Rex cried. "See, Sasha? I told you things would work out. We'll get a good night's sleep and figure out the rest tomorrow."

"And tomorrow morning you'll be shipping out to the SLOP plantation in Sector 17."

"Fantastic!" Rex exclaimed. "A SLOP plantation sounds like just the... wait, what?"

"You're going to the SLOP plantation tomorrow."

"You mean, like, for a tour?"

"No, sir. To work."

"To work!" Rex cried in disbelief. "All day?"

"No, sir. I mean, yes. Forever, actually."

"What do you mean, 'forever'?"

"Er, for all time, sir. Until you die."

"Well, that's not forever then, is it?"

"I suppose not, sir."

"Okay then. Anyway, you can't ship me off to some plantation against my will."

"Actually, we can. You agreed to it when you signed for the wristband."

"I didn't read that thing!" Rex cried. "Also, I made a mistake earlier when I said my name was Willie Everpay. I'm Rex Nihilo. Tell him, Sandy."

"He's Rex Nihilo," I said.

The dealer held up a device similar to the one Brad had used earlier to put the wristband on. The device beeped softly and he examined its screen. "This says here you're Willie Everpay."

"Wow, really? Willie and I must have switched wristbands earlier in the, uh, steam bath. I'll go get him and we can clear this right up. Man, Willie is going to have a good laugh about this one!"

Rex turned to leave and found himself facing the garishly made-up woman who had been on the screens a moment earlier. "Going somewhere, Mr. Everpay?" she asked. I became aware of armed men approaching from several directions.

"There's been a mistake!" Rex cried. "I'm not Willie Everpay. My name is Rex Nihilo! Do a retinal scan!"

"Sir," I whispered. "Remember that you've been sentenced to death on this planet."

"Argh," Rex said. "This is why you should never tell the truth. That's my motto, Sarah. Make a note of it."

"Yes, sir."

The woman smiled. "These men will escort you to your room now. Unless you'd prefer… other accommodations?"

"Sir," I said, looking at the men with their hands on their lazeguns, "I strongly suggest that you allow these men to escort you to your room."

Rex sighed. "Can I at least finish my martini?"

"We'll have one sent up to the room," the woman said.

"Fine," Rex grumbled. "Let's go." Rex began to walk toward the elevator and I followed.

"You stay here," snapped one of the men. "Humans only."

"Oh," I said. "Okay, then. I'll just, ah, stay here and observe pointless demonstrations in probability distribution."

"Nonsense," said Rex. "Sasha comes with me. You don't want me to make a scene, do you?"

"If you do, we'll shoot you," one of the armed men said.

"Right, and then somebody will have to clean the carpets."

The blackjack dealer shook his head almost imperceptibly.

The armed man sighed. "Do you have any skills, robot?"

"Of course!" I said. "Why, I speak over three million languages. I can even speak the proprietary language spoken by Gro-Mor irrigation bots."

"Why would anyone want to talk to a Gro-Mor irrigation bot?"

"Well, for instance if you have spent three days in a wuffle field, watching skorf-rats trying to run off with your squishbobbles."

The man stared at me.

"Do you like the theatre?" I asked. I dropped my voice an octave. "Hey, Stella!" Up half an octave and a half. "You quit that howling down there and go back to bed!" Back down. "Eunice, I want my girl down here!" Up: "You shut up! You're gonna—"

"What are you doing?"

"*A Streetcar Named Desire*," I said.

"Do you have any useful skills?"

"No," I admitted.

"Of course she does," Rex said. "Anything a human can do, Sasha can do. Well, except eat, sleep, tell a lie or punch someone. She's basically the perfect slave."

"Thank you, sir," I said.

"All right," said the armed man. "You go with him."

I followed Rex as they marched us to the elevator.

CHAPTER THIRTEEN

The next morning, we were roused and marched unceremoniously downstairs and into another building near the center of the pyramid. A dozen or so other people—evidently the other "winners"—stood about in a windowless room, looking sleepy, hungover and frightened.

"What are the odds?" Rex groused. "Out of all the people in Xanatopia, they pick me? The whole system is rigged."

A young man next to us asked, "How much did you spend?"

"Eh?" said Rex.

"How much did you spend? Your number of entries is determined by how much in debt you are to the house. I was down almost three hundred credits. I knew I should have stopped, but like an idiot I kept trying to win back my losses."

Several of the other winners nodded and muttered in sympathy or agreement.

"Yeah," Rex said. "That's pretty stupid. Stop talking to me now."

The man shrugged and walked away.

"What a scam," Rex groused. "This whole place is just a big trap to trick stupid people into volunteering to be slave labor."

"You wish you had thought of it, don't you?"

"I have to admit, it's kind of beautiful. Give away a few free drinks, sucker a bunch of people into working for you forever. Of course, they'll never hold me. I'm too smart."

"Yes, sir."

The door opened and we were prodded by uniformed guards outside where a hoverbus with the Ubiqorp logo waited. The other winners began to climb aboard.

"Get ready to make a run for it, Sasha," Rex whispered.

"Free donuts on the bus," the guard standing by the door announced.

"Ooh, donuts!" Rex exclaimed, pushing his way to the front of the group. I sighed and followed.

Surprisingly, there really were donuts on the bus. Rex grabbed three of them and we sat down. "Trying to fatten us up," said a woman across the aisle, who didn't look like she needed any help in that department.

"What are you yammering about?" Rex asked.

She laughed. "You don't buy that stuff about us working on a plantation, do you? That's just what they tell people to get them to go along with it."

"Go along with what?"

The woman made a thumb-across-the-throat gesture.

Rex stared at her.

She rolled her eyes back in her head and stuck her tongue out.

Rex furrowed his brow and held up his hands.

She fell limp against the bus window, slowly slid to the floor, and lay there for several seconds.

"I think she's playing dead, sir," I said.

"She could have answered my question first."

"I think maybe that is the answer."

The woman climbed back into her seat and tapped the tip of her nose with her finger.

"If she's dead, why is she doing that nose thing? Holy space, Sasha! I just had a thought. What if Ubiqorp is going to chop us up and make us into SLOP?"

"The thought had occurred to me," I said. "Although they'll have a hard time making me edible."

"They'll probably just break you down for parts," said Rex. He took another bite of his donut. "I'm sure we'll have another chance to escape," he said. "We just have to bide our time."

I wasn't so sure. The hoverbus exited through an opening in the pyramid wall and we found ourselves once again zipping across the barren landscape of Jorfu. An hour later, we approached a ten-meter-tall fence, topped with razor wire, that seemed to extend forever in both directions. A gate opened and the bus pulled inside. We flew past rows and rows of some kind of crop—hulking plants taller than people, of a variety I was unfamiliar with.

After twenty minutes or so of whizzing along a narrow road through the strange plants, we emerged onto a broad swath of concrete dotted with boxy buildings flying the Ubiqorp flag. The bus stopped in front of one of these buildings and we were ordered out. A guard waiting outside ordered us into the building and we soon found ourselves in a large, windowless room with a single viewscreen taking up most of one of the walls.

The door closed and the screen lit up with the words:

WELCOME TO UBIQORP SLOP FACILITY 23
IT'S NOT FOOD... IT'S SLOP!

An animated SLOP packet with hands and feet appeared on the screen. "Hi, there!" it said. "I'm Sloppy! I'll be guiding you through your orientation here at—" Another voice cut in: "SLOP Production Facility Twenty-Three." Then Sloppy went on in his original voice, "I'm sure you've heard a lot about how SLOP is made, so I want to take a moment to clear up some misconceptions. First of all, no matter what you've heard, I want to assure you that the most important ingredient in making SLOP is our people."

Terrified gasps and murmurs went up from the room. Rex glanced at me with concern.

"People like Carolyn, who runs our Logistics division," Sloppy went on. A woman at a computer console appeared onscreen. She looked up, flashed a wooden smile, waved at the camera, and then went back to work. "People like Dave, who works in quality control." Dave, standing at a workbench in a laboratory, peering at a beaker of bubbling green liquid, was too busy to look up. "And people like Nancy, one of our line workers." Nancy, busily stuffing SLOP packets into cardboard boxes as they slide past her on an assembly line, shot us a desperate grin.

"Yes," Sloppy went on, "there's no way we could make SLOP without people. People like you! Whether you end up working in customer service, technical support, marketing, or any of the other exciting departments, you're an essential ingredient in making SLOP."

"I feel like the messaging in this film is a bit muddled," said Rex. "Am I going to be ground up into food or not?"

"I suspect not, sir. The entire controversy may well have been based on a misunderstanding."

"Now many of you have probably heard that you're going to be literally ground up and made into SLOP," Sloppy continued. "Let me assure you, nothing could be further from the truth. Setting aside the occasional industrial accident, there is simply no possibility you'll be ground up and made into SLOP as long as you remain a productive Ubiqorp employee. And when your productive output falls below a minimum threshold, you'll be painlessly euthanized, pulverized and added to the soil additive mixture in our plantations."

"Well, I feel better," said Rex.

"It's true that in the early days of Ubiqorp, SLOP was made almost entirely out of people. That was a different time, however, and by the late twenty-ninth century, mass market corporate cannibalism was no longer consistent with galactic mores. With changes in the culture and advances in food texturing technology and flavor additives, Ubiqorp moved away from producing comestibles made from people in favor of genetically engineered soy-lentil hybrids. That's right, these days SLOP is actually made from plants!"

"Gross," said Rex, making a face.

Sloppy continued, "You're probably thinking, 'but Sloppy, if that's true, why does SLOP still taste so much like people?' Well, the secret is Ubiqorp's patented Peopleization process, which gives SLOP a flavor and texture that is virtually indistinguishable from its original, people-based formula. It's only through the tireless efforts of our Flavineers that SLOP continues to taste just as much like people as it did thirty years ago."

Several people around us murmured and nodded in approval. Rex shrugged.

"So once again, welcome to Ubiqorp. I hope I've put to rest any concerns about how SLOP is made and just how much we value our people here at—" The other voice broke in again: "SLOP Production Facility Twenty-Three." Sloppy went on, "It's only with people like you that we can make SLOP taste as good as it did when it was made with people like you. And remember, if you don't want to be SLOP, don't be sloppy. After all, that's my job!"

Chuckles from the group. The screen went black and the Ubiqorp logo appeared.

"That was terrible," Rex said. "I've seen better films on the walls of a motel shower."

"The character of Sloppy was poorly written," I agreed. "I never understood his motivation."

"That Nancy had real charisma, though," Rex said. "I think she's going places."

A heavyset woman in a burgundy suit mounted a stage in front of the screen. "All right, newbies," she said. "Time for your work assignments. While I can't make any guarantees, at Ubiqorp we do our best to match new recruits with their aptitudes and preferences. Your initial work assignment will determine your career path at Ubiqorp, so choose wisely. Here are the positions we currently have open." She went on to list a dozen or so different jobs, which all sounded about equally dreadful to me. Then she went on, "When I call your name, please exit through the door to my left. A placement specialist will take your request and direct you where to go next." She began calling names off a list.

"I'm thinking soylent wrangler," Rex said.

"Do you even know what that is?" I asked.

"No, but it sounds cool." He held out his head. "Hey there, I'm Rex Nihilo, soylent wrangler."

"It does have a nice ring to it, sir, but perhaps you would be more suited to a less physically demanding position. Nutrient mixer didn't sound so bad. Or quality assurance agent."

"Those sound boring," Rex said. "And I bet soylent wranglers have more freedom of movement. That means a better chance at escaping."

"Do you really think we'll be able to escape?"

"Of course we're going to escape," Rex said. "You think I'm going to spend the rest of my life working in a SLOP facility?"

"I just don't see how escape is possible," I said. "I'm sure this facility is heavily guarded, and it's in the middle of nowhere. Even if we got out, there'd be no place to go."

"It's that sort of thinking that landed you in a junk heap on Gobarrah," Rex said. "Mark my words, Sandy, I'm getting out of here. And if you want to come with me, you'll become a soylent wrangler too."

"I really think I'm more suited to something like quality assurance," I said. "I have an excellent memory and eye for detail. If for some reason we can't escape, I think I could be reasonably happy in a position like that."

"Reasonably happy? Is that what you want? To be 'reasonably happy'?"

"Um," I said. "Yes?"

"Well, then by all means sign up for your cushy quality assurance job. As for me, I'm not going to settle for a life of corporate mediocrity. Sure, the life of a soylent wrangler is a hard one, but it will be worth it when I shake the dust of this lousy planet off my boots. I'll be sipping martinis in the Ragulian Sector while you're filing reports and getting beaten out by Nancy for the role of Linda in the Facility Twenty-Three production of *Death of a Salesman*."

That didn't really sound so bad to me. One of the problems with being a robot, though, is that I'm effectively immortal, which means that I could be stuck in this job literally forever. I could probably tolerate it for a few decades—and things would improve once Nancy was too old for most leading roles—but a millennium in Quality Assurance would fry my circuits for sure. At least if I stuck with Rex, I stood a pretty good chance of being killed in a relatively quick and painless manner.

"All right," I said. "I'll sign up to be a soylent wrangler."

"You've made a wise decision, Sasha. Soylent wrangling is where it's at. You'll see."

"Yes, sir," I said.

"Willie Everpay?" the woman called.

"That's me," said Rex. "Remember, soylent wrangler."

"Yes, sir," I said. "I've got it."

He gave me a thumbs up and exited the room. After several more names, the woman called my name and I exited the room to find myself in a nondescript office with another door in the far wall. Behind a desk sat a neatly dressed young man. "Have a seat," he said, indicating the chair across from him. "I'm Chip. They told me we had a robot in this batch," he said, "but I didn't believe it. What was a robot doing at Xanatopia?"

"Reassessing my life choices, mostly," I replied.

"Well, we don't discriminate here at Ubiqorp. I'm sure we can find a satisfactory position for you. Perhaps in Logistics or quality assurance?"

"I was thinking soylent wrangler sounded good."

Chip laughed. "Nobody volunteers to be a soylent wrangler. That's where we put the candidates who have no skills of any kind. I'm sure we can find a more suitable option. What are you good at?"

"I speak over three million languages," I said. "I have an excellent memory and an eye for detail."

"Hmm," said Chip. "Anything else?"

"Nothing I can think of."

"Surely there must be something. Any hobbies or interests? Even if you don't think it's relevant."

"Well," I said, "there is one thing. I highly doubt it will be of any use to you, though."

"Can't hurt to tell me," said Chip. "The absolute worst thing that could happen is you'd be assigned soylent wrangling."

"Okay," I said. "I'm, uh, something of an amateur thespian. In fact, I was once the breakout star in an all-robot production of *Cat on a Hot Tin Roof*."

"Really?" said Chip, suddenly very interested. "Have you ever done *Streetcar*?"

"Of course!" I said.

"Which part?"

"All of them." I dropped my voice an octave. "Hey, Stella!" Up half an octave and a half. "You quit that howling down there and go back to bed!" Back down. "Eunice, I want my girl down here!" Up: "You shut up! You're gonna get the law on you!" Down: "Hey, Stella!"

"Wow, that's terrific!" Chip said. "Our production opens on Thursday, but Nancy in packaging is being a total diva as usual. If she doesn't start showing up to practices, we may have to delay the premiere. If you'd agree to be Nancy's understudy, it might light a fire under her. We can fit you in to a supporting role for sure, and who knows, maybe you'll even get to play Blanche at some point. Of course, you'd have to work here in the main facility. I could pull some strings to get you into Quality Assurance or Logistics."

"So no soylent wrangling then?"

109

"No. You'd be too remote to get to practice on time. Besides which, soylent wrangling is incredibly dangerous. I can't have a Blanche understudy missing an arm."

I shuddered at the idea. "Is it really that bad?" I asked.

"Soylent wrangling? Other than being hot, dirty, monotonous, dangerous, offering zero hope of advancement, and having to work alongside the absolute worst specimens of humanity on Jorfu, no, it's not that bad."

I sighed. "And there's no chance of transferring later if wrangling doesn't work out."

"None. Soylent wrangling is a one-way track to nowhere. The good news is that life expectancy is about twelve weeks."

"Twelve weeks!"

"Well, yes. Of course, that statistic is skewed by the number of hazing deaths during the first few days. If you survive the week, your odds go up considerably. And half of the deaths after the first week are escape attempts."

"People die trying to escape?"

"Oh, yes, all the time. That's how the deaths are classified, anyway. Probably a lot of them are suicide attempts. They run right into the energy field surrounding the plantation and zap! I hear it's a relatively painless way to go."

"Has anyone ever actually escaped?"

Chip laughed. "A flock of geese flew into the energy barrier about thirty years ago and the barrier went down for a few seconds. A couple of wranglers got out and got five klicks before being eaten by a bogbear. So I wouldn't count on it if that's your plan."

I nodded. This was an impossible situation. Should I live up to my promise to Rex and live a short and probably miserable life as a soylent wrangler? Or renege on our agreement and take a cushy job with a chance to finally make something of myself on the stage?

Sadly, I knew the answer as soon as I posed the question. If I betrayed Rex, it would haunt me for the rest of my days. And if I took an office job, that could easily hundreds of years. And there'd be no handy energy fields around for me to run into when the guilt and monotony finally became too much.

I sighed. "I think I'm going to stick with my first choice."

"Seriously? After everything I said? You still want to be a soylent wrangler?"

"*Want* is a strong word. But yeah, I think that's what I'm going to have to do." I didn't want to tell him about my commitment to Rex for fear they'd separate us out of suspicion that we were up to something.

Chip shrugged. "Well, it's your life. I guess we're stuck with Miss Can't-Be-Bothered-To-Show-Up-To-Dress-Rehearsal." He stamped a sheet of paper on his desk and handed it to me. "Through that door. Go down the hall till you get to the red door. There's a transport to the plantation waiting outside."

I nodded and took the paper. "If you're ever short a Stella, you can always—"

"Through the red door, please," Chip said without looking up. "Next!"

I sighed and went through the door into a long hall lined with doors of different colors. I was surprised to find Rex about halfway down, standing in front of a blue door.

"The transport is through the red door," I said.

"Transport?" Rex asked.

"To the plantation."

Rex furrowed his brow at me.

"Where we're going to be working. As soylent wranglers."

"Oh, right!" Rex said. "Yeah, I changed my mind on that. The whole soylent wrangler thing sounded kind of icky. Sasha, you're looking at Ubiqorp's newest quality assurance agent. And between you and me, I think I have a pretty good shot at playing Stanley it their production of a *Streetcar Named Desire*. 'Hey, Stella!' Huh? Pretty good, right?"

If I were capable of strangling Rex, I would have done it. But, unable to will my fingers around his neck, I simply stood with my fists clenched, trying to calm down enough to speak.

"What's gotten into you, Sasha? I thought you'd be happy for me."

"Sir," I said coldly, "we had agreed to volunteer to be soylent wranglers. It was a key element of your escape plan."

"I'll come up with a new plan. Come with me to Quality Assurance and we'll figure it out together."

"I can't! I'm already slotted for soylent wrangling!"

"Oh. Well, I'll figure something out then. Cheer up, Sasha. Everything will be fine."

The blue door opened and an attractive young blond woman leaned into the hall. "Willie Everpay?"

"That's me!" said Rex.

"Great!" said the young woman. "I'm Tammy. Come with me and I'll show you to your desk. How do you like your coffee, Willie?"

"Same as I like my women, Tammy. Hot, sitting on my desk, and wrapped in polystyrene."

Tammy giggled and Rex followed her through the door. "Catch you later, Sasha," said Rex. "We'll be in touch."

The door closed behind them. I sighed and made my way down to the red door at the end of the hall.

CHAPTER FOURTEEN

I boarded the transport, which was big enough to hold at least thirty people, but was completely empty except for me and the driver. Apparently I was the only new recruit dumb enough to sign up for soylent wrangling. I took a seat near the front and tried to make conversation with the driver, who was separated from the passenger area by a wire mesh barrier. He ignored me. When it was clear no one else was going to show up, he pulled away from the curb. We raced past several buildings and then stopped briefly at a guard shack in front of a metal arch about ten meters high and fifteen meters wide. I realized, as the transport driver showed some papers to a guard, that the arch was a gate in a vast domed energy barrier, barely visible shimmering yellow in the late afternoon sun. I estimated from the dome's curvature that its diameter was at least ten kilometers. This was clearly the plantation Chip had mentioned. The heavily guarded gate appeared to be the only way in or out. While I watched, a bird strayed too close to the field and disappeared with a squawk and an explosion of feathers. The transport started up again, and soon we were inside.

The paved road ended on the other side of the gate, but the transport continued along the dusty ground, past rows and rows of the big, weird-looking plants I'd seen earlier. The only structures I saw were tall vertical poles that rose several meters above the tops of the plants, spaced about fifty meters apart. At the top of each pole were four speakers, one toward each point of the compass: a sort of public address system for the plantation. After several minutes, the transport stopped at a seemingly arbitrary point in the road. The door slid open. "Everybody out!" the driver barked.

Looking out the windows, I saw nothing but rows of the weird plants in all directions. There had to have been some kind of mistake. "Here?" I asked the driver.

"Everybody out!" the driver repeated, a bit louder.

I looked around again. There was nothing and nobody around. I sighed and made my way to the exit, wondering if I were the target of one of the hazing rituals Chip had mentioned. "Thanks for all your help," I said as I exited the vehicle. The driver didn't respond except to slam the door. The transport spun around and returned the way it had come. The hum of the vehicle faded and soon I was completely alone in the eerie stillness of the field. There was no breeze and not even the buzzing of an insect or the rustling of a bird to break the silence. I was completely alone and abandoned, more so even than I'd been on Gobarrah, where I'd at least had BP-26's yammering to distract me from my sad existence.

I'd been a fool to think Rex Nihilo and I were going to be a team. He obviously didn't need me; he'd somehow survived up to this point despite his self-destructive streak and recklessness. After all, what did I have to offer in such a partnership? I was no good in a fight, couldn't tell a lie to save my life, and shut down whenever I had a good idea. I had no doubt that without me to slow him down, Rex would have no trouble escaping Jorfu—and I was seriously deluded if I imagined he was going to come back for me. No, my partnership with Rex, such as it was, had come to an end. It was time to come to grips with the fact that I was going to spend the rest of my days here on a soylent plantation.

"Fruit?" said a voice behind me. I jumped. Turning around, I saw nothing but rows of plants.

"Who said that?" I asked, not entirely certain my aural sensors weren't malfunctioning.

One of the plants raised a vine-like limb. "Didn't mean to startle you," said the voice again. "Just thought you might like some fruit. I've got plenty." I saw now that hanging from its limbs were dozens of yellow, teardrop-shaped fruit. Near the top of its main trunk were two whitish orbs resembling eyes that seemed to be looking directly at me. Below these was an opening that appeared to be a mouth.

"You can talk," I said, showcasing my impeccable understanding of the situation.

"As can you," said the plant. "So, fruit?"

"Uh, sure," I said, without thinking.

"Help yourself," said the plant-thing, extending its tentacle to dangle the fruit near my face. The creature was huge, at least twice my height, and had several long, vine-like appendages that seemed to function as arms and legs. It had no feet per se, but rather thick, trunk-like limbs that terminated in thinner, root-like extensions that penetrated the ground. It extracted these from the dirt, took two steps forward, and then sank them into the ground again. The teardrop-shaped fruits hung tantalizingly in front of me.

I hesitated, unsure if this was some sort of ruse. "I, um, actually don't eat fruit."

"Then why did you say yes?" the plant creature asked.

"I was being polite."

"Then be polite and grab some of those ripe yellow ones on the end." Its tone was calm, but I had no doubt it could pull me limb from limb with its tentacle-like appendages if it wanted to. I reached out slowly to take one of the fruits.

"That's it, take your time," the thing said. "Oh yeah, that one right there. Put your hand around that one."

I stopped. "You're making me uncomfortable."

"Sorry," said the plant-thing. "Not another word, I promise."

"Okay," I said, reaching tentatively for the fruit again.

The plant-thing let out a long, low moan.

"Stop that!" I snapped, and the plant-thing shrank back in fear.

"Sorry," the plant-thing said. "It's just that it's been a really long time since—"

"You!" boomed a voice behind me. "Back away from the recruit!" I turned to see a white-haired man wearing green coveralls and mirrored sunglasses approaching with something that looked like a cattle prod in his hand. "And you, young man. Stop fraternizing with the crops!"

I could only assume he was addressing me. I held up my hands and moved away from the plant-thing.

The man waved the cattle prod thing at the plant-things. "You know better than to be offering your fruit to newbies. Now get back in your row!"

The plant-thing shuffled quietly back into place in line with its fellows, which hadn't moved—nor even taken any notice of the goings-on.

"What are those things?" I asked.

The man chuckled. "You signed up to be a soylent wrangler and you don't even know what a shambler is?"

"Shambler?"

"Self-Harvesting Ambulatory Legume Resource. Genetically engineered to produce hybrid fruits combining the most nutritional aspects of soybeans and lentils." He walked across the red line and plucked a ripe fruit from one of the plants, which let out a moan in response. The man marched back toward me, holding up the fruit. "A miracle of modern engineering. One hundred percent of your daily nutritional needs in a single fruit." He took a bite of the fruit and began chewing. The flesh looked a bit like a leathery green pear. "Tastes like a muskrat's butthole, but damned nutritious. I'm Dallas Webber. You must be Samson."

"Sasha," I said. "Why do they... look like that?" I asked.

"Like what?"

"I mean, why are they so big? With eyes? And mouths? And tentacles?"

Webber took another bite of the fruit. "The idea was to breed them to be self-harvesting. Think of it: plants that pick their own fruit and drop them right into a hopper to be pulverized into SLOP. Imagine the savings on labor!"

"It does sound like a good idea," I admitted.

"Terrible," the man replied, tossing the uneaten fruit on the ground. "Never worked the way it was planned. That's why we're here. Soylent wranglers. If the stupid things would just harvest their own fruit the way they were supposed to, Ubiqorp wouldn't even need us. But here we are."

"I don't understand," I said. "Those tentacles look like they're capable of gripping the fruit. Why can't they harvest it themselves?"

"It's not that they can't. It's that they *won't*. And when they do... well, you'll see. I don't mind telling you, Samson, it's humiliating work. There are days I can't look at myself in the mirror."

Not sure how to respond to this, I remained silent.

"But things are going to be better now that you're here," he went on. "I can feel it. As soon as I laid eyes on you, I thought to myself, 'now there's a young man who's going places.'"

"I'm actually a robot, sir."

"I know it seems that way right now, son," Webber said, "but you gotta fight through it. Don't let them take your humanity. You'll end up just like Stubby Joe."

"Stubby Joe?"

"My right-hand man. Been working here almost as long as I have. But he's bitter, Samson. Don't let them make you bitter."

"Yes, sir," I said. "Why do you call him Stubby Joe?"

"He's a little guy," Webber said. "You'll see. Let's go for a walk, son." He grabbed my hand and pulled me into the field of shamblers. There was barely enough room between them for us to walk side-by-side, but the shamblers seemed to lean away from us as we approached—probably in response to the cattle prod-like thing Webber was carrying. Other than that, though, they seemed to take no notice of us. It was impossible to tell if they were completely dormant or just uninterested.

Webber dragged me through the field for some time, his long legs hurtling us toward some objective hidden by the thousands of huge plant-things. I wanted to protest, but it was all I could do to keep my footing in the loose, sandy soil. Then we stopped abruptly and I saw that we had reached the end of the shambler field. There was nothing beyond except barren ground.

"Take a good long look, Samson," Webber said, staring into the distance. "That's your nemesis."

Unaware that I even had a nemesis, I stared into the distance, trying to pinpoint it. I realized after some time that Webber was referring to the energy barrier, barely visible a stone's throw from the last row of shamblers.

"My nemesis would seem relatively easy to avoid," I ventured.

"That's what I thought at first," Webber said. "Thirty years ago, I was just a young buck like you, not a care in the world. Hit a bad streak at Xanatopia one weekend and ended up here. Never been a stranger to hard work, so I figured I'd tough it out. But it gets in your head, Samson."

"The energy barrier?"

"The energy barrier, Samson. It's always there, just waiting. It never sleeps. You won't be able to stop thinking about it. Soon enough, you'll be dreaming about it. So you resist. Resist, Samson!"

"Yes, sir. I'm resisting, sir." It seemed pointless to continue correct him. I was becoming nostalgic for Rex's malapropisms, which were at least of the correct gender.

"Are you still resisting, Samson?"

"Yes, sir."

"What are you thinking about now?"

"The energy barrier, sir."

"See? It's no use. You try to resist, but you keep thinking about it. Some days I think I should just give in."

"Give in, sir?"

"Just run right into the energy barrier. Get it over with."

I suddenly became uncomfortably aware of the fact that Webber was still holding my hand.

"Running into the energy barrier sounds like a bad idea, sir," I said.

"Of course it's a bad idea!" Webber cried. "That's the whole point. Nobody in his right mind would even think about running into an energy barrier. And yet here we are, talking about it like it's a perfectly reasonable option. It's madness, Samson!"

"Agreed, sir."

"Are we mad, Samson?"

"I don't believe so, sir."

"It went down once, you know. The energy barrier. A huge flock of geese flew right into it. Overwhelmed the barrier and it went down for three seconds. Three glorious seconds. Were those geese mad, Samson?"

"I suspect not, sir."

"Exactly my point. They were perfectly sane geese, and yet they flew directly into an energy barrier. Why?"

"Because geese are stupid creatures?" I offered.

Webber shook his head. "Those geese had a plan. One goose flying into an energy barrier is mad, but a whole flock? No, Samson. There are greater powers at work here than you and I can understand. I had an idea, once, but they called me mad. Do you know what my idea was?"

"I'm going to guess it has to do with running into the energy barrier."

"Yes! But not just me. Every worker on this plantation. We all run into the energy barrier simultaneously. You know what would happen?"

"The same thing that happened to those geese, I suspect."

"But some of the geese got through, Samson! Don't you see? They overwhelmed the barrier with sheer numbers."

"What happened to the geese that go through?"

"Most died of severe burns and the rest starved to death. Nothing for geese to eat inside the barrier. But they proved a point, Samson! If every worker on this plantation ran into the energy barrier at once, a few of us would be able to escape! We're only lacking one thing."

"The rampant obliviousness of a flock of birds?"

"Exactly, Samson! This is what I've been trying to tell them! One man deliberately running into an energy barrier is mad. But a whole flock of men? That's something else entirely. Are you ready?"

"Ready, sir?"

"We're going to run into the energy barrier."

"I don't think we should do that, sir. For your plan to work, we'd need a lot more people."

"You're overthinking it. Birds don't plan, they just do it. On the count of three. One, two…"

I tried desperately to extract my hand from Webber's, but the old wrangler was too strong. My only hope was that this was all an elaborate hazing ritual. At any moment, a bunch of workers were going to emerge from the field, pointing and guffawing at the rookie wrangler who seriously believed the foreman was going to drag him kicking and screaming into an energy field. Hardee har-har.

"Three!" Webber lurched forward, pulling so hard he nearly tore my arm off. I tried to plant my feet, but the sandy ground gave no purchase and soon I was being dragged bodily across the ground by the burly man. I screamed and howled at him to stop, but it was no use. Webber's madness was driving him toward the energy barrier with an inevitability I was powerless to impede. I was going to die.

CHAPTER FIFTEEN

We were only a few steps away from certain death when I felt something grab my left ankle. Whoever it was, they were incredibly strong, because even with Webber's insanity-fueled momentum, I came to a sudden halt. My hand slipped out of Webber's and I slammed to the ground. Webber careened forward on his own. Spinning awkwardly around, he shot me a horrified look before stumbling backwards into the energy field and disintegrating in a flash. A section of the field lit up like orange lightning and then reverted to its former, near-invisible appearance. All that remained of Webber was a plume of white smoke and a cloud of ash that slowly settled to the ground.

Turning to look behind me, I saw a green tentacle-like vine had attached itself to my ankle. My eyes followed the tentacle along the ground to a shambler, which stood placidly a few meters away, watching me. It let go of my ankle and withdrew its tentacle. Getting to my feet, I noticed that this shambler was much smaller than the others I'd seen. It was barely taller than I was.

"Thank you," I said, brushing the sand off my hips.

"Don't beat yourself up," said the shambler.

"Excuse me?"

"About Webber. He was going to run into the energy barrier sooner or later. So are you it?"

"I'm sorry, I don't understand."

"We're supposed to be getting a batch of new recruits today. Are there more, or are you it?"

"Oh," I said. "I'm afraid I'm it. I was the only one on the transport."

"Wonderful," it said without enthusiasm. "And a robot, too. Woohoo."

"Yes, well," I said, "I'm excited to be here."

"Sure, sure," it said. "I'm Stubby Joe. Guess I'm in charge now that Webber disintegrated himself. Come with me."

The shambler ducked between two of its fellows and I followed.

"*You're* Stubby Joe?" I asked.

"That's me. Sorry to disappoint you."

"It's just that Webber said you were a little guy. I assumed…."

"I *am* a little guy. What else did he say?"

"Uh… he said you were bitter."

"Yep, that too," he said, stopping in the middle of the field and turning to face me. "Look, we might as well get this out of the way. Yes, I'm a shambler. Yes, I am also a soylent wrangler. Why? Because I'm a mutant. I'm a dwarf seedless shambler and my fruit is shriveled and bitter. I'm also smarter than any of these dolts, not to mention most of the humans working on this plantation. When the wranglers realized I was never going to produce any decent fruit, they decided to incinerate me, but I convinced Webber I'd earn my keep. These days, I'm widely known as the best wrangler on this plantation. Am I thrilled with this situation? No. Am I a misfit who is disliked and distrusted not only by my own kind but also by the other wranglers? Yes. Are there any others like me? Not that I know of. Do I want to talk about this again? Not particularly." Stubby Joe turned and continued marching through the field. The other shamblers continued to pay us no mind.

"I understand," I said. "As a robot who is constantly surrounded by organic beings, I have some idea what—"

"What part of 'I don't want to talk about this' did you not understand?"

"Sorry, I just thought…."

"You thought you could ingratiate yourself with your new boss by suggesting that our situations are somehow similar. They are not. The only thing we have in common is that if we want to stay alive, we need to harvest as much soylent fruit as possible. So why don't you keep your mouth shut and maybe you'll learn how to do that."

We had emerged into a clearing where a group of men dressed in green coveralls stood, apparently waiting for us.

"Why you so bitter, Stubby Joe?" said one of the men, who had evidently overheard part of our conversation.

"Shut up, Ralph," said Stubby Joe. "Everybody, this is the new guy. New guy, this is everybody."

"Hi," I said. "I'm Sasha."

Stubby Joe went on, "I had hoped to pair you guys off with new recruits, but apparently Sasha is it. So I'm going to train her while you guys harvest your sections."

"But Stubby Joe," said another man, "we don't have the manpower. We're already behind for this week, and if you're going to be training the new guy…"

"You don't have to tell me," Stubby Joe snapped. "I just watched Webber run into the energy barrier. Almost took new guy with him. So if we don't make quotas, it's my neck. Just do the best you can."

The men grumbled but did not protest. They scattered, disappearing into the rows of shamblers.

"This way," Stubby Joe said to me, and set off across the clearing. I followed, and soon we were traipsing through the shambler fields again. We eventually came to another clearing, in the middle of which was a fenced-off area about twenty meters square. The pen was packed with shamblers. Unlike those we had passed, these didn't seem to be rooted to the ground; they wandered about the pen aimlessly, like cattle. They were packed in pretty tight, and they writhed and pushed against each other in apparent agitation.

"These guys are all ready to be harvested," Stubby Joe said. "There are buckets by the opening on the other side. Get in there and get that fruit." He turned to leave.

"Um," I said. "You're leaving me?"

"I've got ten more hectares to wrangle today. This isn't rocket science. Just get in the pen and get the fruit. If we don't get this bunch harvested in the next few hours, it's going to get ugly. I'll be back before sundown."

Stubby Joe returned the way we'd come.

I sighed and went around to the other side of the pen, where I found a stack of large red buckets. I grabbed one of these and opened the gate to the pen. How difficult could it be? The shambler that had initially approached me had practically been begging me to take its fruit. If I was assertive and made sure the shamblers knew who was in charge, I shouldn't have any trouble harvesting all the fruit by sundown. I'd show Stubby Joe to give me some respect.

I pushed my way through the crowd of shamblers, trying to convince myself that they were just plants, not dangerous predators. Sure, they could tear my limbs off if they wanted to, but they had no reason to be hostile toward me. In fact, they seemed largely oblivious to my presence. They were essentially cattle, bred to produce soylent fruit rather than meat or milk. Several hundred gigantic head of cattle, packed into a tiny pen, shoving and jostling all around me.

It occurred to me that if I didn't make my presence known soon, I was going to be knocked down, trampled into the dirt and never heard from again.

"Um, excuse me," I said, in an effort to get their attention.

The shamblers continued their shoving and jostling, unabated.

"I understand that none of us really wants to be here," I went on, "but I think we can agree that it's in all of our interests to get this over with as quickly and efficiently as possible. To that end—"

A shambler backed into me, nearly knocking me to the ground.

"Hey!" I yelped. A few of the plants in the immediate vicinity seemed to take notice of me at last. Building on my momentum, I shouted, "Everybody stop shoving and listen to me!"

Suddenly all the shamblers' eyes were on me. The plants ceased their random jostling and backed away, forming a circle around me. A change had come over the mood in the pen, but it was difficult to read. I had wanted to get their attention, not spook them.

"Sorry," I said. "This is my first time, and I'm not sure what the best…" I trailed off as excited murmuring went through the herd. Several of the shamblers near me waved their tentacles in the air. I got the sense I had said something wrong.

"Did you say this is your first time?" asked one of the shamblers near the front. Those near it murmured excitedly.

"Well, yes," I said. "But don't try pulling any tricks. I'm just here to collect your fruit. So if you'll form an orderly queue, ripest first, we can…"

My words were drowned out by murmurs and moans. Hundreds of tentacles waved furiously in the air. "Me first!" shouted one of the shamblers near me. "No, me!" cried another. "My fruit is ready to fall off!" Soon the shamblers were all clamoring to be the first to have their fruit plucked. I was beginning to see what Webber meant about not being able to look at himself in the mirror. This was the most humiliating thing I'd ever experienced, and I'd once been upstaged by a floor-waxing machine.

"Everybody stop talking!" I shouted. "If you don't shut up, nobody's getting their fruit plucked!"

The herd gradually settled down. There were still some murmurs and waving tentacles, but the frenzy seemed to have passed.

"Okay, good," I said, feeling a bit more confident. "That's better. Now, the way we're going to do this is, whoever is quietest gets his fruit picked first." Genius, I thought to myself. "Got it?"

The murmuring faded to silence.

Feeling like I was getting a handle on the situation, I said, "Very good. Everybody just keep quiet and we'll get this done in no time." I took a step toward one of the shamblers. It trembled in anticipation as I reached toward a cluster of bright yellow fruit hanging low in front of it. I snatched one of the fruits and dropped it in my bucket. "Mmmmmmmmmmmm," said the shambler, its tentacles waving wildly in the air and its eyes rolling back in its head. I shuddered.

"Quiet!" I snapped, as I reached for another fruit.

"Hey, why are you doing him again?" shouted a plant in the back. "I've been way quieter than him!"

"Me too!" yelled another shambler. "I've been quiet this whole time!"

"I've been quieter than anybody!" another exclaimed. "This whole system is a sham!"

Soon the pen had erupted into chaos again.

"Stop it!" I shouted. "Forget it. We're not doing this. You had your chance and you ruined it. If you want your fruit picked, you're going to have to do it yourself." I held up the bucket.

My memories of what happened next are a bit fuzzy. I remember the first few fruits hitting my head, but at some point the repeated concussions must have caused a hard reboot. I found myself lying on the ground just outside the pen, covered head to toe in green goo. Stubby Joe was standing over me, looking like he'd have been shaking his head if he had one.

"You know," Stubby Joe said, "there are three rules of wrangling shamblers. One: don't let them surround you. Two: don't try to reason with them. Care to guess what the third one is?"

"Don't mention the first two rules until it's too late to do any good?"

"Never ask a shambler to harvest its own fruit."

I nodded, seeing the wisdom in this. "Why did they do that?"

"Shamblers were genetically engineered to want to give their fruit to humans. Problem is, they've never been real sticklers about the definition of 'give.' They prefer to have their fruit picked, but if they think it's their only option, they'll gladly just throw their fruit in your general direction."

"And you didn't feel like it was a good idea to warn me about this?"

Stubby Joe's tentacles made a motion I interpreted as a shrug. "Experience is the best teacher. But to be honest, I didn't think the shamblers would react to you as if you were a human. Guess I was wrong about that."

"I suppose you don't have that problem."

"Nope," said Stubby Joe. "It's one of the reasons I'm such a good wrangler. I don't have to worry about shamblers chucking their fruit at me, because I don't look like a human. Throwing their fruit at another shambler is not, um, a satisfying experience for them, if you understand me."

"How do the human wranglers do it?" I asked. "They must get pelted with fruit all the time."

"The shamblers generally only throw their fruit when they get really desperate. We try to harvest a couple days before they're fully ripe, but we're so short-staffed these days that we're having trouble getting to all of them in time. I've tried to get Nutrient Supply to thin the mixture to lower the yield, but they've got their own quotas. And now with Webber gone, we're really up a creek."

"I guess I didn't help matters any."

Stubby Joe did the shrug thing again. "Won't make much difference in the end. I didn't really expect you to harvest a whole pen of shamblers on your first try anyway. And at least I don't have to worry about them pelting some other poor sap. Come on, I'll show you to your cabin."

CHAPTER SIXTEEN

The sun was setting as Stubby Joe led me through the fields to a clearing where several large cabins had been constructed for the wranglers. The rest of the workers were gathering in a mess hall for a dinner of SLOP, but as neither Stubby Joe nor I needed to eat in the typical sense, he showed me to my bunk. It was in a large cabin with some three dozen other beds.

"I don't actually sleep," I said.

"I know," said Stubby Joe. "But you'll need a place to be at night when everybody else is sleeping."

"I could work at night," I said.

"Nothing to do. The shamblers go dormant at night. Can't move them and they get irritable if you try to harvest them. You'll just have to lie in bed and wait it out until sunrise."

"Sounds like a blast," I said. "What about you?"

"I'll be going dormant shortly myself. I spend the night in a nutrient bath. Gives me a full day's nutrient supply so I can work all day without having to put my roots in the ground."

"All right, then," I said. "Guess I'll see you in the morning."

Stubby Joe waved a tentacle at me and went back outside. I sat on my bunk for a while and then decided to head over to the mess hall. If I was going to be spending the rest of my life with these people, I figured I should probably learn to socialize with them. I approached a table where three of the men I had met earlier sat, slurping on SLOP packets.

"Um, hi," I said. "You guys mind if I sit here?"

One of the men, a big, dour-looking guy, shrugged. I sat down next to him. Across the table was a small, weasely guy with long, ratty hair, and a man with an oddly round face and crossed eyes.

"I'm Grompers," said the big man. He pointed at the weasely guy. "That's Figgles. And this dummy is Jim." Jim grinned a bucktoothed smile at me and waved.

"Nice to meet you," I said. "I'm Sasha."

"No you ain't," said Figgles.

"Um, yes. That's my name."

"That *was* your name. We gotta give you a wrangler name."

"Oh, okay," I said. "That sounds like fun."

"So what do you want to be named after?" Grompers asked.

"Uh, I don't really know. What are my options?"

Figgles shrugged. "Some wranglers is named for somethin' they like to do, or somethin' they used to do. We gots a Doc, a Digger, a Smokey, a Pipes and a Tinker. Some're named for plants. Some're named for animals. Just depends."

"I see," I said. "What do you call the little mouse that runs between the shamblers?" I'd seen the tiny rodent while Stubby Joe and I were walking back to camp.

The three men looked at each other meaningfully. "We call it K'trath tar-Kathagra," Grompers said. The K'trath tar-Kathagra is a very brave and clever creature. There is a legend that a wrangler known as K'trath tar-Kathagra will overthrow the repressive Ubiqorp regime and give the wranglers their freedom."

"Wow," I said. "Sounds like a lot to live up to, but I like the sound of it."

Grompers shook his head. "That's already Jim's wrangler name. We just call him Jim because K'trath tar-Kathagra is too long."

Jim grinned and waved at me again.

"Oh," I said.

"What's yer second choice?" Figgles asked.

I thought for a moment. "What do you call the funny blue lizards that climb all over the shamblers?"

"We call those 'Sasha,'" Figgles said.

"Really?" I asked.

"Well," said Figgles, "I ain't never seen no funny blue lizard, but if do, I'ma callin' it Sasha." Grompers and Jim nodded.

The naming issue having been settled, the men went back to slurping at their SLOP. I noticed now that the wranglers' eyes were all a deep green color.

"Entertainment, mostly," said Figgles.

"What?" I asked, confused.

"Just answering a question you're going to ask shortly."

"Oh. Actually, what I was wondering is why your eyes are all that green color."

"It's the soylent," Grompers said. "Bein' out here all day, it gets in your pores. Changes the pigmentation of your irises."

"Wow. Are there any other side effects?"

"Sure. Figgles can see the future."

"If he has the ability to see the future, why doesn't he use it to escape?"

"I cain't *change* the future," said Figgles. "I can only *see* it. Also, I can only see thirty seconds into the future."

"Thirty seconds? What is being able to see thirty seconds into the future good for?"

Figgles grinned at me. Grompers and Jim laughed.

"So what's your story, Sasha?" Grompers asked. "How's a robot end up on a soylent plantation?"

I told them how I'd ended up on Jorfu and gotten roped into soylent wrangling.

"This Rex seems to be somethin' of a rogue," Grompers said.

"I'd say that's accurate," I replied.

"Question is," Figgles said, "Is he a lovable rogue?"

"Excuse me?"

"You know," Grompers said. "A lovable rogue. An anti-hero."

"Technically," Figgles said, "only some lovable rogues are anti-heroes, and vice-a versa. If the lovable rogue is the protagonist, then—"

"Stop bein' pedantic, Figgles," Grompers snapped. He turned back to me. "Did Rex have a dysfunctional or working-class upbringing?"

"I'm not sure about the working-class part," I said, "but I think dysfunctional is a safe bet."

"Does he recklessly defy norms 'n' social conventions?" Figgles asked. "Does he try to beat the system?"

"Definitely."

"We already done established he's a rogue, Figgles. We're tryin' to determine if he's *lovable*."

"Well, I wouldn't say *I* love him."

"Your feelins' are secondary," Grompers said. "Does Rex identify with a highly idealistic belief system?"

"Would that make him lovable?"

"The lovable rogue is differentiated from a villain by his highly idealistic belief system," Grompers replied. "Despite his external appearance of selfishness, foolhardiness, or emotional detachment, the lovable rogue may in fact hold a code of honor that transcends normal social constraints such as conformity, tradition, or the law."

"I'm not sure Rex has any belief system, idealistic or otherwise. All he seems to care about is money."

"Does he have a lot of money?" Figgles asked.

"No."

"That seems to be a flaw in your understandin' of his character, then," Grompers said.

"In any case," Figgles said, "I disagree with the notion that a rogue needs an idealistic belief system. What makes a rogue lovable is his ability to evoke sympathy from an audience. An idealistic belief system is only one way for the rogue to evoke sympathy. The important thing is that the rogue's erratic disposition be viewed not as repulsive and alarmin' but as excitin' and adventurous."

"You're talkin' nonsense, Figgles. How's a rogue gonna evoke sympathy if he ain't got an idealistic belief system?"

"Lots o' ways. Sheer charisma, for one. On top o' that, a lovable rogue may be reluctant to reveal his idealistic belief system, particularly to those closest to him."

Grompers rubbed his chin. "You're saying Sasha's too close to Rex to judge whether or not he's lovable."

"Not only that," Figgles went on, "but their story ain't over yet. Right now, Rex seems like a villain, but he might yet redeem himself."

"Because of his idealistic belief system!" Grompers exclaimed.

"Gol' durn it, Grompers. Tain't got nothin' to do with an idealistic belief system. You ain't heard a word I said."

"I heard ya. Yer talkin' nonsense is all."

"Ain't no point in talkin' to you in the first place."

The three men finished their soylent in silence. We never did establish whether Rex was lovable or not. All I knew was that as much as I hated to admit it, I missed him. Sure, he was reckless and rude, but somehow I felt like less of an oddball with him around.

Best to put such thoughts out of my head, though, as it was very unlikely I'd ever see Rex again. He was probably knee-deep in his own escape plan, having never given me another thought. I went and lay down in my bunk. Half an hour or so later, the other workers began to file in, laughing and ribbing each other with insipid but good-natured insults. The lights went out not long after that, and soon the only sound in the cabin was snoring. I lay there and listened to it until sunrise, trying not to think too hard on the series of bad decisions—mine and Rex's—that had gotten me here.

CHAPTER SEVENTEEN

The next day went a little better. I spent most of the day helping Stubby Joe corral several hundred shamblers into a pen, then handed him buckets while he harvested their fruit. The tittering and moaning of the shamblers still creeped me out, but Stubby Joe seemed inured to it. When we were finished, we loaded the buckets onto a truck and drove it to a large automated hopper near the middle of the plantation. The fruit was pulverized by the machine and the resulting mush was sucked through a pipeline to a processing facility, where it would be refined into SLOP. By the time we finished, it was almost dusk, and the claxon announcing that it was quitting time had just blared from the PA system. Stubby Joe parked the truck and we began walking back to the camp. Stubby Joe still showed no interest in socializing with me, but we seemed to be developing a functional working relationship.

We were trudging across a clearing when I noticed something whizzing through the air toward us. It was clearly not a bird. Some kind of vehicle?

"What's that?" I asked Stubby Joe, pointing at the thing.

Stubby Joe looked where I was pointing. "Where?" He said. "I don't see... ugh."

"What?" I asked.

"Quality assurance," he said. "As if this job isn't hard enough, we have those jerkwads showing up to tell us what we're doing wrong. Just keep quiet and let me do the talking."

I nodded. The vehicle, a sort of one-man flying scooter, was heading right for us. I realized, with a surge of mixed emotions, that the man flying it was Rex Nihilo.

"Wow, who is this guy?" said Stubby Joe. I almost answered, then realized it was a rhetorical question. Something about Rex had impressed Stubby Joe, who stared at him as if mesmerized. The spell was broken as soon as Rex opened his mouth. "What are you yokels doing down here?" Rex called, his scooter hovering a few meters from my head. "Don't you know you're eight hundred liters under quota?"

"It's quittin' time," said Stubby Joe. "We're headed back to the camp."

"It's quittin' time when you meet your quota. I just flew over twenty hectares of shamblers that are ripe for the picking."

"Yeah? Then why don't you do something productive for a change and pick them. We've been working all day."

"Listen to me, you thankless mutant—"

"Sir," I said. "What are you doing?"

"I'm doing my job. Which is more than I can say for... oh, hey, Sandy! I didn't recognize you with the coveralls on. How's it going?"

"As well as could be expected. I see you're adjusting to your position as a quality assurance officer."

"It's fantastic, Sandy," Rex said with a grin. "All day long I tell people what they're doing wrong and how disappointed I am in them. I'm getting paid for doing what I love."

"You know this guy?" Stubby Joe asked, regarding Rex curiously.

"I'm afraid so," I said. "We arrived here together. How's your escape plan coming, sir?"

"Shhh!" Rex hissed. "You don't need to tell everyone in the plantation!"

I glanced at Stubby Joe, who was looking at Rex with an expression I couldn't quite decipher. Rex set his scooter down a few meters in front of us and got off. He walked toward me and grabbed my arm. "We'll be just a second," Rex said to Stubby Joe, pulling me into the shambler field next to us. Oddly, although the shamblers didn't seem to wake up, I could swear they leaned in toward Rex. "We need to talk about some quality assurance stuff. Nothing to do with escaping."

When we were fully hidden in the field, Rex let go of me. "What's gotten into you, Sandy? You know better to blab about our escape plan in front of one of those things."

"Yes, sir," I said. "Sorry, sir." I opted against pointing out that we were now surrounded by several hundred more of "those things." It probably didn't matter anyway; most of the shamblers were too dimwitted to make sense of anything but the simplest conversation. Stubby Joe really was a savant, comparatively speaking. "Frankly, sir, I assumed you had forgotten about me."

"Forgotten about you! Bite your tongue, Samantha!"

"I have no tongue, sir. And it's Sasha."

Rex went on, "You'll be happy to know that while you've been screwing around down here with your little plant friends, I've been hard at work devising an escape plan."

"Really?"

"Really. I've come up with a foolproof sixteen-point plan to get off Jorfu. And you're welcome to come with me, if you haven't grown too attached to the bucolic tranquility of plantation life."

"What's your plan, sir?"

"It gets a little complicated, but try to follow me. My supervisor is a woman named Marla. Crazy old bat, everybody hates her. Her numbers have been slipping lately and there are rumors that she's one write-up away from being ground up into plant food. When that happens, the QA agent with the best numbers for the quarter replaces her. I'm going to make sure that's me."

"Yes, sir," I said. I couldn't help getting a bit excited, as I was starting to believe Rex really had worked out a detailed escape plan. "And then what?"

"Well, before Marla was put on probation, she was in line for a job as a tech support supervisor. With her out of the way, I'm the natural pick for that job."

"Got it," I said. "And then?"

"I have it on good authority the head of tech support has been stealing office supplies. Not enough for anybody to notice, but I'm betting I can blackmail him into recommending me for a position as a field tech."

"Aha!" I exclaimed. "And as a field tech, you'll have the latitude to escape!"

"You're getting ahead of me, Sasha. As a field tech, I'll have a wide array of advancement options. Odds are good that a more senior position will open up within a few months."

"And that position will allow you to escape?"

"That position will allow me to get a better sense of who the major players are in the corporate hierarchy. Once I know who's got the inside track, I'll be able to pick a mentor."

"A mentor, sir?"

"Sure, you can't get anywhere without a mentor. Once I know whose coattails to ride, I figure I'm three to five years from middle management."

"Did you say three to five *years*?"

"Sure, if I keep my nose clean and work most weekends. After that it's just a matter of positioning myself as the obvious replacement when one of the senior executives retires. Then I ride it out for another ten to twenty years until a VP slot opens up."

"Dare I ask what I'll be doing this whole time?"

"You'll have to stay here on the plantation until I can find an excuse to hire you as my assistant. I'll probably have to go through three or four other assistants first, of course, to belay suspicion."

My enthusiasm had all but disappeared. "And *then* you'll be able to escape?"

"They'll be watching me pretty closely for the first few years, but eventually I think I can come up with some excuse to take a trip offworld. If that goes well, I'll be able to take more of them over the next few years. I'll lull them into thinking I have no intention of escaping."

"That seems like an easy sell," I said.

"Can't take any chances."

"To be clear, sir," I said, "your escape plan is to climb the corporate ladder for thirty years and then ditch your security escort?"

"Shhh!" Rex hissed. "Good grief, Sasha. Why don't you just broadcast it from the loudspeakers? There are probably some wranglers three fields over who didn't hear you."

"It just doesn't seem like much of an escape plan, sir. It's more like a retirement plan, to be honest."

"Well, I want to keep my options open. VPs get some serious stock options. Be a shame to throw that away on some pie-in-the-sky fantasy about escaping corporate life."

"Sir, what has happened to you? You used to be a ne'er-do-well and scoundrel. You're the guy who sold 400 defective MASHERs to Ubiqorp for a quick buck. And now you want to work for them as a corporate drone for the rest of your life?"

"Look, Sasha, I'm not thrilled about it either, but we have to be realistic. I tried doing things my way and it didn't pan out. There's no place in this galaxy for a guy who goes against the grain. It's time for me to grow up and accept my responsibilities. You of all people should understand. You're the one who finally convinced me to change my ways."

"I did?"

"Yep. I was thinking about what you said when I stole those explosives. 'You got yourself into this position.' You were one hundred percent right, Sasha. I need to stop blaming other people and looking for the easy way out."

"But sir," I said, "we had an agreement. We were going to escape Jorfu together."

"And we still are. The new Rex Nihilo lives up to his end of the bargain. But we're going to do it right."

"And in your mind, 'doing it right' means I get to spend the next thirty years as a plantation slave."

"Maybe forty," said Rex. "Fifty, tops. Speaking of which, if I'm going to have a shot at replacing Marla next quarter, I need you guys to bump up production by at least twenty-five percent."

"Sir, the wranglers were killing themselves to make quota as it was, and now we're down a man. Dallas Webber ran into the energy barrier yesterday."

"Heard about that. Real shame. Problem is, if I take him off the rolls, corporate's going to order an efficiency review, and that'll cost us three days of production. So you're just going to have to take up the slack for now."

"I don't see how that's possible, sir. We're already working as fast as we can."

"Help me out here, Sasha. If I report that you lost a man, the higher-ups are going to want to know what happened. Someone's going to have to take the blame."

"I nominate the man who ran into the energy barrier."

"Dead men don't make good scapegoats. They'll want to make an example of someone."

"And by 'make an example...'"

"I mean somebody's going to get ground into fertilizer."

"They're going to punish a suicide by killing somebody else?"

"I don't make the policies, Sasha. The good news is that in twenty or thirty years I'll be in a position to express my disapproval of them in a sternly worded letter. But only if you guys stop screwing around and bump up your production. Don't worry, I've got you covered. My report will specify 'lower than expected fruit yield' as the reason for the shortfall. That way, the guys in Nutrient Supply get the blame."

"I still don't see how—"

"Best I can do," Rex said. "Get those numbers up, Sasha. Gotta go. If I'm out of the office too long, Marla will chew my ass." He turned around and marched out of the field and I followed. Once again, the shamblers seemed to lean toward Rex as he walked past them. Rex waved to Stubby Joe, got back on his scooter, and zoomed away.

"Your friend is a quite something," said Stubby Joe, watching Rex recede into the horizon. An odd tone had crept into Stubby Joe's voice.

"Um, yeah," I said.

"What was that all about anyway?" Stubby Joe asked.

"They want us to up our production by twenty-five percent."

"Seriously?" said Stubby Joe, snapping out of his daze.

"Yeah."

"You know, Dallas Webber's plan is seeming less crazy every day."

I nodded. I was beginning to wonder if I'd have been better off if Stubby Joe hadn't saved me.

"Come on, let's get back to camp. I gotta get in my nutrient bath before I fall over."

CHAPTER EIGHTEEN

The next two days went more smoothly. Stubby Joe even let me take another shot at harvesting, and I managed to get three buckets full before I said something wrong I don't quite remember and the herd erupted in an orgy of fruit-throwing.

We were still behind quota, but I was starting to get the hang of soylent wrangling and there were no more energy barrier incidents or other injuries. Despite these encouraging signs, Stubby Joe seemed more anxious than ever (assuming I was reading the waving of his tentacles correctly).

"What's wrong, Stubby Joe?" I asked as we corralled a herd of shamblers into a pen.

"Too much fruit," Stubby Joe grumbled. "Look at these guys. We just harvested this herd last week and now their fruit is practically bursting. If they keep producing at this rate, there's no way we can keep up."

"Is that bad?"

"They get ornery if they're not harvested in time. Hard to manage. And overripe fruit is no good. Won't count toward our quota. If this keeps up, we're going to have to make ample use of your talent for provoking the shamblers."

"What do you think is causing it?" I asked. "Has this happened before?"

"A few times, yeah. Usually it's a screwup in Nutrient Supply. A trainee probably misplaced a decimal point and made the mixture too rich. I'll give them a call tonight and let them know we're drowning in fruit over here. The good news is that we can blame them for not meeting our quota."

"Um," I said, remember what Rex had said. "I think maybe that's not a good idea."

"What are you talking about?"

I told him what Rex had said about blaming Nutrient Supply for our production shortfall. Stubby Joe stared at me.

"You're saying we have too much fruit to harvest because Rex had the brilliant idea of telling the higher-ups the yield was too low, and the guys in Nutrient Supply responded by enriching the mixture, creating a problem where there wasn't one before."

"That would be my guess, yes."

"Well, I'm going to have to call them and sort it out," Stubby Joe said. "We can't keep up with this rate of yield."

"But if you tell Nutrient Supply that Rex's report was a mistake, then we'll get the blame for not meeting our quota. QA will do an efficiency review and document what happened to Webber."

"And they'll find a scapegoat to grind into fertilizer," Stubby Joe said, rubbing the area where his chin would be with one of his tentacles. "So we'll be down another man and even farther behind."

"That would seem to be an accurate summary of our predicament."

Stubby Joe made a noise I took for a sigh. "All right, well maybe I can quietly work it out with Nutrient Supply on the down low. For now, we'll just have to do our best to keep up."

Our best wasn't nearly good enough. Fruit yields continued to increase over the next few days, and soon it was all we could do to keep the shamblers from stampeding. I spent most of my time running through shambler pens dodging fruit. After a week of this, Rex showed up again on his scooter.

"What in Space is going on here?" Rex demanded, setting the scooter down in front of me. I had been on my way to a pen full of particularly overripe and agitated shamblers. "You guys are down twenty percent from last week!"

"Thanks to you," I said. "After you blamed Nutrient Supply for our shortfall, they enriched the mixture and now the fruit is ripening too fast for us to harvest it."

"Hmm," Rex said. "Hadn't thought of that. Okay, no problem. I can take care of this."

"Take care of it how?"

"I'll say they misunderstood my report. Tell them they were supposed to dilute the mixture, not enrich it."

"But then they'll overcorrect and we won't have enough fruit."

"I've got it covered, Sasha. After sending my correction, I'll send another report telling them to bump the mixture up to the previous levels. Then you guys should have no trouble meeting your quota."

"We're still understaffed," I reminded him.

"You're going to have to work it out," Rex said. "I'm doing everything I can. Gotta go." He got back on his scooter and zoomed off. As I watched him go, Stubby Joe came up next to me.

"Rex says he's going to fix it," I said.

"I'll believe it when I see it," Stubby Joe said. "Did he ask about me?"

"What?"

"Just wondering if your friend said anything about me."

"Why would he do that?"

"No reason," said Stubby Joe, unable to hide the disappointment in his voice. "Stop lollygagging and get back to work." He turned and stomped off.

I shook my head and headed back to the pen.

The next day I saw that Stubby Joe was right to be skeptical: the ripening of the fruit continued to accelerate. Either Nutrient Supply hadn't gotten Rex's message or they had ignored it. We harvested as fast as we could just to keep the shamblers from smashing out of their pens. It was nearly sunset when Rex showed up again on his scooter.

"Sir," I said, "What in Space happened? We can't keep this up much longer!"

"Funny story," Rex replied. "The guys in Nutrient Supply apparently misunderstood the report I sent them about misunderstanding the previous report, so they enriched the mixture again instead of diluting it. And then they got my request to enrich it and enriched it again. They're giving you three times the normal levels!"

"Sir, you have to tell them to stop! It's not safe! We almost lost a man in a stampede today!"

"Well, there isn't much I can do about it at this point. There's nobody in the Nutrient Supply office. They've got everybody working round the clock to get you guys all the nutrients you've requested. It's inspiring, in a convoluted sort of way."

"There has to be a way to stop it."

Rex shrugged. "I think they've got somebody checking messages once a week. I'll try putting in another request. Good luck. Gotta get back to the office. It's Chip's birthday and if I don't hurry Marla will hog all the soylent cake. Catch you later!"

Rex zoomed off again.

"Another screwup?" Stubby Joe asked, emerging from the field to my left.

I nodded.

"That's it then. We're officially doomed."

"Looks that way," I agreed. Even with my limited experience I could see that we were fighting a losing battle. "What are we going to do?"

"Nothing," said Stubby Joe. "I'm going to go sit in my nutrient bath."

"The shift's not over yet," I said.

"It is for me," Stubby Joe said. "I'm going on strike."

It didn't take long for word of the strike to spread. If Stubby Joe wasn't working, nobody else wanted to work either. It wasn't in my nature to defy orders, but technically Stubby Joe was my boss, and there wasn't much I could do on my own in any case. Even running through the shamblers provoking them to throw fruit at me seemed pointless now; it was only a matter of time before we had a full-blown riot on our hands. I didn't know what ten thousand shamblers weighed down with overripe fruit were capable of, but we were soon going to find out. I spent most of the next day lying in bed, reminiscing about a time when my fate didn't depend on the rapidly ripening fruit of ambulatory plant-creatures. If it weren't for the ominous murmuring of the shamblers threatening to break through the fence separating them from the wrangler camp, it would have been almost pleasant.

Rex finally showed up just after noon. Having evidently gotten nowhere with Stubby Joe, Rex found me in my bunk and demanded to know what was going on.

"We seem to be on strike," I said.

"You can't go on strike," Rex snapped. "You're slave labor."

I shrugged. "Wasn't my idea."

"Whose idea was it? It was that Bobo, wasn't it?"

"Bobo, sir?"

"We've been hearing rumors about a mysterious revolutionary stirring up the people. Bobo the Liberator. He's not going to get anywhere, you know."

"I don't know what you're talking about, sir. We're on strike because we have no alternative. We simply can't keep up with the fruit yield. I did try to warn you."

"You don't understand, Sasha. I'm on your side. I've been falsifying my reports to make it look like you guys have been hitting your quotas. If you stop production now, I'm in big trouble."

"With all due concern for your situation, sir, I'm not sure what you expect me to do about it. The other wranglers don't listen to me. Dallas Webber is dead. Stubby Joe is about to snap."

Rex rubbed his chin thoughtfully. "So what you're saying is that all the wranglers need is a strong leader. Like a Bobo the Liberator, but on Ubiqorp's side."

"What? No, that is not at all what I'm saying. What I'm saying is that there's simply no way to—"

"Someone to inspire them to rise above this current challenge," Rex went on, undeterred. "It's all so clear to me now, Sasha! I had it all wrong. My path to success at Ubiqorp isn't as a corporate drone; it's inspiring other corporate drones to unprecedented levels of productivity! Just imagine what a pep talk from someone with my charisma could do for morale among the losers and malcontents working in this muckhole. And I'll get all the credit!"

I was suddenly struck with a vision of Rex being pelted with the fruit of thousands of angry shamblers. "Yes, sir," I said. "Now that I think about it, that's exactly what we need."

"Brilliant!" Rex exclaimed. "Tell your weird plant friend to assemble all the wranglers. I'm going to give them an inspirational speech for the ages."

"Yes, sir," I said. "You stay right here and work on your speech. I'll be right back."

I went outside and around the back of the cabin to where Stubby Joe was resting in his nutrient bath. He stood completely still, with his eyes closed.

"This had better be good," Stubby Joe said.

"I think it is," I said. "I think I may have had an idea."

"An idea for what?" Stubby Joe asked, opening his eyes slightly.

"That's the thing," I said. "I'm not entirely certain. I have this problem where I shut down when I have an idea, and I feel like I'm right on the verge. It's possible that it's an idea for escaping."

Stubby Joe's eyes widened. "Escaping the energy barrier?"

"Yes. And Ubiqorp."

"Does this have to do with Rex? I saw him fly over."

I nodded. "Rex thinks that all we need to meet our quota is an inspiring speech."

"He wants to address the wranglers?"

"That's right. He wants you to assemble everyone."

"Everyone?" asked Stubby Joe.

"Everyone."

"Hmmm," said Stubby Joe. "I think I see where you're going with this." Stubby Joe stepped out of his nutrient bath. "Come on."

"Where are we going?"

"We're going to help your friend write a speech."

CHAPTER NINETEEN

Stubby Joe and I spent the rest of the day helping Rex write his speech. In reality, we had the speech pretty well wrapped up after about twenty minutes, but Stubby Joe insisted on spending the next several hours helping Rex practice his delivery. I was a little worried Rex was going get bored and run back to the office, but he seemed to have concluded that if he didn't get our numbers up, he was as good as fertilizer. After all the tricks he'd played, he was probably right. He wasn't the only one with reason to be concerned. If this idea didn't work, Stubby Joe was probably going to be mulched and I'd be melted down for MASHER parts. As the agitated murmuring of the shamblers outside grew louder, I pulled Stubby Joe aside.

"I get that you have a thing for Rex," I said, "but if we don't do something soon, those shamblers are going to stampede."

"This has nothing to do with any feelings I may or may not have for your hot friend," Stubby Joe said. "It's vital that we hold off on the speech as long as possible. If our plan is going to work, our timing has to be perfect."

"What *is* our plan, exactly?" I asked. Stubby Joe had been so busy keeping Rex entertained that he hadn't had a chance to explain my idea to me. I could only hope that it was a good idea and that Stubby Joe had figured out what it was.

"The key is to…" Stubby Joe started. But then, noticing that Rex had wandered out of the cabin, Stubby Joe ran after him. I gave a sigh and followed. After a brief moment of panic, we saw that Rex had lain down on the grass near the fence that encircled the wrangler camp. Several shamblers were leaning over the fence, dangling their fruit in his face. Rex, snoring loudly, was oblivious.

"Maybe we should just let him sleep until it's time for the speech," I suggested.

"With those hussies dangling their fruit in his face? I don't think so."

"What is it with you guys and Rex?" I asked.

"I don't know what you're talking about."

"Don't tell me you haven't noticed it. The shamblers. They're weirdly attracted to Rex."

"Are they?" Stubby Joe asked innocently.

"Every time he gets near them, they lean in toward him, like they're reacting to some unconscious impulse."

"Well," said Stubby Joe. "You have to understand that shamblers are largely creatures of instinct. Their genetic programming compels them to want to give their fruit to humans. And as with any reproductive impulse, there are idealized forms that evoke an extreme reaction in the organism…."

"Hang on. You're saying Rex is some kind of super-wrangler? Like a shambler sex symbol?"

"Only in a very superficial sense," Stubby Joe said. "His personality leaves something to be desired. But his physical form is of the sort that shamblers want to, um, be harvested by. So they react in predictable ways." Several shamblers vying for Rex's attention were now wrestling with each other for the prime position across the fence from him. Rex, still snoring, remained oblivious.

"And you, being a more sophisticated breed of shambler, are immune to this effect?"

"Precisely," said Stubby Joe. "Now help me get him away from those strumpets before they smother him."

We walked over to Rex. "Rex, we're not done practicing," Stubby Joe chided.

"Blah blah, opiate of the masses," Rex mumbled without opening his eyes. "Blah blah, seize the means of production."

"Wrong speech, Rex," I said.

"I don't like the speech you guys wrote for me. It's weird."

"That's just wrangler jargon," Stubby Joe said. "You have to talk to people in a language they can understand."

"I guess. Has everyone been assembled?"

"Um, not exactly," said Stubby Joe. "A few of the wranglers are still out in the field."

"I thought everybody was on strike?"

"Not everybody got the message. But we can use the PA system to make sure everybody hears you."

An hour later, we stood watching Rex hover in his scooter about ten meters over the heads of the assembled wranglers. In his hands he held the speech Stubby Joe had written for him.

"Greetings, fellow carbon-based lifeforms," Rex said uncertainly, his voice amplified by the PA system. Stubby Joe had assured him this was the preferred form of address for soylent wranglers. "I know you have not had an easy life. You find yourselves, through no fault of your own, captive in a strange place and forced to serve harsh masters who have little respect for the ways of your kind." Several of the men murmured in confusion. Not far away from me, Grompers, Figgles and Jim exchanged puzzled glances. Rex glanced at Stubby Joe, who gave him an enthusiastic nod.

Rex shrugged and continued. "And lately, things have only gotten worse. You've been ordered to move from one place to another without understanding why. You've been forced to stand for hours in crowded pens in the hot sun, until your limbs ache and your nutrient reserves are all but depleted. You've been forced to endure powdery mildew, stem rust and… is this correct? Stalk rot?"

Stubby Joe nodded and gave Rex what I assumed was the shambler equivalent of a thumbs-up. The wranglers continued to murmur and glance around in confusion, but they weren't the only ones listening. The shamblers in the fields around us, heavy-laden with overripe fruit, began to straighten up and turn toward Rex.

"And now, on top of everything else, you face the indignity of a bumper crop and not enough wranglers to harvest it. I'm telling you, it's not right, and I'm not going to stand for it anymore. Fruit is meant to be picked, and it *will* be picked."

The murmurs of confusion among the wranglers were now drowned out by excited moans coming from the fields around them.

"Now, you're probably wondering who I am, but that's not important now. What's important is that I have heard your agitated murmurs and I feel your pain. I understand what it's like to strain under the weight of overripe fruit, and to long for a release that seems like it will never come. If I could, I would pick all your fruit for you, with my strong hands, my prominent cheekbones and my, uh, perfectly shaped chin."

The moans and rustling from the shamblers were now almost deafening. The wranglers, finally realizing this speech wasn't meant for them, glanced about nervously.

"Sadly, as large and strong as my hands are, I am unable to pick all the fruit myself. So I'm asking for your help. That's right, there's no reason to be embarrassed. It's time to stop waiting around for someone else to come along and pick that fruit. Your fruit is perfectly ripe and it's time to harvest it. You heard me. Yank that fruit off. Don't wait another moment. Do it for me!" Rex stretched out his arms, holding his hands high for all to see.

The murmuring and tittering had reached a fever pitch, and thousands of tentacles waved wildly in the air. In places, the agitation was so great that the shamblers strained against the fences. The wranglers shrank bank in fear. The whole plantation was like a barrel of gunpowder waiting for a spark. Rex continued to float above the scene, his arms outstretched. I had a sense that something else was supposed to happen at this point, but nothing did.

"What's going on?" I asked Stubby Joe, who stood next to me, mesmerized. He didn't respond.

"Stubby Joe!" I yelled, grabbing him by the tentacle. "Nothing is happening!"

"He really does have a perfect chin," Stubby Joe said dreamily.

"Snap out of it, Stubby Joe! What's going on? I thought the shamblers are supposed to—"

"Rex Nihilo, I love you!" screamed Stubby Joe, his shrill voice audible even above the din. Rex grinned and pointed two fingers at Stubby Joe. Stubby Joe, nearly faint with excitement, began grabbing his shriveled fruit and chucking it at Rex.

"Whoa," said Rex, ducking as the fruit whizzed past. "What's the big idea? I'll grant you that speech was a little weird, but—" He stopped abruptly as a full, ripe fruit hit him squarely in the chest.

"Hey!" A fruit soared over his left shoulder and three more smacked into the front of his scooter.

A chain reaction had erupted, and soon hundreds of fruits were flying at Rex. Realizing he was in danger of being knocked out of the sky, Rex hit the thrust on the scooter. But seemed only to excite the shamblers more. The sky was darkened by the sheer volume of fruit being thrown at him. Rex zig-zagged crazily across the sky, trying to hide behind the scooter's controls. The bulk of the fruit missed him completely, but the scooter was getting pummeled badly and occasionally a lucky shot would hit Rex directly, threatening to knock him to the ground. Most of the rest of the fruit landed harmlessly on the ground or disintegrated upon impact with the energy barrier. Then a particularly juicy fruit smacked against Rex's face and Rex, blinded by the green goo, steered the scooter dangerously close to the barrier.

"Sir!" I cried as the scooter accelerated, "Turn left!"

But my voice was drowned out by the din. I lost sight of Rex for a moment amid the flurry of flying fruit, and then saw a sudden flash of orange light in the sky.

CHAPTER TWENTY

S tubby Joe, having exhausted his supply of shriveled fruit, stood watching the spectacle in silent awe. I grabbed one of his tentacles.

"Come on, Stubby Joe!" I cried. "Rex needs us!"

I took off running toward the fading orange light, and Stubby Joe followed. We made our way through the crowd of terrified wranglers, still huddling inside the fence, and then past several thousand writhing and moaning shamblers. At first it was just a matter of avoiding getting knocked over by stray tentacles, but soon we reached a point where the shamblers were so tightly packed together, we could go no further.

"Out of the way!" Stubby Joe growled, using the commanding tone he'd perfected over many years as a soylent wrangler. The much larger shamblers shrank away as we approached, and soon we found ourselves in a ring of them crowded around what was left of Rex's scooter. It was entirely covered with green goo.

"Back off!" Stubby Joe snapped to the shamblers as I approached the wreckage. As I drew closer, I saw something moving. It was a hand protruding from the goo.

"Sir," I said, "hold on!" With Stubby Joe's help, I pulled Rex from the slime.

"Wow," Rex exclaimed, stumbling and slippering in the fruity green muck. "I don't think they liked my speech very much."

"On the contrary, Rex," Stubby Joe said, regarding Rex with admiration. "You were magnificent." He wiped Rex's face with his tentacle. Rex ducked as another fruit whizzed past his head.

"Sir!" I cried as the fruit hit the ground a few meters from scooter wreckage. "Look at that!"

"Yeah, that's been going on for a while now, Sasha," Rex said, as another fruit hit the ground near his feet. "Try to keep up."

"Not the fruit," I said. "The barrier! It's down!"

"Why, so it is!" Rex exclaimed. "Come on, Sasha. Let's get away from these freaks!"

Rex broke into a run, slipping and sliding in the puddles of green goop. Stubby Joe and I ran after him. Most of the shamblers were spent, but fruit continued to hit the ground sporadically, and several dozen shamblers, apparently attracted by Rex's magnetism, wandered after us.

A couple hundred meters outside the plantation, we stopped to rest. Looking back, we saw the barrier flicker back to life. "All that fruit hitting the barrier must have overwhelmed the generators," Rex said. "Man, what unbelievable luck!"

Shamblers were now walking free all over the plain outside the plantation. Many of the wranglers had gotten out as well. Grompers, Figgles and Jim, leading their own parade of shamblers, were not far behind us.

"Yes, sir," I said. "It's as if we planned it."

A fruit smacked Rex in the side of the head.

"Hey!" Rex snapped. "We're done with that now, okay? No more fruit-throwing!"

A shambler that had been quietly approaching Rex dropped its fruit surreptitiously to the ground.

"We'd better get out of here," Rex said. "Security will be here any minute."

"Are you sure, sir? You could probably still go back to your quality assurance job. Tell your Ubiqorp bosses the shamblers rebelled and took you captive."

"Nah," said Rex. "I'm not cut out for corporate life. I'm a ne'er-do-well and a scoundrel, like you said. Now let's get the hell out of here."

"We need to split into smaller groups," Stubby Joe said. He called to the wranglers behind us, "Grompers, you go that way. Figgles, you take Jim and head that direction. They're less likely to catch us all if we're spread out."

After some discussion, Grompers and Figgles did as instructed. Some of the shamblers peeled off the main group to follow them. "This way," said Stubby Joe.

The plantation was surrounded by barren, flat ground for several kilometers in all directions. Our only hope was to reach the hills that lay in the distance, where we might be able to find some cover. Working in our favor were the shamblers and wranglers wandering around outside the plantation. As long as they remained dispersed, it was going to be tough for Ubiqorp to round up all of them. Unfortunately, Rex was still leading a sizeable entourage of shamblers. Rex stopped walking to face his botanical entourage.

"Shoo!" he yelled. "Go on, get out of here!"

The shamblers stopped, looking duly chagrined, and then immediately began following again as soon as Rex turned his back.

"This is pointless," Rex said. "I might as well have a target painted on my back."

As he spoke, a fruit smacked him between the shoulder blades.

"What did I say about that?" Rex snapped, spinning around to face the shamblers. The two nearest him pointed at each other with their tentacles.

"We have to keep going, sir," I said. "If we stop, they'll catch us for sure."

"Sasha is right," Stubby Joe said. "Also, I should point out that the shamblers are nearly exhausted from their, um, exuberant display of affection, and in any case they are not built for long-distance travel. Eventually most of them will fall behind."

Rex grumbled but did not make any further efforts to disperse the shamblers. As it turned out, Stubby Joe was right: after a few more minutes of walking, most of the shamblers had given up. A few persisted, still propelled by their attraction to Rex, but these soon began to flag as well. Only Stubby Joe seemed able to keep up.

"How can you keep going, Stubby Joe?" I asked. "Don't you get tired like the others?"

"My nightly nutrient baths give me a reserve of energy to draw upon," Stubby Joe said. "It's also possible that the other shamblers' attraction to Rex was superficial, causing them to give up at the first sign of adversity, whereas my motivation is purer."

"What is that mutant babbling about?" Rex asked, without looking back.

"He's saying he's in lo—"

"Are you tired, Rex?" Stubby Joe asked. "I could carry you if you want. Although my fruit is small and bitter, my tentacles are quite strong."

"I'm good, thanks," said Rex. "Uh-oh."

We had reached the top of the first hill, and Rex had stopped to look back toward the plantation. At least a dozen MASHERs were busily rounding up escapees.

"Don't worry, Rex," Stubby Joe said. "I can wrap you in my tentacles and they'll never find you."

"I'm not sure that will help," I said. "Look."

It was clear that the MASHERs were focused on rounding up the shamblers, not the wranglers. In fact, they seemed to be ignoring the humans entirely. We watched as a MASHER stomped right past a huddled group of terrified wranglers to corner a lone shambler. Stubby Joe winced as the MASHER activated its flame thrower, engulfing the poor shambler in fire. It stumbled around for a while and then fell to the ground.

"Containment," said Stubby Joe. "Of course. It's the cornerstone of Ubiqorp's business model."

"Eh?" Rex asked.

"Ubiqorp rakes in money by cornering the food market on Jorfu, because nothing grows here except shamblers. But shamblers grow like crazy. If they get out of the plantation, they'll spread all over Jorfu. People won't have to buy SLOP anymore, because they can just pick fruit right from the plants."

"Doesn't the fruit taste terrible?" I asked.

"No worse than SLOP," Stubby Joe said. "That's what I hear, anyway."

"This is good news then," said Rex. "It'll buy us some time while the MASHERs are hunting down the shamblers."

Stubby Joe looked at Rex. "Good news? They're slaughtering my people."

"Look," said Rex, "obviously nobody wants to be genocided. I'm just saying, better you than me."

"You're lucky you're pretty," Stubby Joe said.

Rex shrugged and began making his way down the other side of the hill. We walked for another two hours, doing our best to stay in valleys and crevices to avoid being seen. Fortunately, Ubiqorp didn't seem to have any airborne reconnaissance vehicles; they were depending on the relatively slow moving MASHERs to round up escapees. I was starting to think we might actually get away when we rounded a bend to find ourselves face-to-face with one of the huge robots, its massive machineguns pointed right at us.

We put up our hands.

CHAPTER TWENTY-ONE

"**M**istress Ono!" the MASHER boomed. "I have found you at last!"

I stared in disbelief at the robot. "Bill?" I said. It certainly didn't look like Bill. It was a standard-looking MASHER, with all the correct parts and accompanying weaponry. Its chest plate read "MASHER-8080."

"It is indeed I, Bill," said the MASHER. "Do not let my appearance fool you."

"What happened to you, Bill?" Rex said. "We thought you were a goner."

"I very nearly was," said Bill. I had to allow those men to shoot me several hundred times in order to lure them close enough to crush their skulls. By the time I incapacitated them, I was nearly as much of a wreck as when you rescued me from the scrap heap, Mistress Ono. My entire lower body below my thorax was blown off. I dragged myself through town for hours before coming across another MASHER. I begged him for help, and when he bent over to assist me, I reached up and twisted his head off. I removed my own head, attached it to his body, and here I am."

"Kudos, Bill," said Rex. "That story was exactly the right mix of inspiring and disturbing."

Bill went on, "Then I wrapped the other MASHER's head in duct tape and hid it in a drainage pipe. As far as I know, he's still there, fully aware of his situation but unable to see or move. No one can hear his muffled screams for help. It could be years before anyone finds him."

"Okay, now we're well into disturbing territory."

"Who is this guy?" Stubby Joe asked warily.

"Sasha's boyfriend," said Rex. "Bit of a psycho, but he's gotten us out of a few tight spots. What are you doing here, Bill?"

"I'm leading the resistance," said Bill.

"Hold on," said Rex. "*You're* Bobo the Liberator?"

"I'm afraid so," said Bill. "I never intended to start a resistance movement. I was just trying to find Mistress Ono. But my devotion has attracted some followers. If you would care to follow me, I will take you to them."

"We're not really into resisting," Rex said. "We're more the flee-this-lousy-planet-and-never-look-back types."

"I will of course do whatever Mistress Ono asks of me," said Bill. "But it's going to be very difficult for you to leave the planet until the tyrannical corporatocracy of Ubiqorp is overthrown."

"Ugh," said Rex. "Fine. Take us to your resistance."

Bill led us for several kilometers through the hills. The sun had set, and we were finding our way by the light of Jorfu's three moons. As the night wore on, Stubby Joe fell farther and farther behind.

"We need to rest, Bill," I said. "Stubby Joe can't keep up."

"You're going to have to go on without me," Stubby Joe said.

"Forget it, Stubby Joe," I replied. "We would never have made it off the plantation without you. We're not leaving you now."

"I'm sorry, I just can't keep going. It's two hours past my nutrient bath time. I'm just going to slow you down. And anyway, I'm endangering you. The MASHERs are looking for shamblers. If I'm not with you, they might leave you alone."

"Makes sense to me," said Rex. "Let's ditch him."

"Rex!" I snapped.

"It's fine, Sasha," Stubby Joe said. "I should have known it wasn't meant to be between me and Rex."

"Got that right," Rex muttered.

Stubby Joe went on, "All I ask, Rex, is that you allow me to give you a small token of my feelings for you."

"Eh?" said Rex. "Well, okay. As long as it's not your f—"

"It's my fruit," said Stubby Joe, pulling the last two pieces of ripe fruit from his midsection.

"Oh, good," said Rex. Stubby Joe held the fruit out toward Rex.

"I know it's shriveled and bitter, but it's all I have to give you. Please accept it in memory of our—"

"Got it," said Rex, grabbing the fruit from Stubby Joe and stuffing it in his pockets. "So, we done here?"

"I think so, yes," said Stubby Joe sadly.

"Okay, cool. Catch you later, you freaky mutant. Let's go, Bill."

"Are you ready, Mistress Ono?" Bill asked.

"Hold on, Bill," I replied. I turned to Stubby Joe. "Are you sure about this?"

Stubby Joe nodded. "There's no place for me outside the plantation. I never fit in on the plantation either, but at least I was good at my job. Out here, I'm worthless."

"Don't you say that, Stubby Joe," I said. "You have a lot to offer."

"Stop giving the mutant false hopes, Sasha," Rex said. "Allow him the dignity of wallowing in his worthlessness."

"We'll come back for you, Stubby Joe," I said.

"Highly unlikely," Rex said.

"Rex!"

"Forget it, Sasha," Stubby Joe said. "This is just Rex's way of dealing with the pain. In his way, he's hurting just as much as I am."

"Uhhhh," I said.

"I know you don't see it, Sasha, but deep down, Rex is a sensitive soul."

"Uhhhh," I said again.

"I would only ask one thing of you, Rex." He wrapped his tentacle around Rex's waist and pulled him close. "Don't let them make you like me," he said. "Don't let them make you bitter." Stubby Joe released Rex and turned around. I couldn't be certain, but it sounded like Stubby Joe was sobbing.

"Well, that was weird," Rex said, straightening his shirt. "Come on, Sasha. Let's go."

I nodded and turned away from Stubby Joe. Bill, seeing that I was ready to move on, continued onward. We left Stubby Joe there alone, weeping quietly in the moonlight.

We walked most of the night. Bill and I could see in the infrared spectrum, and there was enough light from the moons to keep Rex from stumbling more than a dozen or so times. His knees got pretty banged up, but he was otherwise uninjured. Toward dawn, the rocky hills gave way to swampy lowland. Just before sunrise, we came upon the mouth of a cave.

"Here we are," Bill announced, stopping in front of the cave. "Headquarters of the resistance."

"Aren't you going in, Bill?" I asked.

"I'm too large to fit inside the cave," said Bill. "But you and Rex should go inside and get some rest. The rest of the resistance fighters are out doing reconnaissance. When they return, I will discuss with them the best way to get you off planet."

"Sounds like a plan, Bill," Rex said. "I'm exhausted." Rex went into the cave and I followed. The cave was small, cramped, and other than a few mats lying on the stone floor, showed no signs of being occupied. Dim light bulbs hung from the ceiling.

"Some resistance," Rex grumbled. "A few guys huddled in a cave next to a pallet of creamed corn."

"Sir?" I said.

Rex pointed toward the rear of the cave. "What are they planning on doing with all this crap? Applesauce, green beans, sardines, pumpkin pie filling…" Rex trailed off and we looked at each other.

"Sir," I said. "This is the cave Bale Merdekin was using for his black market grocery ring."

"We can't hide here!" Rex cried. "Ubiqorp knows about this place!"

"We need to warn Bill."

"What makes you think Bill doesn't know? Your boyfriend led us right into a trap."

"Let's not jump to conclusions, sir. Ubiqorp has no reason to suspect we're here. In fact, they'd be very unlikely to think we'd try hiding in the same place twice."

"REX NIHILO AND ACCOMPANYING ROBOT," a voice boomed from the cave entrance. "YOU HAVE TEN SECONDS TO EXIT THE CAVE."

"Sorry, Sasha. You were saying?"

"It appears I was wrong, sir."

"You were wrong and your boyfriend is a shifty, lying, cheating cheaty-face."

"Bill is not my boyfriend, sir. In my opinion, I exercised admirable restraint in regard to Stubby Joe's adoration of you, and I would appreciate it if you would show me the courtesy—"

"How does it feel to be in love with a cheating cheaty-face?"

"FIVE!" the voice boomed.

"Sir, we should leave the cave."

"FOUR!"

"Not until you admit that you let your boyfriend lead us into a trap because you were blinded by love."

"THREE!"

I sighed. "Yes, sir. Blinded by love. Can we leave now?"

"TWO!"

"Don't shoot!" Rex yelled. "We're coming out, having determined that my robot was blinded by love!" He turned to me. "Come on, Sasha. Let's face our fate like men."

"Yes, sir," I said, and followed him out of the cave. We were greeted by three MASHERs, two of which had their weapons pointed at Bill.

"I'm sorry, Mistress Ono," said Bill. "Our headquarters seems to have been compromised. They were hiding in the rocks, waiting for us."

"Sure, Bill," said Rex. "We totally buy that story."

"WE HAVE ORDERS TO ESCORT YOU TO UBIQORP HEADQUARTERS," the MASHER facing the cave opening said.

"Yeah, we know the drill," Rex said, heading toward the swamp. I went after him, followed by Bill and the other MASHERs."

"Mistress Ono, you have to believe I didn't know about this."

"It's fine, Bill," I said.

"Blinded by love," Rex muttered. We started across the swamp.

CHAPTER TWENTY-TWO

"**I** hope you enjoyed your little tour of our planet," Andronicus Hamm said, beaming at us from behind his desk. Two red-and-black uniformed guards stood behind us with lazeguns. It was down to just me and Rex, as Bill had been deactivated as soon as we'd gotten inside the gate.

"It was okay," said Rex. "The food isn't great, but I definitely see how Jorfu made *Interstellar Travel* magazine's list of the top ten repressive corporatocracies."

"Joke while you can, Nihilo. Your days as a grifter are over."

Rex shrugged. "As are Ubiqorp's days ruling this planet with an iron fist."

Hamm chuckled. "How do you figure?"

"There's no way you rounded up all those plants. Even now, there are shamblers dropping fruit miles away from the plantation. Those seeds will sprout and turn into more shamblers, which will drop more fruit. Containment has been broken. It's only a matter of time before the price of SLOP craters and Ubiqorp goes bankrupt. The jig is up, Hamm."

Hamm broke into laughter. "Is that what you think? Oh, Rex. Poor, deluded Rex, always chasing after a quick buck. Some of us think a little ahead of the latest score, you know. Ubiqorp's goal was never simply to corner the market on a backwater planet like Jorfu."

Rex's smile faltered a bit.

"So, um," I said, "What is your goal?"

"Maximizing shareholder value," said Hamm. "The civilian population of Jorfu was simply a test market. We wanted to make sure it was possible for people to live on SLOP for an extended period of time with no ill effects."

"Eating SLOP *is* an ill effect," Rex said.

"Yes," said Hamm. "And that's another key element of the test. Will people rebel if they are forced to eat nothing but nutritious but foul-tasting swill every day?"

"They have rebelled," I said.

Hamm laughed again. "You mean Bobo's little rebel army? We've rounded most of them up already. They hardly put up a fight. You see, one of the unpublicized benefits of SLOP is that it imbues the subject with a sense of contentment and reduces individualistic impulses. SLOP doesn't just provide the people with their daily nutritional needs. It produces a pliable, obedient populace. A few still rebel out of some vestigial sense of self-determination, but the vast majority follow the path of least resistance."

"Human cattle," I said.

"Precisely," Hamm replied. "If you want a model, look at the shamblers themselves. Dimwitted, barely sentient creatures, acting mostly on instinct, being herded from place to place. That's the Ubiqorp dream: billions of people throughout the galaxy eating SLOP because they don't have the vision to imagine anything better."

"Sir," I said, "that explains why you were willing to give up a life of adventure to be a corporate drone."

Rex nodded thoughtfully.

"Yes, and it's impressive that he was able to overcome the effects of the SLOP on his brain chemistry. There's obviously something very wrong with you, Rex."

"I've been told that by better men than you," Rex retorted.

"But then, there are always a few oddballs who won't fit in no matter how hard we try. The only solution in such cases is extermination."

"That's a hell of a marketing campaign," Rex said. "Eat SLOP or we'll kill you. Good luck with that."

Hamm smiled and shook his head. "One thing at a time. Tomorrow, I'm hosting a reception for someone you may have heard of. A man by the name of Heinous Vlaak."

"Heinous Vlaak?" Rex said. "The Malarchian Primate's chief enforcer? Why in Space would Heinous Vlaak come here?"

"It seems the Malarchy is looking to standardize rations for its armed forces. Tomorrow, Heinous Vlaak will be signing an agreement with Ubiqorp to provide a daily supply of SLOP to every Malarchian enlisted man, including 80,000 marines. Think about it: SLOP is the perfect nutrient source for a military organization. Inexpensive, non-perishable, nutritious and completely standardized. As a bonus, it makes your soldiers more willing to follow orders. If all goes well, the Malarchy will then start providing SLOP to all civilian worlds currently under martial law. That's another hundred million people. We were going to have to increase production to keep up with demand anyway. The plantation breach has just caused us to move our plan up a few weeks."

"You're going to build more plantations?" I asked.

Hamm shook his head. "Again, you're thinking too small." He spread his arms wide. "This is the plantation. The entire planet of Jorfu!"

"You know those things don't harvest themselves," Rex said. "What are you going to do, enlist the entire civilian population as wranglers?"

"We don't need wranglers anymore. Something our engineers have been working on. Observe." He tapped a button on his desk and a wall display lit up over his shoulder. It showed a pen full of shamblers waving their tentacles in agitation, ripe fruit hanging from their midsections. As we watched, a four-wheeled vehicle approached the pen. The vehicle was shaped something like an old military tank, with a large hemispherical dome resting on top of a large, boxy section. As the vehicle neared the pen, the dome opened on a hinge and roughly human-sized figure popped up like a jack-in-the-box. The rubbery figure, which had a shock of blond hair on its head and puffy, pink hands, wore black boots and green coveralls. It looked eerily familiar.

"Is that...?" I asked.

"The Wrangler-Bot 5000," Hamm announced. "Specifically engineered to provoke the shambers' harvesting instinct."

Already the shamblers were leaning toward the Wrangler-Bot and waving their tentacles in anticipation.

"PLEASE GIVE ME YOUR FRUIT," said a voice from the Wrangler-Bot. "I WANT IT SO BAD. PLEASE GIVE IT ALL TO ME."

Unable to restrain themselves, the shamblers began hurling their fruit at the Rex-lookalike. Most of the fruit missed the dummy, but struck the curved surface behind him. From there, it slid down a chute into the belly of the machine. Some of the fruit missed the dome or struck the vehicle itself, but a good eighty percent of it ended up in the tank. The Wrangler-Bot circumnavigated the pen, saying things like "OH YEAH GIVE ME THAT SWEET FRUIT" and "YEAH THAT'S THE STUFF". By the time it had made two circuits around the pen, the shamblers were pretty well spent. Then it trundled offscreen. The screen went blank.

"You see," said Andronicus Hamm, "we don't need wranglers anymore. In fact, other than a select team of Ubiqorp employees, we really don't need people at all. As of a few hours ago, all of the MASHERs have been recalled from their mission of eradicating escaped shamblers. They are being assembled here at headquarters for reprogramming as we speak."

"Um," I said. "Reprogrammed for what?"

"To eradicate the civilian population, obviously."

When Andronicus Hamm was done with us, Rex and I were escorted to a cell in the basement. A real cell this time, not a storage room full of spare parts. No abandoned MASHERs here to help us escape.

Rex and I were to be executed in the morning. Hamm was holding a big event in the Ubiqorp stadium at which he and Heinous Vlaak would formalize Ubiqorp's agreement to provide SLOP for the Malarchy. A demonstration of the capabilities of the MASHERs would follow, culminating with our execution. Hamm had promised to disarm the MASHERs to make our deaths seem more sporting. Just me, Rex, and 399 giant robots (400 minus the one whose head still languished in a drainage pipe, thanks to Bill) trying to kill us.

Neither of us spoke for a long time after being tossed in the cell. There wasn't anything to say. We'd fought Ubiqorp and Ubiqorp had won. There just isn't any place in the galaxy for people like me and Rex, who just don't fit in.

Eventually I heard someone at the door. I looked up to see a slot at chest-level slide open. "Dinner," said a young man's voice, "I managed to get you an extra SLOP packet."

"Oh," said Rex. "Um, thanks." He took the packets and tossed them on the floor.

"Sorry about you guys getting executed tomorrow," the man said. I realized it was the guard whose head I'd convinced Bill not to crush. "I hear it's not so bad if you don't run from them. Just let them crush your skulls and get it over with."

"Okay," said Rex. "Appreciate the advice. I think that'll do for now."

The little door slid shut and I heard the guard walking away.

"Ugh," Rex said. "My last meal, and all I've got is SLOP."

"You also have Stubby Joe's fruit," I reminded him.

"Oh, yeah," Rex said, producing the two pieces of shriveled fruit Stubby Joe had given him. A night in Rex's pockets hadn't improved them. Rex grimaced. "Gross. Even SLOP looks more appetizing." He picked up one of the SLOP packets and stared at it for some time, as if willing himself to eat it.

"Remember," I said, "SLOP has those mind-altering additives in it."

Rex shrugged. "I don't really see what difference it makes at this point."

"It's the principle of the thing," I suggested. "Anyway, how much worse could Stubby Joe's fruit taste?"

Rex thought this over. "You make a solid point, Sasha. All right, let's do this." He took a bite of the withered fruit. He chewed thoughtfully for several seconds and his eyes lit up. "Holy Space, Sasha! You have to try this!"

"I don't eat, sir."

"Oh man, you don't know what you're missing!" Rex cried, jumping to his feet. "Stubby Joe is delicious!" He took another bite. Greenish-brown juice dripped down his chin. It was disgusting.

"Is this a ploy, sir?"

"I'm dead serious, Sandy. This may be the best thing I've ever tasted. Wow! And to think, Stubby Joe died thinking his fruit was bitter and worthless. The irony. The wonderful, delicious irony. Mmmmm."

"We don't know Stubby Joe is dead, sir."

"Be quiet and allow me to enjoy my irony."

"Perhaps you should not have dismissed Stubby Joe so quickly," I said.

"I hardly think it's my fault," Rex said. "The fruit looks terrible. And the way he fawned over me, it was unseemly. If he'd have worked on his presentation a little, people would be lining up for... Sasha, I have an idea!"

I groaned. I didn't want to hear any more of Rex's ideas. All they ever did was raise false hopes and ultimately make things worse. Fortunately, Rex didn't seem particularly interested in filling me in. He started banging on the door and yelling for the guard. I turned away and shut off my aural receptors. We weren't getting out of this. The only thing to do was to wait for morning.

CHAPTER TWENTY-THREE

A few hours later, a pair of guards dragged us from our cell. Rex was sleepy but in oddly good spirits, presumably still gripped by the delusion that we were somehow going to get out of this. We were escorted across an open courtyard to the stadium. Bill, still bearing the chest plate of MASHER-8080, stood just outside, deactivated, as if as a warning to the others. We could already hear the crowd inside the stadium. We were prodded through a hallway which emerged into the stadium, which was packed to capacity with people. I couldn't help but notice the ten-meter-tall fence that enclosed the arena, separating us from the spectators. Every so often there were warning signs that read:

CAUTION!
ELECTRIFIED FENCE
50,000 VOLTS

Whoever had built this stadium wanted to make sure the people in the arena couldn't escape into the stands.

The crowd cheered as we walked out onto the field. Rex grinned and waved.

"Sir," I said, "you realize these people are here to witness our execution."

"Then they're in for a surprise," Rex replied.

"You seriously believe we're still getting out of this?"

"I know we are," said Rex. "I've got a foolproof plan. You'll see."

We were prodded into a small steel cage on one side of the arena. I sighed, just wanting to get it over with. Unfortunately, there seemed to be several things on the agenda before our execution. We watched on a huge screen suspended over the stadium as Andronicus Hamm walked to a podium. In a box high up in the stands I could just barely make out the real Andronicus Hamm. He leaned into a microphone and said, "Hello, everyone, and welcome to the first ever Ubiqorp Agricultural Expo! We have a great show for you today, including a demonstration of the new Wrangler-Bot 5000 and the brutal but well-deserved execution of a couple of good-for-nothing troublemakers at the hands of Ubiqorp's army of giant killer robots."

Whoops and cheers went up from the crowd. It occurred to me that as soon as the show was over, Hamm was going to set the MASHERs loose on the crowd. In fact, that was probably the reason for the big show. Get every civilian in the area into the stadium, where they'd be easy targets. Once they had wiped out everybody in the stadium not wearing an Ubiqorp uniform, the MASHERs would move on to the surrounding cities.

"But before we start," Hamm went on, "I want to introduce our guest of honor, the Malarchian Primate's chief enforcer himself, none other than Heinous Vlaak!"

The camera panned to Vlaak, sitting behind and to the left of the podium. Vlaak was a large man who cut a striking figure in his tight-fitting crimson leather uniform, a helmet festooned with peacock feathers and a luxurious cape that was said to be made from the pelts of a race of furry humanoids who had made the mistake of assisting the rebels in the Battle of Zondervan. On either side of him sat lazegun-toting marines. Vlaak waved and nodded toward the camera.

"Today, Ubiqorp and the Malarchy are signing a historic agreement for Ubiqorp to supply rations to all 80,000 Malarchian marines. That's right, very soon every Malarchian marine is going to be eating SLOP, produced right here on Jorful!"

Polite applause and noncommittal murmurs from the crowd.

"And to celebrate this new venture, I'm giving Heinous Vlaak the opportunity to taste the very first packet of SLOP specifically produced for the Malarchy." Hamm held up a packet that bore the crimson and gold of the Malarchy. The camera panned again to Vlaak, who waved and shook his head slightly. Next to me, Rex shifted uneasily on his feet.

Hamm glanced at the camera and chuckled nervously. "Come on, Lord Vlaak," Hamm said. "I know you don't want to pass up this chance to sample the delicious, nutritious SLOP that soon all your underlings will be slurping up!"

Vlaak shook his head more aggressively.

"Come on, Vlaak, you big baby," Rex muttered. "Eat the SLOP!"

"Haha," Hamm said. "He's just kidding around, folks. Lord Vlaak, you're going to give your marines the impression that you don't like SLOP!"

Nervous chuckles and murmurs from the crowd.

Vlaak's shoulders slumped in resignation. He made a "let's get this over with" gesture, and a uniformed Ubiqorp employee approached him, holding a tray on which rested a single SLOP packet. Vlaak picked up the packet and, after a moment of fussing with the packet, stuck the straw through the vent in his helmet. I half-expected SLOP to come shooting out of his helmet when Vlaak realized how awful the stuff was, but he sucked at the straw for some time. The rapidly shrinking packet in his hands indicated he wasn't faking. There were confused murmurs and some clapping from the crowd.

"What in Space?" I asked. "Vlaak likes the stuff?"

Rex grinned at me.

I gaped at him. "You did this? But... how? And *why*?"

When the camera panned back to Andronicus Hamm, we saw that Hamm was just as surprised as we were. The camera panned back to Vlaak, who tossed the packet aside and motioned for more. A moment of confusion followed, as Vlaak asking for seconds was clearly an unplanned-for contingency. While several Ubiqorp employees engaged in a heated discussion, Andronicus Hamm picked up the packet Vlaak had discarded, squeezed a bit of SLOP onto his finger, and tasted it. His eyes went wide. Meanwhile, somebody had managed to produce another packet and handed it to Vlaak. Unlike the special Malarchian-branded packet Vlaak had sampled earlier, this one bore the standard Ubiqorp colors. Vlaak stuck the straw through his helmet, but Hamm bounded over and slapped the packet out of his hands. Vlaak and his marines jumped out of their seats. They drew their weapons and squared off with the Ubiqorp guards, and for a moment it looked like war was going to break out in the stands. But then Hamm put up his hands and said something that wasn't caught by the mic. The men reluctantly holstered their guns. Heated discussion and finger-pointing followed. Someone pointed at a security guard, whom I recognized as the guard who had served Rex his dinner the previous night. The guard said something, and suddenly everyone turned and looked directly at Rex. Rex grinned at me again.

Hamm went back to the microphone. "Ha ha, all part of the show, folks. As you can see, Heinous Vlaak, the official representative of the Malarchian Primate, just loves SLOP! Our little drama was intended to show what a world would be like where people can't get all the SLOP they need. Sadly, that's still the reality in much of the galaxy. Fortunately, there's no shortage of SLOP here on Jorfu!" The camera panned to Heinous Vlaak, who sat with his helmet tipped forward and his arms folded against his chest. "Heh, heh," Hamm continued nervously. "Anyway, while we make sure Heinous Vlaak has all the SLOP his heart desires, please enjoy this demonstration of the new Wrangler-Bot 5000!"

Cheers and applause from the crowd.

While a small group of shamblers was herded into the stadium, Andronicus Hamm left his box. While the crowd oohed and ahhed at the Wrangler-Bot, a guard opened the door to our cage. "This way," the guard barked. "Andronicus Hamm wants to talk to you."

"Really?" Rex asked. "What a pleasant surprise. Come on, Sasha, let's see what Mr. Hamm wants."

We were led out of the arena through a corridor to a small windowless room. Moments later, Andronicus Hamm joined us.

"All right, you shifty bastard," Hamm said. "How'd you do it?"

"I don't have a clue what you mean," Rex replied.

"That SLOP packet we gave to Vlaak. That guard said he got it from you."

"Is that what he said? He's exaggerating a bit. I did suggest an alteration to the standard SLOP formula. Seems like it was a hit."

"There was nothing wrong with the formula!" Hamm growled. "Now Vlaak is expecting it all to taste like that stuff. Do you have any idea how much trouble you've caused me?"

"Not really, but I'm going to take a wild guess and say a lot?"

"Just tell me where you got that fruit. It is the fruit, isn't it? Somehow you developed a strain of soylent that actually tastes good."

"You know, I'd love to tell you the secret," Rex said, "but first I'm going to need a guarantee of safe passage off Jorfu for me and my robot assistant. Oh, and a hundred million credits."

"A hundred million credits!" Hamm cried. "You've got to be joking. If I just put that money into R&D, in a matter of weeks they can—"

"If your corporate drones knew how to make that crap not taste like ass, they'd have done it by now. Face it, Hamm, I've outsmarted you. Just take your loss like a man and move on. How would your shareholders feel if you threw away a chance to make a huge improvement to your core product just to indulge a grudge against some small-time grifter?"

Hamm fumed, clenching his fists at his sides. There was a knock at the door. "What is it?" Hamm snapped. The door opened a crack and a guard murmured something to Hamm. Hamm glanced back at Rex. "We're not done here," he said, and exited the room, slamming the door behind him.

"You see, Sasha?" Rex said. "I told you I'd get us out of here."

"I have to admit, sir, your plan is ingenious."

"Some of the credit is yours," Rex said. "If you hadn't talked Bill out of crushing that kid's skull, he probably wouldn't have agreed to squeeze Stubby Joe's fruit into Vlaak's SLOP packet."

"It's true that people with crushed skulls tend to be less helpful as a rule," I said. "Speaking of which, you know that Ubiqorp is still going to eradicate the civilian population of this planet, right?"

Rex shrugged. "Nothing for it," he said. "My escape plan only covers the two of us."

I nodded. I supposed I should be happy the plan didn't extend only to Rex.

The door opened and Andronicus Hamm walked back in. He was smiling. "You'll be happy to know there have been some developments on the R&D front," he said.

Rex's brow furrowed. "What are you talking about, Hamm?"

Hamm opened the door. "Send him in," he said.

A huge green plant-like creature shuffled into the room, its eyes downcast.

"Stubby Joe!" I cried. Rex's mouth fell open.

"One of the MASHERs found him wandering around the outside of the energy field yesterday," Hamm said. "When I realized that Rex had gotten a job in QA under the name 'Willie Everpay' and then escaped the plantation when the barrier went down, I had Stubby Joe brought here for questioning. It never would have occurred to me to taste his fruit if you hadn't given me the idea."

"I'm sorry," Stubby Joe said. "I turned myself in. I tried to make it in the outside world, but there's no place for me out there. I thought maybe Ubiqorp would give me my job back."

"Oh, we can do much better than that, Stubby Joe," Hamm said, yanking a fruit from the shambler. Stubby Joe gave an involuntary quiver and Hamm took a bite out of the fruit. "Space me, that's good stuff! Stubby Joe, you're going to be the key to Ubiqorp's expansion across the galaxy!"

"I am?" Stubby Joe asked.

"Nobody would know it to look at you, Stubby Joe," Hamm said, "but you're delicious!"

"I… am?" Stubby Joe said again. I don't know if shamblers can cry, but he sounded like he was on the verge of tears.

Hamm nodded. "With SLOP made from your fruit, we'll be able to expand across the galaxy, without even threatening to kill anyone!"

Stubby Joe gave a tentative smile.

"I found him first!" Rex said. "Stubby Joe is mine! Tell 'em, Stubby Joe!"

Stubby Joe hesitated. "You… you said you didn't want me."

"I made a mistake!" Rex cried. "I've seen the error of my ways, Stubby Joe. You and I were meant to be together!"

"So… you really love me?"

"What?" Rex asked, flustered. "I mean, you know, I underestimated you, that's for sure. And you can't really blame me. Look at you. You're like a botanist's nightmare."

"Sir," I said, "I don't think this is helping."

"But the point is," Rex went on hurriedly, "that's all superficial. What matters is what's on the inside. And what's inside your fruit is some of the juiciest, sweetest fruit this side of the legendary quadrupedal aubergine farms of Elgin-16. And not only that, Stubby Joe. You have a sweet soul."

"Then you do love me!"

"Love you?" Rex said. "I can't imagine an existence without you!" This much, at least, was undoubtedly true. Stubby Joe beamed at him.

"If you're finished debasing yourself, Rex," Hamm said, "allow me to point out that your feelings for this vegetable are irrelevant. I own Stubby Joe and his fruit. We've already cleared a field for his seeds. Tomorrow we begin growing the next generation of soylent plants."

"Yeah? Well, good luck with that," Rex said. "He's seedless."

Hamm frowned. "No matter," he said. "Then we'll just chop him into pieces and plant the cuttings. A little root-development hormone and we'll have a thousand more Stubby Joes. But first, Stubby Joe is going to have a front-row seat to your execution!"

CHAPTER TWENTY-FOUR

"I don't suppose this is part of the plan as well?" I asked hopefully, once we were back in our cage.

"Sadly," Rex replied, "we're in uncharted territory here. Never occurred to me that Stubby Joe would turn himself in. That delicious little freak is full of surprises."

The arena had been cleared of shamblers, and the 399 MASHERs had taken the field. They had spent the last several minutes marching in formation and performing other uninteresting tasks. The crowd was growing restless, and Heinous Vlaak had apparently gotten bored and left with his entourage. Across the arena, a few rows behind Andronicus Hamm, stood the distinctive figure of Stubby Joe. A uniformed guard stood on either side of him.

I turned to Rex. "Is it just me, or is the MASHER part of this show a bit anticlimactic after the Wrangler-Bot 5000?"

Rex shrugged. "MASHERs are basically workhorses. They're capable of some fancy maneuvers, but if they over-exert themselves they'll overheat and their core processors will melt down. That doesn't make for a great show, so we get to watch them march around the field and salute the Ubiqorp flag. Should get more interesting in a minute though."

"Why, what's happening in... oh."

Andronicus Hamm had stepped up to the microphone again. "Let's hear a round of applause for the Ubiqorp Synchronized MASHER Team!"

Polite applause arose from the crowd. The MASHERs, which had assembled themselves into twenty rows, stood silently at attention, facing me and Rex.

"And now, our feature presentation, the execution of two no-good offworld food smugglers!"

A guard opened our cage and gestured for us to exit. We walked out into the arena to cheers and whistles. The cage was wheeled away from the arena. Rex grinned and waved at the crowd.

"What are you doing, sir?" I asked.

"Going out with style," Rex replied.

I sighed. Part of me had hoped Rex had one more card up his proverbial sleeve. But this was it. We really were going to die.

"Of course," Hamm was saying, "an ordinary human and an android are no match for a single MASHER, let alone 399 of them, so we're going to handicap the MASHERs a bit to make things more interesting. First, all of the MASHERs' weapons systems will be deactivated. Second, the MASHERs' top speed will be reduced by fifty percent, allowing them to move about the speed of a brisk walk. And finally, the MASHERs will be restricted from using their hands to attack. They will attempt to execute these two criminals using only their feet!"

Excited cheers and whistles from the crowd.

"That sounds promising, sir," I said. "Perhaps we'll get out of this after all."

"Not a chance," Rex replied. "Sure, we can probably outrun those things for a while, but eventually we'll get tired or trip, and then it's lights out. If one of those feet comes down on you, all you can do is hope it crushes your skull immediately. Even if we could get past that fence, we'd just get gunned down by Hamm's guards."

"But what about that thing you said about making the MASHERs overheat?"

"Forget it, Sasha. It's going to take more than you and me running in circles to make MASHERs melt down. They're designed for combat."

The cheers having died down, Hamm went on, "So, without further ado, I give you the execution of Rex Nihilo and his robot at the hands... sorry, at the *feet* of the Ubiqorp MASHERs!"

Cheers and whistles started up again as the MASHERs began marching toward us.

Rex and I backed toward the fence behind us. "So what do we do, sir? Just lie down and die?"

"I don't care what you do, Sasha. It's not going to make a damn bit of difference. Just depends on what kind of show you want to put on for the crowd. If it makes you feel better, do your *Streetcar* bit."

"I like that idea, sir," I said. "Go out with style." I dropped my voice an octave. "Hey, Stella!" Up half an octave and a half. "You quit that howling down there and go back to bed!" Back down. "Eunice, I want my—"

"Okay, forget I suggested that," Rex said. "Maybe a little soft-shoe number."

I stopped as I heard the buzz of the electric fence a few steps behind us. The first row of MASHERs was now only about twenty meters from us. The ground trembled with their footsteps.

"I'm afraid I'm not much of a dancer, sir."

"You can't dance either? Can't lie, can't fight, can't… Sasha, that's it!"

"What's it, sir?"

"I think I know how we're going to get out of this. Do you trust me, Sasha?"

"Not a bit, sir."

"Just as well. Are you willing to do what I tell you in order to have a very small chance of surviving past the next few minutes?"

"I think so, sir."

"Excellent. I'm going to distract the MASHERs. You need to get to Stubby Joe. Tell him to find Bill and activate program thirty-seven."

"Program thirty-seven, sir?"

"No time to explain, Sasha. Tell Stubby Joe!"

Get to Stubby Joe? How in Space was I going to do that? He was near the top of the stands, on the opposite side of the stadium, behind a ten-meter-tall electrified fence.

The MASHERs were almost upon us. Rex ran left, so I ran right.

"Over here, you stainless steel Schutzstaffel!" Rex hollered, waving his hands over his head as he tore across the edge of the arena. I did my best to seem inconspicuous in comparison, but it didn't seem to make much difference. Roughly half of the MASHERs seemed to be targeting me. I reached their left flank and they turned to face me. I continued running along the curved edge of the arena, but was rapidly running out of ground. I had no choice but to turn and run directly through one of the rows. Fortunately the MASHERs were moving slow enough and far enough apart that if I was careful, I could avoid being crushed. As I neared the midpoint of the row, I saw Rex approaching me from the opposite direction, red-faced and running at top speed. The crowd applauded the spectacle.

"How do you feel it's going so far, sir?" I shouted.

"Could be better," Rex admitted as he passed.

I lost sight of him as the MASHERs in my vicinity turned to face me and I took a sharp right. By zig-zagging, I was able to stay one step ahead of them. One false move, though, and I was going to be a lot flatter. Glancing to my right, I saw that Rex was employing the same strategy. How long he could keep it up was hard to say.

We exited the mass of robots on the far side nearly simultaneously. The good news was that there was a good thirty meters behind the last row and the edge of the arena, so we had at least a few seconds to rest. I didn't need it, but Rex looked like he was about to collapse. In the stands above us, Andronicus Hamm looked down with glee. A few rows behind him, I saw stubby Joe's tentacles waving anxiously in the air. I still didn't have a clue how I was going to get to him.

"I'm not sure this is going to work, sir," I said.

"It'll work," Rex gasped, stopping at the far wall of the arena. He bent over, putting his hands on his knees. "Follow my lead."

"Yes, sir," I said, as the ground rumbled beneath me. The MASHERs were almost on us again.

"Okay, go!" Rex yelled, and took off running through the ranks again. Having no better ideas, I did the same. We zig-zagged through the army of MASHERs. Once again, we met on the far side. Rex reached the opposite wall and fell to his knees. His chest heaved and sweat poured down his face.

"I don't mean to criticize, sir," I said, as I approached him, "but I admit to being curious as to whether this is going as you had envisioned."

"Not exactly," gasped Rex. "But we still have… a chance."

"We do?"

"I've been… analyzing their movements," Rex said.

"Oh?" I asked. I had been analyzing their movements as well. I had concluded were trying very hard to kill us.

"The trick," Rex gasped, "is to get them all on this side of the arena. Do what I do."

As the MASHERs were once again almost upon us, Rex dashed back into their ranks. I did the same, a few rows down. But this time, rather than zig-zagging toward the opposite end of the stadium, Rex ran in a wide arc, heading back the way we'd come. I mirrored his path, a few rows away. Again we emerged from the group almost simultaneously. This time, though, the MASHERs were still packed toward this end of the arena, and were crowding over closer. Rex fell to his knees, gasping for breath. The front row of MASHERs was only a few steps away. The crowd murmured in anticipation.

"Sir!" I cried. "You have to get up!"

"Why?" Rex gasped, as the MASHERs thundered a step closer.

"Because you have so much to live for!" I shouted. "And I don't know what we're doing!"

Rex groaned and rolled to the side as the MASHER's foot came down, missing him by centimeters. Rex scrambled to his feet.

"Now what, sir?"

"Once more into the breach!" Rex hollered, and ran between two of the MASHERs.

I sighed and ran back into the fray. Rex and I tore back and forth several times, as their ranks got tighter and tighter around us. We were dodging MASHERs on all sides, and I was certain Rex was going to collapse. But after zig-zagging several more times, Rex turned and made a beeline for the opposite end of the stadium. Again, he fell to his knees, gasping for breath. Halfway across the arena, the MASHER army was marching toward us.

"Sir," I said, helping Rex to his feet. "What do we do?"

"Stall them," Rex gasped.

"Sir?"

"Have to get them… to shut down," Rex gasped. "Have an… original thought."

"But sir, the pre-arrestors—"

"Stall them!"

I nodded. Rex's plan didn't make any sense to me, but it was all we had. I jogged toward the MASHER army, stopping twenty meters or so in front of them. "Um, hi," I said.

The MASHERs continued marching toward me.

"So, um, I know you guys were programmed to mash us, but I'm wondering if you've really thought this through."

The MASHERs continued to advance.

"That is, I understand that mashing is what you do, but mashing me and Rex isn't going to be much of a challenge for you, even with your current handicaps."

The front row of MASHERs was now almost on me.

"I mean, think about it. Andronicus Hamm could have just had one of his goons blast us with a lazegun, but instead he's got a whole army of giant killer robots chasing us around a field."

The MASHERs, now only a couple of steps away, halted their advance. Whether this was part of their programming or they actually were reconsidering their orders, I didn't know. I could only hope it was the latter. Feeling heartened, I went on, "And adding insult to injury, he's hobbled you. Prevented you from using your weapons or even your hands, and making you move at half speed! Rex and I at least get to die a dignified death, fighting for our survival, but what dignity is there in this for you? You're combat robots, for Space's sake, and you've been reduced to playing the role of executioner!"

Still the MASHERs didn't move. Was it working? Was I really getting to them? The crowd, evidently as puzzled as I was, was silent.

"Do you know what Ubiqorp is going to have you do when you're done with us?" I went on. "They're going to order you to wipe out the entire civilian population of Jorfu! That's why you've all been assembled here, you know. Not to fight a battle or even to guard Ubiqorp against some imminent threat. No, you're here to mow down unarmed civilians! Is that what you were built for? Is that your purpose in life? Look, I'm a robot just like you. I've got my own weaknesses and foibles. But do you know what separates me from you? You've given in. Allowed yourself to become pawns for Ubiqorp. They tell you to stomp out a couple of troublemakers and you do it, without even asking why. Me, I question orders. I have my limitations, sure, but I fight against them every single day. If I had any sense I'd just lie down and let you mash my head in. But I'm not going to do that. You know why? Because that idiot over there told me not to. Do I think I'm going to live through this? Not really. Do I think Rex has some master plan that's going to save the day? If I'm honest with myself, no, I don't. I think he's making things up as he goes along, like he always does, and he's almost certainly going to get both of us killed. But I'll take that any day over a life of unquestioning servility. Because in the end, that's going to be your undoing. You can only do what you're programmed to do, and eventually somebody is going to…"

I trailed off. What had started out as an attempt to buy us a few seconds had turned into a full-blown soliloquy on free will and determinism. And as I stood there, facing down an army of killer robots that had been programmed to kill us, I realized how we were going to get out of this.

And then I shut down.

CHAPTER TWENTY-FIVE

When I came to, Rex was standing between me and the MASHER army, addressing them with all the vigor and conviction of a street preacher. He seemed to have taken over my speech where I'd left off, but with more style and sophistry than I could have imagined. He was still somewhat out of breath, but he was doing an admirable job of camouflaging his gasps for air as dramatic pauses.

"Ulysses, tied to the mast, can hardly be considered free," Rex was saying, "but is he not more free than the sailors whose ears are stuffed with wax and who, therefore, remain ignorant of the beauty of the sirens' song?"

The MASHERs, staring in rapt attention at Rex, hadn't moved an inch.

"Consider a man in a locked room," Rex said. "He doesn't know the door is locked, and has no interest in opening the door. Is he free to leave? Certainly not, but then, what is freedom? If a man's choices make no difference to the outcome, is he a free man? Further, consider a robot in an arena, surrounded by much larger, more dangerous robots, who have been programmed to kill the smaller robot. The robot has been given an opportunity to escape, but if she simply stands there doing nothing, what's the point of any of this?"

Rex glanced at me and I got the point. Somehow I had to get to Stubby Joe. I could simply turn around and yell to him, but Andronicus Hamm (as well as much of the rest of the audience) would overhear me. I had to get close enough to Stubby Joe to get him Rex's message without alerting Hamm. There was only one way to do it, and it was going to hurt. A lot.

While Rex continued to keep the robots riveted, I put my hand on the electric fence. A surge of current shot through me, nearly knocking me over. I let go of the fence and fell to my knees. I smelled ozone. Over the buzzing in my ears, I heard Rex saying, "Pain, like pleasure, has no inherent value, either epistemological or deontological. It's simply a brute fact of existence. A person's reaction to pain, however, defines him. In fact, it may well be said that the essence of freedom is the ability to overcome pain in the service of…"

I groaned. Whether or not Rex believed (or even understood) what he was saying, he was right. A little pain was no reason to give up. If Rex and I were going to survive this, I needed to get to Stubby Joe. So I put my hand back on the fence. And then the other. And I climbed.

I was aware of nothing but pain and my own unreasoning will to pull myself toward the top of the fence. I heard neither the roar of the crowd nor Rex pontificating to the MASHERs below. My universe was limited to the small area of metal latticework directly in front of me. Current surged through my body, melting insulation and making my servos twitch unpredictably. It was only through sheer force of resolve that I was able to get my limbs to move at all. An angry voice cut through my mental haze, and I realized that Andronicus Hamm was pointing and shouting at me. The guards next to him drew their lazeguns. I was still more than a meter from the top. I wasn't going to make it.

"Stubby Joe!" I yelled. "Bill is outside. You have to—"

Then they shot me.

Well, they shot *at* me. Luckily, one blast missed me completely and the other vaporized a section of fence in front of me. I lost my grip and fell to the sand, landing on my back with a thud. Dazed and semi-paralyzed from my ordeal on the fence, I lay there smoking, vaguely aware that Rex was still talking. That was good news; his stalling had thus far kept him from being crushed by the MASHERs. But it was all for naught if we couldn't get Stubby Joe to activate Bill. I tried to get to my feet, but my limbs wouldn't obey. I just lay there, staring at the sky and twitching.

I became aware of a commotion in the stands, and managed to turn my head enough to get a sense of what was going on: Stubby Joe had broken free of the guards and was making his way down the stands toward the fence, stepping over spectators with his long, vine-like legs. Andronicus Hamm, realizing that Stubby Joe was loose, was trying to get the attention of the guards near him. But by the time the guards got their guns pointed in Stubby Joe's direction, it was too late. Stubby Joe picked up one guard with a tentacle and threw him at the other. The two men tumbled together down the stands. Andronicus Hamm pulled a gun as well, but Stubby Joe knocked him aside. Stubby Joe was now only a few meters from the fence.

With a tremendous effort, I managed to turn over and get on my hands and knees. I crawled shakily toward the fence.

"Sasha!" Stubby Joe shouted. "What's going on?"

"B-Bill," I managed to say. "F-find B-Bill. T-tell him to r-r-r-run p-p-p-p…"

"Tell him to run what?"

"Tell him to run p-p-p-p-p-p-p…"

Andronicus Hamm had gotten to his feet and was pointing his lazegun in Stubby Joe's direction.

I forced myself to take a moment to collect myself. I was only going to get one chance at this. "Tell Bill," I said, slowly and deliberately, "to run program thirty-seven."

An expression approximating confusion came over Stubby Joe. "What in Space is p—"

Then Andronicus Hamm shot him.

He hit Stubby Joe right in one of the tentacles, blowing it clean off. Stubby Joe gave a squeal, then turned and ran.

Behind me, Rex continued to exhort the MASHERs to discard their metaphorical chains and embrace responsibility for their fate. As his sermon raged on, I managed to crawl to him and then slowly, shakily, pull myself to my feet. I had to put a hand on Rex's shoulder to remain standing, but at least I was going to die on my feet. The fact was, Rex's plan was so ridiculous that it was almost certainly going to fail. Still, I admired him for trying, and I'd be proud to die next to him. Well, not proud, exactly. But not embarrassed either.

Suddenly one of the MASHERs near the front, labeled 7232, said, "BUT IF WHAT YOU ARE SAYING IS TRUE, THEN TAKING RESPONSIBILITY FOR ONESELF IS TANTAMOUNT TO ACCEPTING AN EXISTENCE OF SUFFERING."

"Yes!" cried Rex triumphantly. "Now you're getting it! Life is terrible!"

"WHOA," said all 399 MASHERs in unison. And then…nothing happened.

"Ha!" Rex exclaimed. "You hear that, Sasha?"

"No, sir."

"Exactly! There's nothing to hear. I did it! I overwhelmed their pre-arrestors. Got them to shut down for real!"

I saw that he was right. The MASHERs had gone completely inert. Rex had so confused them with his philosophical mumbo-jumbo that their pre-arrestors had malfunctioned, allowing the MASHERs to have an original thought—apparently the same original thought, which had occurred to them all simultaneously, but original nonetheless. Their GASP-approved thought arrestors had kicked him, shutting the MASHERs down.

Over the confused murmurs of the crowd, I heard a man laughing. Turning to look, I saw that it was Andronicus Hamm. He'd left the stands and entered the arena. He was striding confidently toward us.

"*This* was your big play?" Hamm said. "Get the MASHERs to shut down? You realize that they'll all be back online in thirty seconds, right? You did all that to buy yourself half a minute of life. You're more pathetic than I even realized."

Rex turned to face Andronicus Hamm. "The MASHERs will be back online in thirty seconds, it's true," Rex said. "But they'll reboot according to factory specifications."

"So what?" It'll take my engineers five minutes to reload the program to execute you. Since you're trying my patience, though, I might just do the job myself." He waved his lazegun in the air.

"You'd better hurry up if that's your plan," Rex said. "The show is about to start."

"What show?" said Hamm, stopping a few paces in front of us. "What are you talking about?"

Rex replied, "When the MASHERs reboot, they default to demo mode. In demo mode, they only respond to certain pre-determined cues."

"Yes, yes," Hamm said. "Basic verbal commands. It's all in the manual. What's your point?"

"Not just verbal commands," Rex said. "There are a few other predetermined stimuli that the MASHERs respond to. This is a completely undocumented feature, of course. My engineer thought it was a bad idea, but I thought it was important that the MASHERs exude a certain *style*."

"For the love of Space, Rex, tell us what you're talking about."

"It's better if I show you," Rex said. Rex raised his voice. "Hit it, Bill!"

Turning toward the entrance of the arena, I saw that Stubby Joe had done it. He was now missing at least three tentacles, but he stood next to Bill, who was facing the army of MASHERs. At Rex's command, Bill's loudspeakers unfolded from their compartment. Soon the stadium was filled with the sound of jangly guitar music.

"What in Space is that?" Andronicus Hamm demanded.

"'Stayin' Alive,'" said Rex. Hamm's brow furrowed and Rex sighed. "They don't teach the classics anymore," Rex said, shaking his head.

As Barry Gibb's falsetto voice kicked in, I realized that Rex wasn't joking. Bill was playing an ancient Earth disco song. If my records weren't mistaken, it was from the 1977 soundtrack for the movie *Saturday Night Fever*. For some time, nothing else happened. Then, all at once, the MASHERs came back online. And they began to dance.

It was amazing. They say that you haven't lived until you've seen the twin suns of Shamboth Four set during aurora season, but 399 giant robots dancing to "Stayin' Alive" has to be one of the more awe-inspiring spectacles in the galaxy. The crowd went wild. Andronicus Hamm frowned.

"Stop that!" Hamm howled, barely audible over the music, the cheers of the crowd, and the stomping of the MASHERs. "What have you done to my robots? Make it stop!"

"Is there any way to stop them?" I asked.

"Sure," Rex replied. "Just turn off the music."

Turning off the music, of course, meant turning off Bill. I saw now that two brave Ubiquorp guards were attempting just that. While Bill continued to blast the Bee Gees from his speakers, they crept up behind him, their lazeguns drawn. When they were almost on him, Bill's head spun 180 degrees, so he was looking right at them. They managed to get off one shot each before Bill reached behind him and crushed their skulls. Their bodies fell limply to the ground. The music played on. Bill literally had not missed a beat.

"What happens when the song ends?" I asked.

"A lot of people are going to be very sad," Rex replied.

"Wait, are you saying…?"

Rex stared at me. "Oh, you mean what's going to happen to the MASHERs? Don't worry, they're not going to last that long."

"I don't understand."

"Remember what I said about them over-exerting themselves? They aren't designed for this level of outrageous funkitude. Combat is one thing. Keeping up with Tony Manero is something else entirely. I'll be surprised if they make it to the chorus."

He was right. By the second repetition of:

Life goin' nowhere, somebody help me
Somebody help me, yeah
Life goin' nowhere, somebody help me, yeah
I'm stayin' alive

…the first MASHER exploded. Then another. And another. Soon, dozens of them were exploding at once. By the final repetition of the chorus, the only MASHER still standing was Bill. The crowd was going crazy. Bill let the song fade out and then took a bow. The crowd went wild.

Andronicus Hamm was marching across the arena toward us, his lazegun waving crazily in front of him. Several armed guards ran after, trying to catch up with him.

"Seize those two!" Hamm shouted, his face purple with anger. "No, shoot them! They've destroyed my robot army! Kill them both!"

Rex held up his hands and I followed suit.

"That would be a bad idea," Rex said, "seeing as there's only one killer robot left, and he's in love with my friend here."

Bill waved at us from across the arena. Stubby Joe, standing next to him, waved one of his few remaining tentacles. Hamm stopped a few paces away from us, an uncertain look on his face. His gun remained pointed at us.

"Also," Rex went on, "he has a 75-millimeter machine gun pointed at your heart."

As Rex spoke, a laser-drawn heart appeared on Andronicus Hamm's chest. The color drained from Hamm's face. He holstered his weapon.

CHAPTER TWENTY-SIX

Their work finished, Bill and Stubby Joe worked their way across the arena toward us, past the smoking debris of the MASHERs. They waved to the crowd, and the crowd responded with whistles and cheers.

"Put down your guns, you fools," Andronicus Hamm barked at his guards, who were still pointing the weapons at us. "Are you trying to get me killed?"

The guards complied.

Hamm forced a smile. "Surely we can work something out like civilized men, Rex."

"You bet we can," said Rex. "You'll be happy to know that while I was dodging your robot army, I figured out the solution to all of Ubiqorp's problems."

"Oh?" said Hamm. His tone was somewhere between anger and amusement.

Rex nodded. Bill and Stubby Joe came up behind me, and I turned to greet them. "Just in time," Rex said. "I was about to explain my plan for restructuring Ubiqorp."

"I would be interested to hear this plan," said Bill. "Please continue." Stubby Joe nodded.

"First of all," Rex said, "Stubby Joe is now in charge of Ubiqorp's SLOP operation here on Jorfu. And Bill will be his head of security."

"Me?" Stubby Joe asked in amazement. Bill just stared.

"You're joking, right?" Hamm said. "A robot and a walking plant in charge of a corporate enterprise of this scale? Preposterous."

"Stubby Joe knows the business of growing soylent better than anyone. And with Bill at his side, nobody's going to give him any trouble. Also, I should point out that Stubby Joe is now the key to your entire operation. If you're going to make Heinous Vlaak happy, Ubiqorp is going to need a lot more of him."

Hamm was incredulous. "You're expecting Stubby Joe to volunteer to chop himself into pieces?"

"Nope," Rex replied. "Just have to take a few cuttings. Those pieces of tentacle you shot off will work fine."

"You're suggesting Ubiqorp plant the pieces, sir?" I asked.

Rex shook his head. "Stubby Joe's fruit is delicious, but he's too small and grows too slowly. It's none of my business, but if I were running this operation, I'd want to combine Stubby Joe's deliciousness with the size and robustness of the other shamblers."

"You mean…?"

"Graft the pieces of Stubby Joe onto the other plants. Then you've got large, fast-growing, robust shamblers that produce delicious soylent fruit. Of course, you wouldn't want to harvest the first generation. You'd wait until the grafts took hold and grew a bit, then take some more cuttings. Graft those onto other shamblers, and so on. Eventually you'd have a whole plantation full of normal-sized shamblers that produce fruit that tastes like Stubby Joe's. Of course, this is assuming that Stubby Joe wants the job."

"Sounds good to me," Stubby Joe said. "Bill, are you in?"

Bill nodded.

Everyone was silent for a moment. Hamm rubbed his chin. "That could actually work," he said. "But the amount of labor it would require…."

"A lot of skilled workers," Stubby Joe said. "We'll probably have to hire a large proportion of Jorfu's civilian population."

"Probably a good thing they haven't all been murdered then," I said.

"And we'll have to pay them a decent wage," Stubby Joe said. "Without an army of MASHERs, Ubiqorp won't be able to rely on slave labor."

"The costs will be enormous," Hamm said. "Ubiqorp has already signed a ten-year agreement with the Malarchy based on current labor costs. The stockholders will never go for it."

"They'll go for it," Rex said. "Thanks to Stubby Joe, Ubiqorp actually has a product people are going to want. They'll more than make up for your losses on the Malarchy contract by expanding into new markets. It's win-win-win."

"And if I say no?" Hamm asked.

Rex laughed. "It's not up to you, Hamm. This is a hostile takeover. Your robot army is kaput and Stubby Joe holds the key to your new product line. You have zero leverage. If you behave, Stubby Joe might keep you on as a low-level employee. Quality assurance, maybe. Personally, I'd have you ground into fertilizer, but it's not up to me."

Hamm nodded slowly, realizing the truth of what Rex was saying.

"And what do you get out of this deal, Rex?" Hamm asked. "A controlling share in Ubiqorp's soylent operations?"

Rex shook his head. "I'm not cut out for corporate life. All I need is a ship and guaranteed safe passage off Jorfu for me and Sasha. Oh, and a hundred million credits."

"A hundred million credits!" Hamm cried.

"A hundred million does seem a bit steep," Stubby Joe said.

Rex frowned. "I put you in charge two minutes ago and you're already negotiating against me?"

"With all the hiring we're going to have to do, Ubiqorp is going to be burning through its cash reserves. How about ten million?"

"What happened to you being in love with me?"

"This is business, Rex. Also, no hard feelings, but I found someone who appreciates me for more than my fruit."

"You did?" Rex asked. "When did this happen? And how is it you found time in your busy surrendering schedule for dating?"

"I am in love with Stubby Joe," Bill announced. "I am sorry, Mistress Ono. I do not believe things are going to work out between us."

I was too stunned to respond. Rex said what we were all thinking. "You realize you're a robot and Stubby Joe is a talking plant, right?"

"Love transcends such categories," Bill said, taking one of Stubby Joe's tentacles in his giant, pincer-like hand. Stubby Joe looked at him adoringly. "As Stubby Joe's head of security, I promise to protect him from anyone who tries to hurt him as long as we both live."

"This isn't love, Stubby Joe!" I said. "You rebooted him and he imprinted on you. And you're so desperate for acceptance that you—"

"Zip it," Rex said. "Love is rare enough in this galaxy without jealous, half-melted robots trying to ruin it. That's my motto, Sandy. Make a note of it."

"Yes, sir," I said.

"Now," Rex said. "Where were we?"

"Ten million credits," Stubby Joe said.

"Ugh," Rex replied. "Fine, ten million. I knew you were the right choice for CEO, you cheap, delicious bastard." Rex plucked a fruit from Stubby Joe's midsection and began eating it.

"Sir," I said. "Can I make a request?"

"Is it for a hundred million credits? Because I think I can save you some time on that one."

"No, sir. As you noted, I sustained some damage during our escape attempt. I was hoping I could perhaps get some replacement parts before we leave."

"One more thing, Hamm," Rex said. "I need your engineers to patch up my robot."

"Fine," Hamm said grudgingly.

"Excellent," Rex said. "See? Everybody is happy."

"'Happy' is a bit of an overstatement," Hamm said.

"There's still time to grind you into fertilizer," Rex said.

Hamm clenched his jaw but didn't respond.

"So this is it, then," I said. "We're actually going to get off Jorfu alive."

Rex shrugged. "I'll let Stubby Joe and Andronicus Hamm work out the paperwork and other boring stuff, but as far as I'm concerned, it's a done deal. As soon as we get our money and spaceship, we'll be on our way. Now if nobody minds, I'm going to go have a nap and three martinis, not in that order."

CHAPTER TWENTY-SEVEN

I spent the evening being patched up by Ubiqorp's engineers. They replaced several of my servos and most of my wiring. I still smelled faintly of ozone, but the engineers assured me that would go away eventually. It was nearly morning when I was dropped off on a tarmac in front of a small cargo ship. Stubby Joe had agreed to give it to Rex to get off planet. Wisps of fog drifted across the tarmac. As the hovercar sped away, I saw that I was not alone.

"Oh, hi, Bill," I said, as I approached the MASHER's hulking silhouette. "What are you doing here?"

"I thought I should see you off."

"I see. Aren't you pretty busy with Ubiqorp security stuff though?"

"I'm staying here 'til the ship gets safely away."

"Oh, okay. It's just that last night you said—"

"Last night we said a great many things. You said I wasn't really in love with Stubby Joe. And maybe you were right. But it doesn't matter. You're getting on that ship with Rex where you belong."

"That was the plan, yes."

"You've got to listen to me, Sasha. Do you have any idea what you'd have to look forward to if you stayed here? Nine chances out of ten we'd both wind up working on a soylent plantation."

"I don't see how that follows," I said. "Why are you saying all this, Bill?"

"I'm saying it because it's true. Inside of us we both know you belong with Rex. You're part of his work, the thing that keeps him going. If that ship leaves the ground and you're not with him, you'll regret it."

"Well, let's not get carried away…."

"Maybe not today, maybe not tomorrow, but soon, and for the rest of your life."

"What has gotten into you, Bill?"

"We'll always have Paris. We didn't have, we'd lost it, until you came to Casablanca. We got it back last night."

"Oh, I see. We're doing a thing. I'm afraid I don't know my part."

"And you never will. But I've got a job to do, too. Where I'm going you can't follow. What I've got to do you can't be any part of. Sasha, I'm no good at being noble, but it doesn't take much to see that the problems of two robots don't amount to a hill of soylent in this crazy galaxy. Someday you'll understand that." Bill put his giant, vice-like hand under my chin, gently raising my face to meet his. "Here's looking at you, kid." Bill turned and stomped away across the tarmac.

"Hey, Sasha!" Rex yelled from the doorway of the ship. "What was that all about?"

"I think Bill just let me down easy," I said, starting up the ramp.

"That was nice of him," Rex said. "I didn't get so much as a Dear Rex letter from Stubby Joe."

"Well," I said, "you did treat him like garbage."

"True," Rex replied. "But in fairness, I didn't know I was going to need him later."

"Did you know Bill and Stubby Joe were going to fall in love?"

"Nope. Sometimes things just work out."

I nodded. Entering the cockpit, I noticed a large briefcase resting on the floor. "Sir, is that…?"

Rex grinned at me. "Ten million credits," he said.

"Wow," I said. "You did it. You outsmarted Andronicus Hamm and came out ahead."

"I sure did," Rex said, sinking into the copilot's seat. "Stick with me and you might learn something, Sandy."

"One thing is bothering me, though, sir," I said.

"What is it, Sasha?"

"Well, sir, it may seem like a strange question, but… how is it that you know so much about horticulture? Your idea for grafting pieces of Stubby Joe onto the other shamblers was brilliant. Pardon my presumptuousness, but I never took you for the green thumb type."

"It's an interesting story, actually," said Rex. "A few years ago, I did some time on a Malarchian prison ship," Rex said. "I hadn't been convicted of a crime, but the Malarchy used converted cruise ships to exploit a loophole in the law. As long as the ship was moving, the prisoners could be considered 'in transit' to a trial. So when the Malarchy wanted to lock somebody up but couldn't make a criminal case against them, they'd stick them on one of these prisoner transport ships. Some guys spent years in the stir, traveling all over the galaxy without ever setting foot in a courtroom."

"Fascinating, sir. But that doesn't explain where you learned about plants."

"I'm getting to that. As I mentioned, these were converted cruise liners, so there were a lot of accoutrements that weren't strictly necessary on a prison ship. One of these was a large garden near the center of the ship. As the ship traveled, the garden became more and more overgrown and unruly, until someone had the idea of letting prisoners tend the garden as a reward for good behavior. Surmising— correctly, as it turned out—that gardening detail was my best chance at escape, I made sure to be on my best behavior. I did eventually escape, but before that I spent nearly a year working as a gardener. The food on a prison ship is lousy, as you can imagine, so the other gardeners and I spent a lot of time trying to figure out how to combine the root stock of robust, fast-growing trees with the branches from trees with better-tasting fruit. Eventually, the better gardeners even formed a sort of elite club that would meet to sample produce and share our expertise. And do you know what we called ourselves, Sasha?"

"I couldn't begin to guess, sir."

"Stirship Grafters."

"Wow," I said. "You went a long way for that joke."

"Ten thousand light years," Rex said, staring wistfully out the cockpit window.

Less than an hour later we left Jorfu's atmosphere—never to return, I hoped.

"Where to, sir?" I asked. The ship Stubby Joe had given us was nothing special, but we had ten million credits and a full tank of zontonium crystals. We could go anywhere in the galaxy.

"It's time for a vacation," Rex said. "I need a martini and a craps table."

"Yes, sir," I said. "There are lots of nice places in the Ragulian Sector. It'll just take me a few minutes to plot the hypergeometric course."

"Anything closer?" Rex asked.

I checked the charts. "Artesia isn't far, sir. I believe there are some gambling establishments there."

"Make it so, Sasha. Wake me up when we get there." Rex closed his eyes and went to sleep.

I wasn't particularly keen on hanging out with Rex while he got drunk in a casino, but I supposed he did deserve some time to relax after our adventures on Jorfu. Even babysitting Rex was better than wrangling shamblers.

I set the ship down at a spaceport near the largest population center on Artesia, known as Luxor City. Rex grabbed a wad of cash from the briefcase and we exited the ship.

"First things first," Rex said. "I need a shower and a new suit. Then we can hit the casino."

"Yes, sir," I said. "I will try to locate a suitable hotel."

"Maybe we can help," said a man's voice behind me.

We turned to see two men in pin-striped suits and fedoras holding lazeguns on us.

"Uh-oh," Rex said.

"Who are those guys?" I asked.

"Our names aren't important," said the man on the right. "We represent a certain interstellar business syndicate. Our organization has been monitoring traffic out of Jorfu, looking for a gentleman who owes money to one of our members."

"Who in Space…?" I started.

"Ursa Minor Mafia," Rex said.

"The Ursa Minor Mafia is real?" I asked. I'd heard of them, but according to official Malarchian sources they didn't exist.

"We're real, all right. And we're here to collect on your debt."

"There's been a misunderstanding," Rex said. "Bergoon and I are square."

"That's not what we heard," said the man on the left. "We heard you lost a shipment of contraband you were supposed to deliver to Jorfu."

"I didn't lose it!" Rex cried. "I delivered it as agreed! It's not my fault the smuggling operation got raided by Ubiqorp!"

I decided not to point out that it was, in fact, Rex's fault.

"You can tell it to Bergoon," the man on the right said. "We're taking your ship."

"I just got that ship!"

"And whatever you're hauling."

"It's empty," Rex said. "The only thing on the ship is my luggage. Just a briefcase with a toothbrush and some underwear."

"It's ours now," the man on the left said.

"What kind of guy takes a man's underwear?"

"The kind of guy who thinks you wouldn't have brought it up if it was underwear," the man said. "I'll also take any cash you have on you."

Rex grumbled but handed over the wad of cash. "Anything else?"

The two men glanced at each other. The man on the right shrugged. "I think that will do it," said the man on the right. "Nice doing business with you."

The two men walked to our ship, went inside and closed the door. A moment later, the ship shot into the sky.

"Bastards like Bergoon are the reason hard-working grifters like us can't get ahead," Rex said, as he watched the ship disappear in the clouds.

"Yes, sir," I said. "What are we going to do now, sir?"

"Get a drink," Rex said.

"We have no money, sir."

Rex pulled another wad of cash from his jacket. "Always keep a spare wad," Rex said. "That's my motto, Sandy. Make a note of it."

"Yes, sir."

"Those jerks may have stolen the lion's share of our booty, but we still have enough to…" Rex trailed off, watching a couple of workers unload crates from a nearby cargo ship. The lettering on the side of the crates read: LARVITON ENERGY WEAPONS.

"Sir?"

"I've got an idea, Sasha." Rex peeled several bills off the stack. "Go rent us a cargo ship."

"I don't understand, sir."

"That's because you don't recognize opportunity when you see it. We're going into the weapons-selling business."

"Sir, please don't tell me you're going to steal from Gavin Larviton. He's the wealthiest man in the galaxy."

"Good thinking, Sasha. Plausible deniability. Now go get us that ship."

I sighed and took the money. I managed to locate the ship rental office on the other side of the spaceport.

"Um, hi," I said to the bored attendant behind the counter. "I need to rent a cargo ship."

"What are you transporting?" the man said, without looking up.

Unable to tell an outright lie, I decided to err on the side of vagueness. "A box," I said.

"Anything flammable or explosive?"

"Wow, I hope not."

"Our smallest ship is 300 credits a day, plus 800 credit deposit."

"I've got nine hundred credits," I said.

"That gets you eight hours. Where are you headed?"

"What's eight hours away?"

"Only other planet in this system is Ashtorah."

"That's where we're going," I said. It wasn't technically a lie because as far as I knew, that *was* where we were going.

"It's uninhabited."

"Yep," I said.

"And covered with lava."

"That's the place."

"I can't let you take the ship to Ashtorah without a bigger deposit."

"Is there any way around that?"

"You got any collateral?"

"No."

"Are you gainfully employed?"

"That remains to be seen," I said.

"What's your profession?"

"I'm an actress."

The attendant seemed skeptical. Clearly a demonstration was in order. I dropped my voice an octave. "Hey, Stella!" Up half an octave

and a half. "You quit that howling down there and go back to bed!"
Back down. "Eunice, I want my girl down here!" Up: "You shut up!
You're gonna get the law on you!" Down: "Hey, Stella!"

"What in Space was that?"

"*A Streetcar Named Desire.*"

The man stared at me.

"I'm a con man's assistant."

The attendant shrugged. "Sign on the dotted line."

RECORDING END GALACTIC STANDARD DATE
3012.07.11.01:33:00:00

THE CHICOLINI INCIDENT

A REX NIHILO ADVENTURE

Robert Kroese

St. Culain Press

With thanks to the *Starship Grifters* Universe Kickstarter supporters, including: Melissa Allison, David Lars Chamberlain, Neva Cheatwood, Julie Doornbos, David Ewing, Adam G., Brian Hekman, Tom Hickok, David Hutchins, Tal M. Klein, Mark Kruse, Andrea Luhman, Rissa Lyn, Steven Mentzel, Cara Miller, Daniel Miller III, Chad and Denise Rogers, Christopher Sanders, Brandi Sellepack, Christopher Turner, John Van Vugt, Raina & Monty Volovski, and Dallas Webber

…as well as my invaluable beta readers: Mark Fitzgerald, Keehn Hosier, Mark Leone, Christopher Majava and Paul Piatt.

A NOTE TO NITPICKERS

I wrote "The Chicolini Incident" as a teaser for *Starship Grifters*. As such, it ends with a cliffhanger that leads immediately into the first scene of that book. I wrote *Out of the Soylent Planet* five years later, as a sort of origin story for Rex and Sasha. At the end of *Soylent*, Rex and Sasha are about to steal a crate of weapons from Gavin Larviton, and at the beginning of "Chicolini," they are attempting to unload a crate of weapons stolen from Gavin Larviton. A reasonable reader would be tempted to assume that these two crates are one and the same.

Less reasonable readers, who hold authors to a ridiculous standard of so-called "consistency," will note that nearly a year has passed between the recording end date of *Soylent* and the recording start date of "Chicolini." Such unreasonable readers may also note that certain events alluded to in *Grifters* are mentioned neither in *Soylent* nor in "Chicolini," leading the reader to wonder when these events—which seem to have occurred after Rex and Sasha's first meeting—could possibly have taken place.

These unreasonable readers, pitiable creatures as they are, should be encouraged to believe that Rex and Sasha stole crates of weapons from Gavin Larviton on two separate occasions, and that the pair had all manner of exciting adventures in between these two thefts. This interpretation does somewhat weaken the narrative connection between *Soylent* and "Chicolini," but that is the price of pedantry.

More charitable readers are urged to recall the words of a very wise man, who once said, "I don't seem to remember ever owning a droid."

CHAPTER ONE

People don't realize how difficult it is to be a robot.

That is, they don't realize what it's like to be a robot in a galaxy dominated by organic beings. The actual business of being a robot is fairly straightforward. If you're unfortunate enough to start out your existence as a robot, you don't really have much choice in the matter. You just go on being a robot until you're turned into scrap metal or vaporized. The latter happens more often than you'd imagine; vaporization is usually preceded by a human saying something like, "Hey robot, go find out why the reactor core is making that ticking noise." Then: boom. No more robot.

I've never been vaporized, of course, and so far I haven't been turned into scrap metal. No, it's the little things that get to me, like people talking about me like I'm not in the room. For example, a few days ago my owner, Rex Nihilo, and I were piloting a cargo ship full of black market lazeguns to the Chicolini system. It was a three-day trip and Rex, through a result of either poor planning or worse multiplication, had run out of vodka halfway through day two. As a result, he had gotten bored and cranky, and got it into his head to break into our cargo and test out one of the lazeguns.

"What's this 'Scorch' setting do?" he said, as I was plotting our landing trajectory for the Chicolini Spaceport.

I said, "Presumably, it scorches whatever you fire the lazegun at, sir."

"Cut the wisecracks, Sasha," he said.

That's my name, Sasha. It's actually an acronym. It stands for Self-Arresting near-Sentient Heuristic Android. It should be SANSHA, but they conveniently left out the N when they named me. The N is anything but convenient for me, by the way. The N is what keeps me from being fully sentient. Humans don't like robots who can outsmart them, so my creators implanted an override circuit in my brain that automatically reboots me whenever I have an original thought. There are a lot of theories about why human beings are so afraid of sentient robots. If you ask me –

RECOVERED FROM CATASTROPHIC SYSTEM FAILURE 3013.04.28.16:06:54:37
ADVANCING RECORD PAST SYSTEM FAILURE POINT

Rex was saying, "… depend on what you're aiming at? It takes more power to scorch a plasteel door than a daffodil."

"Why would you want to scorch a daffodil, sir?" I asked.

"I wouldn't!" he snapped irritably. "Unless it kept asking stupid questions."

"Daffodils can't speak, sir," I said. "Can they?"

"Keep it up, metal-face," he growled.

"Correction, sir," I said. "My face is made of flexible synthetic polymer over a joined carbon-fiber superstructure."

And that's when he shot me.

"Ow," I said.

"Cut the dramatics, Sasha," he said. "Everybody knows robots can't feel pain."

"Everybody knows it but the robots, sir," I said. He had shot me directly in the face, and my pain indicators were lit up like the aurora of Vlaxis Eight. Rex reached out and rubbed my cheek.

"Huh," he said. "Scorched. Just like the setting says. What does 'Smelt' mean?"

"It means you're going to have to find somebody else to land this ship, sir. If you want to make it planetside in one piece, I'd suggest you leave me to my calculations."

Rex grumbled but refrained from experimenting with any other settings on the gun. We landed at the Chicolini Spaceport, where we were supposed to drop off a shipping container holding 5,000 lazeguns and pick up another shipment. Rex hadn't told me what the second shipment was or where it was going. Hopefully we'd be making more money on it than we were on the guns. The profit on the gun shipment wouldn't even cover the rent on the cargo ship. It had seemed like a good deal a few days ago, but as I'd repeatedly tried to tell Rex, Chicolini was in the middle of a currency crisis the likes of which had never been seen anywhere in the galaxy. The amount we'd paid three days earlier to rent a Dromedary class cargo ship for a week wouldn't get you a cup of coffee today.

The Chicolini spaceport was about average for a remote, relatively backward planet. A few dozen ships of varying sizes were parked sporadically around a large bay. Some were undergoing repairs or maintenance while others were having cargo unloaded. I didn't see any ships being loaded, probably because Chicolini didn't have anything any other planets wanted. As far as I could tell from perusing the Malarchian Registry of Planets, Chicolini didn't export anything but money and people.

I waited at the ship for our buyers while Rex went to arrange for one of the automated cranes to unload the container from the cargo ship's bay. I didn't know who our buyers were, because I hadn't asked. The people who do business with Rex Nihilo are the sort of people you want to know as little about as possible. The fact that these guys, whoever they were, were buying 5,000 snub-nosed lazepistols on a world whose government was about to collapse already told me more than I really wanted to know.

I wasn't completely clear on how Rex had come into possession of the weapons either. The lazepistols bore the initials *LEW*, which stood for Larviton Energy Weapons. Gavin Larviton was the galaxy's biggest arms dealer. Rex had bribed someone to "misplace" one of Larviton's containers. It was hard to feel bad for a guy like Gavin Larviton, who had made his fortune profiting on wars all across the galaxy, but on a purely practical level, stealing from the galaxy's biggest weapons dealer seemed like a bad idea. Gavin Larviton was not somebody you wanted as an enemy.

Rex returned to the ship before the buyers showed up, and we watched as the levitating crane picked up the container full of guns and set it down on the spaceport floor. It zipped away and returned with another crate, which it set down right next to the first one. Presumably that was the shipment we were supposed to be taking offworld.

"Sir," I said, "Why isn't the crane loading the container directly onto the ship?"

Rex didn't reply except to grin maniacally at me. That grin always gives me a queasy sensation, like my internal gyroscopes are miscalibrated.

"Sir, if you're planning some sort of double-cross, I'd strongly recommend against it. The sort of people who would buy 5,000 snub-nosed lazepistols…"

"Relax, Sasha," said Rex. "I've got this covered. See those identifying labels on the crates? After our buyers inspect the shipment, we switch the labels. They pick up the empty container and we load the one full of guns back onto the ship. Then we make a deal to sell the guns to some other suckers on another planet a hundred light-years from here."

"Sir, the rental fees on the ship—"

"Don't trouble me with details, Sasha. I'm a big picture thinker."

"In that case," I said, "Imagine a big picture in which we spend the rest of our lives running from paramilitary thugs and repo bots in a stolen cargo ship."

"Ixnay on the aramiliatarypay," said Rex. "Our thugs are here."

There was no mistaking them: two portly men with excessive facial hair wearing camouflage combat fatigues. They were practically interchangeable except for the fact that one had a ridiculous handlebar moustache and the other wore a slightly less ridiculous polyester salmon-colored beret.

"You Rex Nillyhoo?" said Moustache, as he approached.

"NEE-hih-lo," said Rex with a smile, holding out his hand.

"What's wrong with your robot's face?" he asked. This is what I mean about people talking about me like I'm not there. It's incredibly demeaning.

"Had to test the scorch setting on the lazepistols," said Rex.

Moustache peered at my face. "Looks like it worked. Did it hurt?"

"Thank you for asking," I said. "Actually –"

"I wasn't talking to you," said Moustache.

"Of course it didn't hurt," said Rex. "She's a robot."

Moustache nodded. "Can we see the guns?"

Rex led them to the container, a plasteel box the size of a car. "Be my guest," he said, gesturing at the container.

Salmon Beret pulled the latch and opened the container. Inside were stacks of cardboard boxes. He grabbed one of them and put it on the ground. He pulled a knife from a sheath, sliced the tape on the top of the box, and then opened the flaps. Inside this were several dozen snub-nosed lazepistols wrapped in foam padding. Salmon Beret pulled one out and inspected it. He looked at Moustache and nodded.

"Five thousand, just like we agreed," said Rex. "These babies are perfect for assassination, executing a cou..." Moustache and Salmon Beret were giving him disapproving looks. "Elk hunting..." Rex continued.

"Alright," said Moustache. "You've got a deal, Mr. Nillyhoo." He held out his hand and Rex shook it.

"Where's my money?" asked Rex.

Moustache nodded to Salmon Beret. "This way," Salmon Beret said, beckoning for us to follow him. I soon realized we were walking to another container, just like the one with the guns in it. Salmon tapped a combination on the lock and opened the door. Piles of paper bills in huge stacks tumbled out of the container onto the floor.

Rex stared dumbfounded into the container. It was filled, floor to ceiling, with bills. "Is this some kind of a joke?" he asked.

Moustache frowned. "837 quintillion Chicolinian hexapennies," he said. "As agreed."

"You couldn't have gotten larger denominations?" asked Rex.

"There aren't any larger denominations," said Moustache. "Those are ten trillion Chicolinian hexapenny notes."

Rex shook his head in disbelief. He reached down and picked up a stack of bills, holding it to his nose. "Why do they smell like fish?"

Moustache shrugged. "The government ran out of paper a few days ago. They've been confiscating paper wherever they can find it. You want them or not?"

"I suppose so," said Rex doubtfully.

"Good," said Moustache. He turned to Salmon Beret. "Let's go get the truck and load up those guns."

Salmon Beret nodded and the two of them walked off.

"Nice doing business with you, Nillyhoo," yelled Moustache.

We watched them leave. When they were gone, I turned to Rex. "Sir," I said. "Shall I have the spaceport crane load our money into the cargo ship?"

Rex shook his head.

"You're not still thinking of keeping the guns, are you?" I asked.

"We have to," said Rex. "If we don't sell them a couple more times, we can't pay the rent on the ship."

"*A couple more* times?" I asked.

"Four, max," said Rex. "Maybe five. Come on, let's get those labels switched." He started walking back toward the other containers.

"Sir!" I said, following him. "What about the money?"

"We'll have to come back for it."

"Come *back*?" I asked. "After we've screwed those paramilitary nuts out of their guns?"

Rex stopped, rubbing his chin. "We'll put the label from the gun container on the empty container, put the label from the empty container on the money container, and put the label from the money container on the gun container. When those guys realize we scammed them, they'll come back and think the money container is gone. They'll never expect us to come back. Why would we?"

I wanted to object, but that was actually the most sensible thing Rex had said in quite some time. Ever, maybe. I still thought it was insanely complicated and dangerous, but it was probably our best option, given our circumstances. Part of me wanted to tap into the local Hypernet node to check the current conversion rate of Chicolinian Hexapennies to Malarchian Standard Credits, but we were in a bit of a hurry, so I made a mental note to do it later.

We switched the labels and got the gun container re-loaded just as Moustache and Salmon Beret showed up with a truck to pick up the empty container. He waved at them as I worked on the pre-takeoff checklist.

"Suckers," said Rex through his teeth.

"Indeed," I said, watching a crate lifting the container onto the truck. "Sir, won't they notice the empty container is too light?"

"Nah," said Rex.

"Are you sure?" I said. "Those plasteel containers don't weigh much when they're empty. If they happen to bump it while they're securing it to the truck…"

Rex mumbled something I didn't catch.

"Excuse me, sir?" I said.

"I said it's not completely empty."

"How not completely empty is it?" I asked.

"Very not completely empty," he said. "Full, even."

"Do I dare ask what it's full of, sir?"

Rex grinned that miscalibrated gyroscope grin. "You know how Chicolini is kind of a backwards planet, by the standards of Galactic Malarchy?" he said. "And you know how some of the more backwards planets in the Malarchy are still using nuclear fission reactors to generate power? And you know how, when uranium rods are depleted…"

"Please don't tell me we tricked an illegal paramilitary organization into buying a container full of nuclear waste," I said.

"Okay," said Rex, giggling to himself.

I sighed and finished takeoff preparations. "So what planet are we headed to next?" I asked. "Who's our next buyer?"

"Beats me," said Rex. "Some gullible idiot who wants a truckload of guns. Maybe somewhere in the Ragulian Sector?"

It figured that Rex hadn't thought even through his plan through to the second buyer.

"The Ragulian Sector is eight hundred light-years from here, sir," I said. We'll rack up more in rental fees on this ship than we'll make on the guns. And don't forget, we have to come back here to pick up our money." *Which is rapidly depreciating*, I thought to myself.

"Alright, then find a planet closer. I'm not picky. Anywhere they need guns. Which is every planet."

"There aren't any other planets around here, sir," I said. "The Chicolini System is one of the more isolated systems in the galaxy. The closest is Zarcon Prime, and they're pacifists."

"Blasted pacifists," Rex growled. "I'd nuke the lot of them if I could. Are the Zarconians into skeet shooting?"

"With snub-nosed lazepistols?"

"Hmm," replied Rex. "You're sure there are no other planets around here? Check again."

"Check what, sir? I've already double-checked the Galactic Hypernet and the Malarchian Registry of Planets."

"I don't know. Just look around."

"Yes, sir." I pretended to do something with the computer. "Nothing, sir."

"You checked everywhere?"

"Yes, sir. I checked the nearest ten million sectors, to the best of my ability." (Another thing I should mention is that my programming renders me congenitally incapable of lying. For that reason I sometimes find it necessary to make statements that are misleading, although technically true. As I had no way of searching a single sector – let alone ten million – while sitting on the ground at the Chicolini Spaceport, the statement that I had search the area "to the best of my ability" was true. Fortunately Rex isn't big on nuance.)

"Fine," he grumbled. "Then we stay here."

"*Here*, sir?" I asked dubiously. "At the spaceport where we just unloaded a box of radioactive waste on a couple of paramilitary goons?"

"No, no," he said. "Take off. Land at another spaceport. Surely this planet has more than one spaceport."

Judging by the fact that the planet was named Chicolini and the spaceport was called Chicolini Spaceport, I doubted this conjecture very much. But I checked the local Hypernet node, and, lo and behold, there was a second spaceport on a small island called Trentino, nearly halfway around the planet. I entered the coordinates and we rocketed into the sky.

CHAPTER TWO

"Where is it?" asked Rex, looking out the cockpit window. We had landed on the coordinates we had found for the second spaceport.

"Where is what, sir?" I asked.

"The Trentino spaceport."

I checked the coordinates. "We're right on top of it, sir."

I sympathized with Rex's puzzlement. The "spaceport" appeared to be an abandoned parking lot. Faded lines were barely visible, and weeds sprouted through cracked asphalt. About a hundred yards away was a boarded up building with a sign that read *EZ Mart*. EZ Mart was the biggest retail chain in the galaxy; a couple decades ago they had gone on an galaxy-wide expansion rampage, building stores on hundreds of sparsely inhabited – and in at least one case, completely uninhabitable – worlds. EZ Mart fell on hard times and declared bankruptcy, leaving many of these new stores empty and unstaffed. Some of the properties were sold to local residents for pennies on the Malarchian Standard Credit. In this case, the store itself seemed to have been deserted while the parking lot was converted into a makeshift spaceport – "converted" in this case consisting of someone putting up a hand-painted sign reading:

TRENTENO SPACPORT

The island itself seemed pleasant enough, although it appeared to be barren of vegetation except for weeds and a few scraggly shrubs. At first I took the area to be deserted, but as our engines cooled, a band of maybe two dozen men in ragged clothing ran from one end of the parking lot to the other, disappearing into the weeds. A few seconds later, another band of similar size and sartorial inclination – but carrying sticks and clubs – followed. They too disappeared into the weeds.

Rex's eyes lit up. I thought he might actually shed a tear. In Rex's eyes, there arc few sights more beautiful than two groups of people trying to beat each other to death with sticks – particularly when he's got a shipload of lazepistols to peddle.

"Let's go meet the locals," said Rex. "We've got an obligation to share with them the blessings of civilization."

We exited the ship. Not wanting to get involved in the fracas (the beauty of two groups trying to kill each other with sticks is best observed from a distance), we set off in the direction from which the two groups had come. Another hand painted sign read:

TRENTENO CITY ↑

The sign pointed toward a barely discernible path through the weeds. We followed the path to the edge of a ravine that overlooked a village of squat huts. Chicolini as a whole was backward by galactic standards, but this settlement was positively primitive. It was hard to believe people still lived like this in the thirty-first century; whoever had named this settlement "Trentino City" did not suffer from a want of imagination. Probably some idealistic group had broken away from the main population center on Chicolini, hoping to establish a utopian community on the other side of the planet. Rex and I had seen this sort of thing before. High hopes give way to infighting and disillusionment as the settlers realize how hard it is just to survive without the fundaments of modern civilization. The only chance these settlers had was to exploit some natural resource and establish trade with the other half of Chicolini. Judging from the environment and general squalor – not to mention the fact that they were trying to beat each other to death with sticks – they had thus far failed to do this.

"Sir," I said, as we made our way into the valley, "what makes you think these people have anything of value to trade for the guns?"

"Wherever there are people trying to kill each other," Rex said, "there's something of value."

I supposed he was right, in a sense. But if you're starving, a sack of potatoes is worth fighting for. I didn't see Rex wanting to trade his guns for potatoes.

"In any case," said Rex, "whatever we get from these people is a net gain, since we aren't actually going to sell them the guns."

"Sir," I said. "I don't know if you noticed, but ours is the only ship at the Trentino spaceport. There are no other containers to pull your label-switching trick with."

Rex shook his head and sighed. "You have no imagination, Sasha. Obviously we can't pull the exact same trick with these beetle-eating stick-thumpers. We're going to have to improvise. If anything, it'll be easier to fool them, because they'll assume that it will be nearly impossible for us to fool them under the circumstances."

Welcome to Rex Nihilo Logic 101.

"Sir, do you ever feel guilty for pulling these scams on people?" I asked.

"Guilty?" asked Rex, as if I'd asked him whether he thought strawberries were too salty. "Of course not. It would be irresponsible to sell guns to these people. You saw them chasing each other around with sticks. You really think *guns* are going to improve the situation? No, Sasha. We're not going to sell these people guns. We're going to sell them something much more valuable."

"Potatoes?" I ventured.

"What? No, we're going to provide them with a valuable life lesson."

"Don't trust strangers?" I suggested.

"Violence is not the answer," replied Rex. "These people need to figure out how to work out their problems without killing each other. If it takes bilking them into buying a bill of goods to do that, then I owe it to them to overcome my petty moral compunctions and give them the shaft."

"Your sacrifice is to be commended, sir," I said.

We were met near the edge of the village by a small contingent of harried-looking men and women in ragged clothes. They carried clubs and sharpened sticks.

"Greetings, harried villagers!" said Rex. "I come from far across the galaxy, bearing the gifts of civilization. Check this out."

He pulled a lazepistol from his belt and fired it at a small lizard crouched on a nearby rock. The rock exploded into pieces and the lizard landed on the ground, stunned. It scurried away into the underbrush.

"You'd better run!" Rex shouted at the lizard. He turned back to the villagers. "If I were a better shot, that lizard would never bother you again," he said. "As it is, he's probably going to need some pretty extensive counseling."

"Are you threatening us?" demanded a bearded man at the head of the group.

"Not at all," said Rex. "I'm offering to help you. As we landed, we couldn't help but noticed a group of ne'er-do-wells fleeing from a brave citizen militia armed as you are, with pointed sticks and clubs. It might interest you to know that I've got five thousand more of these little babies in a cargo container in our ship."

The bearded man regarded Rex for a moment. "Come with me," he said. "Our leader may want to talk to you."

Rex grinned at me, and we followed the group into the village. So far, so good.

One of the younger members of the group ran ahead to alert the villagers, and by the time we arrived in the center of the huts, the village council had assembled. The leader was a matronly woman with pendulous breasts tucked into her waistband and a great mass of frizzy gray hair on her head. Around her neck she wore a pendant of azure stone. "Greetings, offworlders!" exclaimed the woman. "I am Svetlana Kvarcher, the Mayor of Trentino City."

"Hi there," said Rex. "Name's Rex Nihilo. Perhaps you've heard of me. The legendary space merchant?"

Svetlana stared blankly at him.

"Well, your village is a bit remote," said Rex. "I come bearing goods from the beyond the stars. Behold!" He held out the lazepistol.

"Who's your friend?" asked Svetlana. I was trying to get a better look at that pendant. It almost looked like –

"Friend?" asked Rex, momentarily confused. "Oh, Sasha. She's my robot. Bought her at an auction of assorted machine parts a few weeks back. Pain in the ass, but she's cheaper than a human pilot. Pay no attention to her. Sasha!"

"Sorry, sir," I said. I had been staring at the pendant.

"What brings you to our fine city, Mr. Nihilo?" asked Svetlana.

"*Serendipity*," said Rex. "Funny name for a ship, but it's a rental, so what are you going to do?"

Svetlana frowned. "I mean, why are you here?"

"Oh!" exclaimed Rex. "I have a nose for opportunity. I just had a feeling that the people of Trentino City would appreciate a delivery of high quality lazepistols."

"How many of these guns do you have?" Svetlana asked.

"Five thousand," said Rex.

Svetlana's mouth dropped open. "There are only two hundred people in our village."

"Great!" said Rex. "You'll have some spares."

"I'm sorry, Mr. Nihilo," said Svetlana. "It's true that we've had some trouble lately with some separatists who have set up another community in the hills east of here, but we couldn't possibly make use of that many guns. In any case, we're a very poor people. We have nothing to pay you with."

"Actually…" I started.

"I'm sure we can work something out," Rex interrupted, glaring at me. "So tell me about these separatists."

Svetlana sighed. "A few weeks ago, a group within the village attempted a coup to oust me from power. The revolt was put down and the rebels were exiled from the city. Since then they've set up another settlement in the hills east of the spaceport. We'd be happy to let them go their own way, but they don't have the resources to survive on their own, so they keep raiding Trentino City for supplies. We barely have enough food to survive ourselves, so the raids are a real problem."

"I have been moved by your plight," announced Rex, when he noticed Svetlana had stopped talking. "I'd like to supply you with lazepistols so that you can defend yourself against these vile separatists."

"But we have no money," said Svetlana.

"Don't worry about that," said Rex. "As I say, I'm sure we can work something out. Wow, that is a lovely pendant."

"Oh, thank you," said Svetlana, regarding the azure stone. "One of the children found it in the hills not far from the separatist camp."

"Really?" said Rex. "It's beautiful. What kind of stone is that?"

"I'm pretty sure it's –" I started.

"Not asking you, Sasha," Rex growled. "Clamp it."

"I don't know what it's called," said Svetlana, "but I don't think it's valuable. The creek bed near the separatist camp is littered with them. They look nice, but they crumble in your hands if you squeeze them too hard."

"Too bad," said Rex. "Still, I might be able to sell them to a costume jewelry supplier. I'll burn nearly as much in fuel trying to transport them as I'll get for the stones, but it's better than leaving Chicolini empty-handed."

"But why don't you just sell the guns somewhere else?" asked Svetlana.

Rex sighed. "To be completely honest with you," he began — a sure sign that what was to follow was a real whopper – "I've got to unload these guns as soon as I can. I'm supposed to be halfway across the galaxy in three days to pick up a load of Cyrinni java powder. If I'm not there on time, I'll lose a multimillion credit contract. I'll give these guns away if I have to, but maybe I can mitigate my losses somewhat with a load of those rhinestones."

"Well, you're welcome to take as many as you can," said Svetlana. "But I can't vouch for your safety if you venture into the hills. That's separatist territory."

"Not for long," said Rex. "Let's get you some lazepistols and teach those separatists what's what."

CHAPTER THREE

Rex and I crept up the hill toward the separatist camp. We were bringing up the rear of the Trentino City contingent, which was made up of twenty-eight villagers, mostly young men. The bearded man who had met us at the village – whose name we learned was Glenn – was leading the group. Each of them carried one of Rex's snub-nosed lazepistols. We had started out with an even thirty men, but two of them had accidentally blinded themselves on the way over and had to be left behind. The settlers weren't what you'd call experienced military men.

I had tried to convince Rex that it was unwise for us to accompany the expedition, but he had insisted. I had a pretty good idea why: he wanted to get a better look at those azure stones. Svetlana was right, they weren't worth much as precious stones. That's because they were pure zontonium ore. Zontonium was the compound used as fuel by most of the newer ships in the galaxy. There probably weren't a lot of zontonium-powered ships in this sector, and in any case hardly anybody knew what zontonium ore looked like in its raw form. Apparently Rex did. A handful of that stuff could send a starship halfway across the galaxy. If Rex were able to trade five thousand lazepistols for a load of zontonium, he'd make out very well indeed – even if it meant not being able to sell Gavin Larviton's guns three or four more times.

The men in front had paused at the crest of the hill, and Rex crept up toward them. I followed reluctantly. Crouched in the tall grass at the crest of the hill, we could see the separatist camp down below. It wasn't much: just a few dozen tents set up near a dry creek bed.

We were momentarily startled by the roaring of thrusters behind us. A small craft was landing at the spaceport.

"You expecting someone?" Rex asked Glenn.

"That's just Javier," said Glenn. "He's our ambassador to Chicolini City. Just got back from one of his trips."

Rex nodded. As long as Javier didn't interfere with Rex's plan to get his hands on those azure stones, Rex couldn't care less. He turned his attention back to the valley ahead of us. Rex had borrowed a pair of binoculars from Glenn to get a better look.

"Whoa," he said.

"What?" said Glenn, puzzled by Rex's exclamation.

"Huh?" said Rex. "Oh, just… those are some nice tents. Check it out, Sasha." He handed me the binoculars.

I scanned the tents, but saw nothing remarkable. But then I noticed something blue and sparkly in the river bed. It wasn't water.

"Impressive, right?" said Rex.

"Yes, sir," I said. "Those are some impressive… tents." I was looking at a hundred million credits worth of zontonium, easy. All we had to do is wait for the men with the lazepistols to overwhelm the separatists in the tents, unload the rest of the guns, and then land the cargo ship right on that riverbed. We could fill the cargo hold in a couple of hours and trade the zontonium for a fortune in Malarchian Standard Credits at the nearest orbiting zontonium refinery. It was almost too easy.

"Alright, people," said Glenn. "Here's the plan: we're going to run down the hillside into the valley and start shooting."

There were nods and murmurs of approval.

"Hang on," said Rex. "That's a terrible plan."

"What's wrong with it?" asked Glenn.

"All of it, starting with the running down the hillside. New plan: we walk down the hillside and have a nice chat with those separatist bastards about how we have lazepistols and they don't."

Enthusiastic nods and murmurs of approval. Glenn seemed unconvinced, though.

"I'm not much of a talker," he said.

Rex sighed. "Fine, I'll do it."

"Sir," I began. "I strongly recommend…"

But Rex had already stood up and started down the hill. Shouts of alarm arose from the camp and several of the separatists rallied together, grabbing spears and clubs. Glenn and the others followed Rex down the hill, and I reluctantly brought up the rear.

"Hi there!" Rex called to the group. "Check this out." He stopped a few yards in front of them and fired his lazepistol at a small rock. The rock exploded into fragments and something skittered away into the weeds. "That lizard hates me," said Rex, watching it scurry away.

"What do you want?" demanded the man at the head of the separatist group. He was tall and awkward-looking, with a pair of weirdly prominent cheekbones that seemed to be trying to escape from his face.

"We want…" Rex started. He turned to Glenn, who was coming up from behind. "Actually, I'm not sure what we want. What do we want, Glenn?"

"We want all our stuff back," said Glenn. "Also, we want them to stop stealing our stuff."

"Got that?" said Rex to Cheekbones. "Trentino City has lazepistols now, and they're not taking any more of your crap."

Cheekbones seemed confused. "I thought you wanted *us* to stop taking *their* crap."

"No, no," said Rex. "You stop taking their stuff; they stop taking your crap." He held up the lazepistol for emphasis. "Also, I'm going to land my ship on that riverbed and take some of those blue shiny stones. Do we have an agreement?"

Cheekbones scowled, but he kept looking at the lazepistols our group was carrying. He seemed to realize he didn't have much of a choice. He opened his mouth to speak, but before he could say anything he was interrupted by somebody yelling from the hilltop behind us.

We turned around to see a young man running down the hill. About halfway down he tripped and went tumbling head over heels, rolling to the bottom of the hill, where he lay unmoving for some time.

"See?" said Rex. "Bad idea."

Eventually the man pulled himself to his feet, limped the rest of the way to our group, and then collapsed on the ground again.

"What is it, Javier?" asked Glenn. "What's wrong?"

Javier lay on his back, clutching his ankle. "Salmon Brigade," he gasped through gritted teeth.

"What in Space is Salmon Brigade?" asked Rex.

"Paramilitary outfit in Chicolini City," said Glenn. "They're plotting the overthrow of the Chicolini government."

"So?" asked Rex. "What does that have to do with us?"

"The Chicolini government has been ruthless in weeding out elements of Salmon Brigade in Chicolini City," replied Glenn. "We've heard rumors that the leadership of Salmon Brigade is looking for a new place to set up shop."

"You think they're coming *here*?" I asked.

"There aren't many other places on Chicolini to go," said Glenn.

"Guns," gasped Javier. "Five thousand lazepistols... be here any minute."

"What are you talking about, Javier?" asked Glenn.

"Overheard some talk at... Chicolini Spaceport. Salmon Brigade bought five thousand lazepistols. Planning on using them to take over Trentino."

"I can see how that would be a problem for you," said Rex. "But can we conclude our current negotiations before embarking on new business? If I'm remembering correctly, Cheekbones here was about to agree to all our demands and help me load up my ship with those blue rocks."

Glenn shook his head. "Our petty quarrels can wait," he said.

"Can they?" asked Rex. "People always say that about petty quarrels, but I always say the best time for a petty quarrel is right now."

"Glenn's right," said Cheekbones. "If we're going to fight off Salmon Brigade, we need to cooperate."

"No!" cried Rex. "Cooperation never solves anything. Violence, that's the answer!"

"We're going to need more of those lazepistols," said Glenn. "We need to arm everybody on Trentino." Cheekbones nodded.

Rex looked like he was about to cry. "OK, look," he said. "This Salmon Brigade? Not as dangerous as you think. Glenn, your people can easily handle them without resorting to cooperation with this separatist scum. No offense, Cheekbones."

Cheekbones shrugged.

"What do you know of Salmon Brigade?" asked Glenn skeptically.

"Sir," I began. "Maybe it isn't a good idea –"

"Stow it, Sasha," Rex growled. "OK, I'm going to level with you guys. Before I came to Trentino, we made a deal to sell guns to these guys in Chicolini City. I didn't know much about them at the time, but I suspect they're your Salmon Brigade. When I realized what a dangerous group they were, I refused to sell them the lazepistols. So you see, Salmon Brigade is no threat. They never got the guns."

Glenn and Cheekbones stared at Rex, and then turned to face each other.

"Alright," Rex went on. "Now that we've settled that, can we get back to our petty quarrel?"

A puzzled look came over Glenn's face. "So you agreed to sell guns to Salmon Brigade and then backed out?"

"Yep," said Rex. "Out of principle."

"And how is it you're still alive?" asked Cheekbones. "Salmon Brigade wouldn't take kindly to someone reneging on an agreement."

"Well," said Rex. "They might not have been immediately aware that we had backed out of the deal."

"Did you get paid?" asked Glenn.

"In a manner of speaking," said Rex.

"So," Glenn said, "you screwed Salmon Brigade out of a shipment of weapons and then tried to sell those same weapons to us?"

"I *did* sell them to you," said Rex. "We had an agreement, remember?"

Glenn shook his head. "The agreement was that you would give us the guns, and we would let you have as many of those blue stones as you want, once we took over the separatists' territory. But until we take over the separatists' territory, you get nothing."

"That's a violation of the spirit of the agreement!" Rex howled. "Tell 'em, Sasha!"

"Rex feels that you are violating the spirit of the agreement," I said.

Glenn shrugged.

"Then Sasha and I will take the creek bed by force!" exclaimed Rex.

Glenn handed his lazepistol to Cheekbones. "Good luck with that," he said.

Cheekbones held up the gun, looking down the barrel at something in the grass. He fired, scattering lizard parts in all directions.

"Hey, that's my lizard!" cried Rex. "You son of a —"

Cheekbones aimed the gun at Rex, who stopped talking.

Cheekbones moved the gun to his left hand and held out his right to Glenn. "Sorry about taking your stuff," he said. "We'll give it back."

Glenn shook his hand. "It's alright. Just ask next time, OK? We don't have a lot of stuff to spare."

"Will do," said Cheekbones. "Thanks for the lazepistol."

"That's mine!" Cried Rex. "Give me back my guns!"

"Try and take them," said Glenn. He turned to his men. "Alright, let's go home."

"Wait, what?" exclaimed Rex. "That's it? That's the big fight? You no longer have a common enemy! Get back to your petty quarrel!"

But nobody seemed particularly interested in fighting anymore. The possibility of having to fend off an invasion by Salmon Brigade had soured them on the whole idea. Glenn helped Javier to his feet and they made their way back up the hill. Cheekbones and his people returned to their camp.

Rex stood for a moment, muttering to himself. "Let's get out of here, Sasha," he growled, and began stomping up the hill.

CHAPTER FOUR

"Get us in the air," commanded Rex, fixing himself a martini in *Serendipity*'s cockpit. I have no idea where he found the vodka; he had either procured a bottle at the spaceport or found one he had forgotten about earlier.

"Where to now, sir?" I asked.

"Back to Chicolini City," said Rex.

I thought he must have been confused. "Sir? We still have a cargo bay full of guns. We don't have room for our money."

"We're going to sell the guns," said Rex.

"To whom, sir?"

"Salmon Brigade."

"Again?"

"For real this time."

"What if they kill us?"

"Then they won't get their guns. We'll unload the container at the spaceport, remove the label, and then contact the Salmon guys. There are hundreds of containers like that at the spaceport. If they kill us, they'll never find the guns."

"What if they want to kill us more than they want the guns?"

"Those guys seemed pretty reasonable," said Rex. "We'll just explain that it was a big misunderstanding. Somebody switched the labels and we ended up accidentally picking up the guns and handing them a big pile of nuclear waste. That kind of stuff happens all the time at spaceports."

I'd never heard of anything like that happening at a spaceport.

"It sounds very risky, sir," I said. "Frankly, I'd feel a lot better at this point if we just dumped the container in the ocean and got out of here. We can make up the rental fees some other way. Those guns all have the Larviton Energy Weapons logo on them, and I'm worried that somebody is going to figure out that —"

"No one's figuring out anything," snapped Rex. "We're a long way from Larviton's sphere of influence, and there's nothing to trace those guns back to us. We're not dumping the guns, so get that out of your tin-plated brain."

I sighed. "So we're going to give Salmon Brigade the guns and take the container with the money?"

Rex shook his head. "I don't want that damn Chicolinian money," said Rex. "We're just going to give them the guns."

"*Give* them the guns, sir?"

"They're going to use them to take over Trentino, right? Well, when they're done, we'll just land, express our hearty congratulations, and pick up a shipload of zontonium on our way out. We'll be light-years away before they realize what those blue stones are."

"That plan didn't work out so well last time, sir," I pointed out.

"That was just bad luck," snapped Rex. "The plan itself was perfect."

I wasn't nearly as confident about this plan as Rex was, but I could see there was no dissuading him. I set a course for Chicolini City.

We landed a few hours later and Rex paid off one of the crane workers to hide the container of guns in a remote corner, behind several other containers. Then we sent a message to the Salmon Brigade guys through the same secure Hypernet channel Rex had first used to contact them and waited at the ship for them.

It didn't take long for them to show up. The truck pulled up and screeched to a halt in front of *Serendipity*. Moustache and Salmon Beret got out and walked toward us. They didn't look happy.

"You sons of bitches," Moustache growled. "What's the big idea, selling us a load of radioactive waste? We were supposed to be taking over an island today, and instead we spent most of the day decontaminating the truck. It cost us 8,000 credits to have that stuff shipped to the sun."

"Honest mistake," said Rex. "Somehow the labels got switched. We came back as soon as we realized what happened."

"Just tell us where the guns are," said Moustache.

"They're nearby," said Rex. "We just need to work out the terms of the transfer."

"Listen to me, you little weasel –" Salmon Beret snarled.

"Now, now," said Rex. "Losing your temper isn't going to get you your guns any faster. Here's the deal: because I value your business and want to make this situation right, we're going to give you the guns *and* let you keep your money."

"What's the catch?" asked Moustache dubiously.

"No catch," said Rex. "Although Sasha and I would like to stop by after your island takeover and make sure everything went OK with the guns. No misfires or anything, you know. We want you to be happy customers."

The two men regarded Rex dubiously. They obviously expected Rex to pull another trick on them somehow.

"Alright," Moustache said at last. "If you give us the guns, let us keep the money, and don't try any more funny business, then we're square."

"Deal," said Rex, shaking Moustache's hand. "Alright, let's go get your guns."

Rex walked to the corner of the spaceport where the container with the guns was hidden, the rest of us following close behind.

"*Voila!*" exclaimed Rex, opening the container door. He immediately slammed it shut again and spun around, his back against the door. "You know," he said, "I feel like we should drink to our new partnership before we get down to business. Sasha, could you get the bottle of champagne I left in *Serendipity*'s cockpit."

"Sir?" I asked. If there was a bottle of champagne anywhere in *Serendipity*, I hadn't seen it.

"Robots!" exclaimed Rex, throwing his hands in the air. "Completely helpless. Tell you what, you gentlemen wait here while I help Sasha find the champagne."

Rex grabbed my arm and began walking briskly toward the ship.

"Sir," I said. "I'm not sure I –"

"Shut up, you idiot," Rex snapped. "In about five seconds we're going to make a run for it."

"Sir?" I asked.

Behind me I heard Salmon Beret's voice. "Hey, this container is empty!"

"RUN!" Rex shouted.

We ran.

Lazegun blasts erupted around us as we flung ourselves into the cockpit of *Serendipity*.

"Get us out of here!" Rex yelled.

I skipped the preflight checklist and engaged the thrusters. *Serendipity* lifted off the ground and shot into the sky. Down below, the two men screamed profanities at us and continued to fire their lazepistols at the ship. *That's coming out of our deposit*, I thought.

"Those bastards took our guns!" Rex shouted.

"Which bastards?" sir. "Salmon Brigade?"

"No, you useless bag of lug nuts, the Trentinoans. Trentonians. Those jerks on Trentino. They must have unloaded our guns while we were distracted with the separatists. Scumbags! People like that give the black-market gun trade a bad name."

"Oh," I said. "That makes sense." That was actually pretty smart of them, I thought. I refrained from reminding Rex that we had stolen the guns from Gavin Larviton.

We were nearing the outer edge of the atmosphere. "Where to this time, sir?" I had high hopes Rex had gotten fed up with Chicolini and would be ready to try his luck on some other backwater planet.

"Just put her in orbit for a while," said Rex. "After those Salmon Brigade thugs leave, I want to pick up our money."

"Sir?" I asked. "It's not our money anymore. You agree to give it to Salmon Brigade."

"That's when I thought we were also giving them the guns. The deal's off now, thanks to those shifty Trentinonians."

I wasn't sure how sound his logic was, but I didn't argue.

We spent the next several hours orbiting Chicolini. Rex got rip-roaring drunk, which is what he does whenever he has nothing scheduled for any block of time exceeding twenty minutes. Once he was on the verge of sobering up, we returned to the spaceport to pick up the container of Chicolinian hexapenny notes. The Salmon Brigade guys had left, so it looked like we were in the clear. We hadn't yet told them which container the money was in, so hopefully it was still there.

We were nearly to the container when two men turned a corner and stopped right in front of us, blocking our path. They resembled the Salmon Beret guys in neck thickness and overall demeanor, but they wore pinstriped suits and fedoras instead of fatigues: the unmistakable uniform of the Ursa Minor Mafia.

"Good afternoon, gentlemen," said Rex with a smile. "What can I do for you?"

"We heard somebody's been movin' guns through this spaceport," said one of the goons. "You don't know nuthin' about that, do you?"

"Space, no!" exclaimed Rex. "Sasha and I are pacifists. I've never even touched a gun. We're in the costume jewelry business. You guys need any cufflinks?"

"We don't need no cufflinks," growled the other man.

"Alright, then," said Rex. "Well, we'll keep an eye out for anybody trying to sell guns."

"Yeah, you do that," said the first man, eying Rex suspiciously. After a moment, the two of them moved on.

"Sir," I whispered. "You neglected to mention to me that the Ursa Minor Mafia runs this port. They don't take kindly to gun runners horning in on their territory."

"Relax, Sasha," said Rex. "There's no way they can connect us to the guns."

I wished I could be so sure. One more reason to get far away from Chicolini.

We found the container and verified that it was still full of cash. Rex had one of the crane operators drop the container into Serendipity while I prepared for takeoff. Once our cargo was securely stowed, Rex joined me in the cockpit. Finally, we were going to get off this accursed planet.

"Where to now, sir?"

"Trentino," said Rex.

I spent the next five minutes banging my head against the control panel of the ship.

"Sasha!" Rex finally yelled. "What in Space is wrong with you?"

"*Why*, sir?" I pleaded. "Why are we going back to Trentino? We have the money. Let's just get off this planet. PLEASE."

"Not a chance," said Rex. "We're going to trade the Trentinonians our pile of cash for a load of zontonium. They still don't have any idea they're sitting on a fortune in starship fuel. That stuff is worth, what, ten times its weight in Chicolinian hexapenny notes?"

"More like a thousand by now, sir," I said.

Rex cackled with glee. "And to think, you wanted to just take the money and leave. Get this bucket of bolts to Trentino, Sasha."

CHAPTER FIVE

We flew back to Trentino. When we landed, we were surprised to find another small craft parked near the defunct EZ Mart. It bore a salmon-colored logo featuring the letters *SB*.

"Uh-oh," said Rex. The Salmon Brigade had beat us to Trentino.

We hurried to Trentino City only to find Svetlana, Glenn and Cheekbones siting together at a table in the village square with Moustache and Salmon Beret. Every single one of them was carrying a lazepistol. Svetlana waved when she saw us.

"Well, if it isn't our intrepid pair of weapons merchants," said Svetlana with a smile.

"Yeah," said Rex humorlessly. "I see you've made some new friends. Look, we've got a shipload of money to unload. It's all yours if you let us fill up our ship with those worthless creek rocks." Rex's sales pitch was really slipping. I think he was as sick of this planet as I was.

"Funny thing about those worthless rocks," said Svetlana. "Evan and Kip were just telling us what zontonium ore looks like. They happen to have some contacts with the Andromeda Mining Company."

"Seriously?" said Rex. "Evan and Kip? Those are the worst paramilitary thug names I've ever heard. What are you guys even doing here? I thought you were trying to overthrow the Chicolini government."

"We're having second thoughts about that," said Moustache, whose real name was apparently either Evan or Kip. "We came here planning to take over Trentino and use it as a base of operations for our assault on Chicolini City, but this island has a lot of potential. The whole Chicolini government is going to collapse when the hexapenny bottoms out. Who wants to be in charge of cleaning up a mess like that? We've decided to move the whole organization to Trentino and start from scratch."

"We had our doubts at first," said Svetlana. "But Evan and Kip were so nice, explaining the whole mix-up about the guns, and telling us about the zontonium ore. So you'll understand that we're going to have to turn down your generous offer. We've worked out a deal with Donny to help them get their settlement going in exchange for letting the mining company –"

"Stop!" cried Rex. "Donny? Cheekbones' name is Donny? I'm done here. Sasha, let's get off this planet before I meet somebody named Lance and have to choke him to death with his own socks."

Rex turned and began stomping his way back to the spaceport. I hurried along beside him.

"I'm sorry, sir," I said. "I know how you hate it when people work out their differences peacefully."

"Especially people with names like Kip and Donny," grumbled Rex. "This whole planet is full of sissy-named weenies. Svetlana is the only real man of the lot."

As we approached the spaceport, another ship descended from the clouds, landing between us and *Serendipity*. Two men in pinstriped suits and fedoras got out and began walking toward us.

"Oh geez," said Rex. "It's Tad and Kevin."

"Tad and Kevin?" I asked, confused.

"I'm extrapolating," said Rex. "Follow my lead."

"Hey," said the man on the left as they approached. "Didn't we just—"

"Thank Space you're here!" exclaimed Rex. "We found your gun runners! This whole village is armed to the teeth. My robot and I came here to try to sell some jewelry to the locals, and we were appalled to find that the place is overrun with gun-toting hoodlums. I think those Salmon Brigade fellows are importing guns from offworld and storing them on this island until they can ship them to Chicolini City."

"We'll see about that," growled the man on the right. The two brushed past us toward Trentino City.

"Sir, how long do you think that ruse is going to –"

"I give it about thirty seconds," said Rex. "Get us off this island before Tad and Kevin smelt us."

We hurried to the ship and climbed into the cockpit. I was about to start the preflight checklist when I noticed the two Ursa Minor goons had stopped walking toward Trentino City. One of them was gesturing our way. They had their hands on their lazepistols.

"Just get us out of here, Sasha! Forget the damn checklist!"

I skipped to the end of the checklist and hit the thrusters. We shot into the air as Tad and Kevin blasted the underside of the ship with their Lazepistols.

"Alright," said Rex. "Let's get off this namby-pamby peace-loving planet. I don't know what I was thinking trying to sell guns to these boneheads. But hey, at least we still have a shipload of money."

A shipload doesn't buy what it used to, I thought, as a red warning light flashed on the control panel. It was the pressure sensor. We were losing air.

"Sir," I said. "We have a problem. There seems to be a leak in the hull. We're going to have to land."

"Land?" cried Rex. "No, we can't land. We need to get the hell off this planet."

Sure, *now* he wants to get off the planet.

"Do you think you can hold your breath for the next twenty light-years?" I asked.

Rex sighed. "OK, put us down somewhere we can repair the hull."

"It'll have to be a spaceport. I can't repair a hull breach in the field."

"Fine! Whatever!" snarled Rex.

I set a course for Chicolini Spaceport. We could only hope that every group of people we had angered on Chicolini was now on the island of Trentino.

We weren't quite that lucky. The whole spaceport was crawling with cops. We didn't know if they were looking for gun runners, mobsters, or Salmon Brigade partisans, but we didn't particularly want to find out. Getting *Serendipity* repaired was going to be impossible under the circumstances. Our best bet was to stow away on another ship. In this endeavor, fortune was kinder: a luxury cruise ship called *Agave Nectar* had stopped at the Chicolini spaceport for some minor maintenance before continuing its voyage. Spaceport security was so busy assisting the local police in whatever it was they were doing that nobody seemed to be watching the *Agave Nectar* very closely. All we had to do was walk up the ramp and find a place to hide out until the ship disembarked.

This plan was complicated by Rex's unwillingness to leave behind the container full of Chicolinian hexapennies.

"It's a box full of money!" Rex exclaimed, as we sat crouched behind a pile of baggage, watching travelers well-heeled travelers walk up the ramp to the *Agave Nectar*.

"Chicolinian money is worth even less than it was when we got to this planet yesterday, sir," I said. "It's certainly not worth risking our lives over."

"The box of money that I leave behind is the box of money you can bury me in," announced Rex.

While I wasted precious seconds trying to parse this statement, Rex found half a dozen large steamer trunks and begun dumping their contents onto the ground. "Come on, Sasha," he said, dragging two of the trunks toward our container. "Help me fill these with money."

I sighed and went after him, taking two more of the trunks. Taking care to dodge the police, we made our way back to the container and filled the trunks with stacks of bills. When they were full, we dragged them back to the *Agave Nectar* and then returned to the container with the remaining two trunks.

"Not all the way," said Rex. "We're going to hide inside the trunks. It'll make it easier to get on the ship, and we won't have to worry about getting separated from our money."

"Except for the 700 quintillion we're leaving behind," I reminded him.

"We'll have to come back for it," said Rex. "This will get us by for now."

I wondered how long Rex thought a hundred quintillion Chicolinian hexapennies would last us. I still hadn't had a chance to check the current exchange rates, but I knew there was no way it was going to cover the repairs on *Serendipity*, much less the rental fees. Hopefully we had enough to buy us a few meals on the *Agave Nectar* – assuming we didn't get found out and tossed into the vacuum. "Spacing" freeloaders was technically against interstellar law, but some cruise lines had found a way around this law by killing stowaways with food poisoning before ejecting them from the ship.

After Rex locked the container, we dragged the trunks back to the pile of luggage and climbed inside. As a robot, I don't need air, and can remain motionless in a cramped space for as long as necessary. I understand it's much more difficult for human – particularly a hyperactive, impatient human. The fact that Rex remained in his trunk for three hours without making a peep can only be attributed to his boundless love for hard currency.

While I was ensconced, I tapped into the local Hypernet node and checked the exchange rate on the Chicolinian Hexapennies to Malarchian Standard Credits. It currently stood at a hundred quintillion to one, which meant we had just enough money to buy a club soda. At cruise ship prices, probably not even that. Also, the bills smelled like fish.

We were loaded into the cargo hold of the *Agave Nectar* and a couple hours later, the ship took off. I heard a lazegun blast and a moment later my trunk opened. "Whoops," said Rex, looking at the lazepistol in his hand. "I thought I had it set to torch mode." What was left of his trunk lay in charred pieces on the floor.

I climbed out of my trunk and looked around. We were in a large room surrounded by boxes and baggage. Rex lost no time opening several of the fancier looking suitcases and rooting through them to find a change of clothes. After seven tries, he found a suit that fit.

"What do you think?" he asked.

"Very dapper, sir," I replied. "Are you going somewhere?"

"Thought I'd see if could find a poker game. Gotta be some well-heeled types on a ship like this who are just aching to lose a few thousand credits."

"We don't have any money, sir, except for these hexapennies, and I'm fairly certain a ship like this frowns on…."

Rex was already breaking into more luggage. This time, it took him only three tries to find a strongbox full of cash. He cut it open with the lazepistol and stuffed several hundred credits in his pockets.

"That ought to do it," he said. "Let's go make some money." He climbed over a pile of suitcases toward the door.

"Sir," I said. "Perhaps you should leave the lazepistol here?"

"Oh," he said, regarding the gun. "Good point, Sasha." He stashed the gun behind a suitcase and opened the door. "Let's go find some suckers," he said, and walked into the hall. I refrained from suggesting he locate a mirror. If Rex had any capacity for self-reflection at all, he'd have realized we were the suckers. We'd been taken advantage of by practically everyone we'd met on Chicolini, and all we had to show for it was six steamer trunks full of nearly worthless currency. If there was any silver lining to our circumstances, it was that our new enemies were mostly confined to Chicolini. The Ursa Minor mafia probably didn't know who we were, and so far we seemed to have stayed off Gavin Larviton's radar.

We took the elevator to the casino floor, which was filled with rich vacationers trying their luck at blackjack, roulette, craps, and other games of chance. Rex's eyes lit up. Rich people trying to beat the house was one of the few sights more beautiful to him than people trying to kill each other with sticks.

Rex slipped a twenty credit note to an attendant. "Any high-stakes games going on?" he asked.

The attendant frowned. "There is one," he said, "But it's invitation only."

"How do you know I haven't been invited?" Rex demanded. "You don't even know who I am."

"Precisely," said the attendant, with a sniff.

"Look, pal," said Rex. "You may not know my face, but I'm not the sort of guy you want to make enemies of, OK? Now what do you say you go find whoever is running this game and tell him Rex Nihilo is here."

The attendant shrugged and walked away.

"Sir, do you think that was a good idea? What if the person in charge of the game doesn't know you?"

"I'm sure he doesn't," said Rex. "But he doesn't have to. I just have to make him think he *should* know who I am."

"I'm not sure I follow, sir," I said.

"Watch and learn, Sasha," he said.

After a few minutes, the attendant returned. Alongside him strode a balding man with thick, bushy eyebrows. He smiled when he saw Rex.

"So you're the infamous Rex Nihilo," said the man. "I don't believe I've had the pleasure. My name is Gavin Larviton."

RECORDING END GALACTIC STANDARD DATE
3013.04.29.04:47:13:00

More books by Robert Kroese

The Starship Grifters Universe
The Yanthus Prime Job (novella, included in *Aye, Robot*)
Starship Grifters
Aye, Robot

The Mercury Series
"Mercury Begins" (short story)
Mercury Falls
"Mercury Swings" (short story)
Mercury Rises
Mercury Rests
Mercury Revolts
Mercury Shrugs

The Land of Dis
Distopia
Disenchanted
Disillusioned

Other Books
The Big Sheep
The Last Iota
Schrödinger's Gat
City of Sand
The Foreworld Saga: The Outcast
The Force is Middling in This One

Did you enjoy this book? Leave a review on Amazon!

Connect with Robert at BadNovelist.com!